PRAISE FOR CASSIE EDWARDS'S
PASSIONATE INDIAN ROMANCES

"Heartwarming, very descriptive, the story will make you think. Clearly essential for your fall reading list!"
—*Rendezvous*

"A fine writer . . . accurate. . . . Indian history and language keep readers interested."
—*Tribune* (Greeley, CO)

"Cassie Edwards consistently gives the reader a strong love story, rich in Indian lore, filled with passion and memorable characters. . . . Wonderful, unforgettable."
—*Romantic Times*

"Edwards puts an emphasis on placing authentic customs and language in each book. Her Indian books have generated much interest throughout the country, and elsewhere."
—*Journal Gazette* (Mattoon, IL)

SILVER WING

Cassie Edwards

A TOPAZ BOOK

TOPAZ
Published by the Penguin Group
Penguin Putnam Inc., 375 Hudson Street,
New York, New York 10014, U.S.A.
Penguin Books Ltd, 27 Wrights Lane,
London W8 5TZ, England
Penguin Books Australia Ltd, Ringwood,
Victoria, Australia
Penguin Books Canada Ltd, 10 Alcorn Avenue,
Toronto, Ontario, Canada M4V 3B2
Penguin Books (N.Z.) Ltd, 182–190 Wairau Road,
Auckland 10, New Zealand

Penguin Books Ltd, Registered Offices:
Harmondsworth, Middlesex, England

First published by Topaz, an imprint of Dutton NAL,
a member of Penguin Putnam Inc.

First Printing, May, 1999
10 9 8 7 6 5 4 3 2 1

REGISTERED TRADEMARK—MARCA REGISTRADA

Printed in the United States of America

Silver Wing is dedicated to a very special, sweet person—Genny Ostertag, an assistant editor who is always there for me! Thank you, Genny, you are truly appreciated!

Always,

Cassie Edwards

I am waiting for my warrior
to come and rescue me.
I'm sitting by the river,
against the white pine tree.
My heart is crying out for you,
A whisper is too loud.
I'm sending kisses on the wind,
Can you hear me, Silver Wing?
Before the storm, is the calm,
And that's what I shall be.
Find me at our lover's place,
Beside the white pine tree.
Mother Earth, she is my friend,
And keeps me company.
Waiting for my Indian love,
To come and rescue me.
We'll walk our paths together,
Our love is as the sun,
Shinning rays of happiness,
And we shall walk as one. . . .

—Julie A. Bergman,
Spirit Woman

1

Thyself prepare to pass the vale of night,
To join forever on the hills of light.
                                            ——Phyllis Wheatley

San Francisco—1840

MAY—*Ah-pah-ahl,* Season of making *Up-pa*
(baked loaf) made from ground *Khousa.*

The stark room had high ceilings with only a few
dusky windows reflecting thin rays of sunshine.

Nuns, dressed in their black habits, ate in silence at
long wooden tables.

Audra Fredericks toyed with the boiled potatoes
and dry piece of beef on her plate, her mind focused
on something else that was more fascinating to her
than the convent's bland, tasteless food. As she had
made her way through the long corridors to the dining
room, she had seen something through a window that
had caused her to hesitate. She was forced to move
onward when a hand took her by an elbow and ushered her along with the others.

"Indians?" she marveled to herself as she plucked
a piece of potato up with her fork, eyeing it specula-

tively. She sucked it into her mouth and chewed, the starchiness of it curling her tongue distastefully.

Why would Indians be at the convent? she wondered, placing her fork on the tin plate.

She had seen several Indians arrive at the church rectory. It was quite peculiar for an entourage of Indians to be at the convent. Yet she had gotten in trouble over speaking her mind to Father John, the priest in charge of this convent, so she knew not to ask any questions.

But she *would* find a way to get answers.

She smiled mischievously at the sister who stood over her table keeping tabs on who did or did not eat. Yes, Audra decided, she would cleverly eavesdrop on the conversation between the Indians and Father John. Surely they would still be in Father John's office when the noon meal was completed. Surely they had been offered food and drink while having their meeting with Father John, since it was the noontime hour for everyone, not only the nuns.

"Finish your meal, Audra, or you will be in line for more punishment," Sister Kathryn said in a warning tone. "Audra, Audra, what are we to do with you? I have never met anyone as rebellious."

Audra wanted to speak up and tell Sister Kathryn her true feelings about having been brought to live at the convent, but knew that it would be a waste of time. She had already decided to quit complaining, for she only received more punishment. Best to take it a day at a time until she could find an opportunity to sneak away.

Knowing that she had no other choice but to eat,

and now having something intriguing to do besides her usual humdrum chores, Audra rushed into the meat and potatoes until her tin plate was empty.

"Now, that's a good girl," Sister Kathryn murmured, patting Audra lovingly on the shoulder. "Run along with the others and resume your chores. As you know, mopping the corridor outside of Father John's study is your assigned duty today."

Again, Audra smiled mischievously at Sister Kathryn, for it was this assigned place that would help Audra get answers she was seeking about the Indians.

Audra scurried from the dining room, then lifted her black skirt up into her arms and ran past the other girls. She avoided their looks of wonder as she brushed past one and then another, then slowed down her pace when she caught Sister Kathryn studying her haste. It was for certain that Audra had never shown this sort of eagerness to mop before. To do so now was quite out of character.

Dropping her skirt, folding her hands demurely before her, Audra walked slower. Then, when she turned a corner and was no longer visible to Sister Kathryn, she broke into a run again and soon left everyone behind her.

Breathing hard, her heart pounding, she went to the supply closet. She sprinkled powdered soap in a bucket, poured water over it, then grabbed up a scrub brush and the bucket.

Rushing from the closet, water splashing on all sides of Audra, she ran from the large, three-storied brick convent. She ran across the spacious courtyard, brightened by spring jonquils and crocuses.

The sun was warm even now on Audra's cheeks. It was the sort of day she would love to have the wind blow through her hair.

Once again she was reminded of her short hair. Getting it snipped short was the first thing she had hated about being at the convent.

Then, one by one, things that she abhorred had mounted each day. Especially the isolation due to her rebellious nature. Scarcely had she been allowed a decent conversation with the other girls because of her constant confinement.

Sister Kathryn wouldn't be surprised to see Audra's antics today. She knew just how badly Audra wanted to leave the convent.

Had Audra aspired to be a nun, that would be a different story. Instead, her uncaring, drunken father forced this on her after her mother had died.

Everything was quiet inside the rectory. The maroon velveteen drapes framed the stained-glass windows, and statues of angels and Jesus on pedestals adorned the sides of the corridor.

Audra's heart pounded when she saw Father John's door. The door was ajar! Even this far away she could hear the drone of voices.

She would soon know why the Indians were there and how long they planned to stay.

She hoped to find a way to leave with them!

It was obvious they were peaceful or they would not have been accepted into Father John's study.

If they were this peaceful, surely they would understand a young woman's pleas to be freed of her confinement at the convent. Surely they knew how it felt to be held captive. Since the white man had come to Indian land, Indians were captive to the white man's rules.

The sun poured through a window on the wall just opposite Father John's study. Audra set her bucket of sudsy water on the hardwood floor, bent to her knees, and began scrubbing the floor in slow circles.

She eyed the door speculatively as she mopped closer and closer to it. She made sure that when she reached it, she positioned herself where neither Father John nor the Indians could see her.

Her pulse racing, she leaned her ear closer and held the brush still on the floor, suds oozing from beneath it.

When she heard footsteps in the distance, Audra's heart froze inside her chest.

She looked guardedly from side to side to make sure no one was coming down this particular corridor.

Thus far, there was no one in sight.

Nor did she hear the footsteps any longer.

Leaning her ear close to the door again, she listened intently to what was being said.

The Indians were Nez Perce, and they could speak perfect English. They had learned the English language from the people who had set up trading posts near the Nez Perce's Wallowa River Valley in Oregon country.

Their precious land was marked by high plateaus and deep, lush river valleys. They called it "The Land of Winding Waters."

The Indian who had introduced himself as Chief Silver Wing seemed to be the spokesperson. He spoke not only of their vast, beautiful, unspoiled land, but also of their great herds of Appaloosa horses.

She then heard Silver Wing tell Father John that his people had been told of a white man's "Book of Heaven." Silver Wing and his four companions had traveled through extensive forests and treacherous Blackfoot country to San Francisco so they could get the mysterious "white man's book" and take it home to their Nez Perce people.

"For many years my people have pondered the mystery of this 'Christian Holy Book,' " Silver Wing said, adjusting his blanket more loosely around his shoulders as he sat in the white man's uncomfortable wooden chair. "It was my decision, as chief, to come to this holy building to ask you, the holy man in charge, for a copy of the book."

"You are speaking of the Bible, I assume," Father John said, unknowingly running a hand slowly up and down the arm of his chair as he sat opposite Silver Wing and his four companions.

"Yes, I have heard it called by that name," Silver Wing said, leaning forward, his eyes locking with the priest's. "Will you part with at least one holy book in exchange for blankets and beads that people from my village have made for the exchange?"

Audra's eavesdropping was quickly interrupted when she heard footsteps approaching again from somewhere in the darker passages of the rectory. She had no choice but to move onward and mop elsewhere, so Audra quickly dropped the brush in the water and lifted the bucket from the floor.

But before she left, Father John hesitated answering the chief's question about the Bible.

She wondered why Father John was postponing giving the Indian an answer?

She could tell that it was on purpose, because he quickly changed the subject by inviting the Indians to stay the night.

She smiled when she heard Silver Wing agree to stay. They did not wish to sleep inside the white man's large lodge, but outside with the moon and stars. Silver Wing also asked permission to build a campfire in the courtyard, which Father John agreed to.

She would sneak out at midnight tonight and meet the Indians.

She could hardly wait to see Chief Silver Wing up close in the fire's light. If his face matched the smooth, dignified manliness of his voice, she expected to see someone brilliantly handsome.

As Audra rushed away from Father John's study, her intrigue of the Indians grew, not only because they were Indians, but because she wanted to hear more about this beautiful land they had traveled from.

Yes, she would sneak from her room tonight and talk with the Indians.

Oh, if only they would sympathize with her for being forced to live a life she never wanted.

If they would take her with them back to their world, she would be forever grateful.

She had lived at the convent for five long years now.

Oh, might this truly be the opportunity she had been seeking?

If she *could* find a way to talk with the Indians, she

would see if she *could* go back with them to their Oregon country.

She could tell by their manner that they were kind and civilized, not the savages most whites defined Indians to be.

What a thrill it was to think of herself among Indians, living the life of an Indian, on land that was described by them as something akin to Heaven . . . their paradise!

2

He spoke of the grass, and flowers, and trees;
Of the singing birds and the humming bees.
——JOHN GREENLEAF WHITTIER

"Holy white man, *will* you part with one holy book in exchange for blankets and beads?" Silver Wing asked, having realized that his question before had been brushed aside as though it were unimportant.

His insides grew tight as he waited for the thin-faced man in black to answer him.

Father John rose from his chair. His long black robe billowing around his legs, he went and stood facing the fireplace, where a slow fire burned on the grate.

His jaw tightened, his eyes narrowed, he swung around and faced Silver Wing again. "I would rather wait and give a Bible to the Nez Perce when I can go to your land and teach it to your people," he said smoothly.

He looked from Indian to Indian, then gazed solely at Silver Wing again. "What is the use of having the book if you do not read or understand the meaning of its words?" he said blandly. "When I have my affairs in order and can find a temporary replacement for myself at the convent, I will come to the Wallowa

River Valley and bring many Bibles and the teachings of the holy word with me."

Silver Wing's spine stiffened. His breathing became shallow, for he had not come to bring white men home with him.

Only a book!

When white men became involved in Indian affairs, nothing good came of it!

Now he felt that he had been wrong to come all of this way for a book that might, in the end, cause trouble for his people.

"All that my people want from you is the holy book, not your teachings from it," Silver Wing said, his voice low and tight.

Father John's chin lifted stubbornly as he gazed intensely into Silver Wing's deep gray eyes. "No, you cannot have a Bible," he said, his own voice as tight as Silver Wing's. "It is best that the Bible is accompanied by a person who can translate its words and meaning correctly to the Nez Perce."

Silver Wing thought through the logic in what the white man said. Just perhaps this man of God was right. What good *would* the book be to his people if they could not translate from it?

And holy men were supposed to be good at heart and trustworthy, so surely no wrong could come from this holy man mingling with his people.

Yet Silver Wing still found himself hesitating.

"Except for trading, when required, the Nez Perce do not mingle with others," he then said. "We prize justice, bravery, generosity, and self-discipline. Those who are not of our tribe might threaten such an existence."

"My presence would not threaten your stability as a tribe," Father John said. "All I would do is bring the Bible and explain its meaning. Some other Indian tribes have even described the Bible as 'Talking Leaves,' seeing the pages as leaves. No harm has come to those I know who have accepted the Bible among their people to grasp its meaning."

"It is a fascinating thing to think about, this book of yours," Silver Wing said, softly kneading his chin.

Then he dropped his hand to his side and tightened his jaw as he gazed into Father John's blue eyes. "Yes, do come, but *xoyim-xoyim,* come alone. Do not bring others with you," Silver Wing said. "Bring only yourself and the holy book."

Father John sat down in the chair again. He arranged the folds of his gown around his legs. He reached up and pulled at the white collar at his long, thin neck and absently cleared his throat. "You must know that I am unfamiliar with your land," he said softly. "I would not be safe traveling alone. And I must have people with me who will see to my meals. I am a man who requires many men around me."

Again, Silver Wing went quiet with thought. He studied the white man and saw how his pale skin seemed to lack sunlight. Yes, it was evident that this man scarcely allowed sun to touch his face, which meant that he was not used to methods to survive in the out-of-doors.

Yes, this man *would* need companionship on the long journey north. Silver Wing had realized the hardships of survival on the long trek from his homeland to San Francisco.

"Yes, you can bring those with you who will make your journey less hazardous," Silver Wing said, rising from his chair. "But do not stay long in our country. We would not want others to follow who might decide to come and check on your welfare."

"I will stay only for as long as I am needed," Father John said, clasping his hands behind him. He smiled. "Thank you for allowing me to visit your lovely land."

Still hesitant about this decision, Silver Wing only slightly nodded.

He turned to walk toward the door, his companions following him, then stopped when Father John came and blocked the way.

"I again urge you and your friends to stay inside tonight instead of sleeping out-of-doors. When the fog rolls in from the bay, it gets quite uncomfortable. Even a campfire will not ward off the chill."

"*Katsa-yah-yah,* thank you, but a campfire will be enough for we Nez Perce," Silver Wing said, smiling slowly at Father John. "We have slept many a night beneath the stars."

"Yes, I imagine you have," Father John said as he thought of their long journey from Oregon country and the hardships they must have had to endure to survive unscathed.

"But I do have one more suggestion," Father John said as he walked from the study with Silver Wing and his companions. "I would like to see you return to your country by a safer mode of traveling than that which brought you to San Francisco. I urge you to travel by way of ship. I will pay your passages."

Silver Wing's eyes widened as he stopped and turned to face Father John. "I have always been intrigued by the white man's water vessels and their large white wings that flap in the wind," he said, even now in his mind's eye seeing the large sea vessels that lined San Francisco's waterfront. "And it would be a much faster way to return to my people. I am chief. I have been gone from my people for too long now."

"Then, you will accept my offer?" Father John asked, gently placing a hand on Silver Wing's bare shoulder.

"Yes, my warriors and I will return home on a white man's ship," Silver Wing said. *"Katsa-yah-yah,* thank you. You are kind for offering."

"It pleases me that you have come so far because of your interest in my religion," Father John said, walking slowly down the corridor with Silver Wing. "Paying your way back home is small in comparison."

As they stepped outside into the sunlight, they were unaware of a man who sneaked quickly away into a grove of maple trees.

Harry Weston, Father John's gardener, hunkered down to make sure he wasn't noticed. He had been standing outside the stained-glass window of Father John's study. It had been open enough for him to hear everything that had been said, and his evil mind desired to know more about this beautiful land that the Nez Perce chief talked of.

Not only the land intrigued him, but the tribe's powerful and many horses! Harry was already plotting how he could get rich by stealing land and horses from the Indians. Having grown weary of being a lowly gardener long ago, he now saw a way out.

But to do so, he would have to gather some close friends to accompany him to Nez Perce country. Only he would go on into their village however. The others would establish a hideout.

Perhaps he could steal a black robe from Father John's closet and pretend to be a holy man as he took many coveted Bibles to the Indians, and song hymnals as well. Harry could tell the Nez Perce chief that Father John had grown ill and sent him there in his place.

But to achieve this plan, Harry knew he would have to leave soon to set things in motion—before Father John could get there.

The Nez Perce chief and his warriors needed time to get back to their village, but he could follow on another boat soon after.

He would already have things under *his* control before Father John even left for Oregon country.

And when Father John did arrive, Harry would make sure he never made it to the Nez Perce's village to spoil things for him!

3

I heard the sounds of sorrow and delight,
The manifold, soft chimes,
That fill the haunted chambers of night,
Like some old poet's rhymes.
——HENRY WADSWORTH LONGFELLOW

The moon sent a gentle silver light through the one lone window in Audra's room. She had a room to herself. It was small and barren of furniture except for a bed, dresser, and chifforobe.

Slowly she opened the chifforobe. The moon's glow revealed the cotton dress she had worn the day she had been brought to the convent. A hairbrush and the shoes she wore were her only other possessions.

"Dare I wear the dress tonight?" she whispered, running her hands over the softness of the fabric. She knew how ugly she was in the nun's attire, even more so with her chopped-off hair. Perhaps at least wearing a decent dress might help her look more normal in the eyes of the Indians—even if her hair was an eyesore.

"Yes, I will wear it," she whispered to herself, taking the dress from its wooden hanger.

Her pulse racing from excitement, Audra hurried into the dress, then winced when she realized just how much she had filled out and had grown since she had last worn it.

Her breasts strained against the inside of the bodice. The waist was tight and puckered.

And the length!

It now was higher than her ankles!

Still believing that she would make a better appearance in a normal dress, she ignored its flaws and reached for her hairbrush. It was a gift from one of the sisters. Quickly she ran it through her tight, short curls. She had been blessed with naturally curly hair, which did help her appearance somewhat. She knew that if the mirror had not been removed from the dresser—the nuns believed mirrors were only for feeding the vain side of women—she might see that she was presentable enough tonight to meet the Indians.

She hated to think of the punishment that lay ahead of her if she were caught by Father John or one of the sisters. Silence was one thing. To be locked up in her room, alone for days, would be another.

Thankful that her door was not locked tonight, Audra placed her hand on the latch and slowly lowered it.

She held her breath as she shoved the door open an inch at a time, then stepped out into the corridor that was scarcely lit with candles burning on wall sconces.

Stiff-backed, she peered from side to side.

When she saw no one, nor heard anyone approaching, she quietly closed the door behind her and ran as softly as possible down the back flight of stairs, then eased her way along the wall until she got past the sisters' living quarters.

Audra then broke into a mad run, left the huge

two-storied building, and followed the light of the campfire until she found the camp.

She stopped and hid behind a thick lilac bush, then peered around and stared at the sleeping Indians on blankets beside the fire. She gained enough courage to move onward, then stopped and knelt beside one of the Nez Perce warriors.

She started to reach over and awaken him but stopped and drew her hand back when, in the soft glow of the fire, she saw how handsome he was. He had such noble, chiseled features, such a strong nose, so sharp and aristocratic.

Where his blanket had fallen away from him, she could see that he wore only a breechclout, which might have embarrassed her at another time, but now, this close, so in awe of him, she could not help but take in his muscled copper body, his broad shoulders and lean waist, his waist-length hair that was as black as all midnight and spread out on the ground beneath him.

When he suddenly awakened and his deep, dark gray eyes found Audra kneeling beside him, she fell away from him with a start, sprawling clumsily on her back. He moved to his knees over her and reached for her waist, helping her back up from the ground. Her face flooded with color, embarrassed for having been caught staring at him.

She was glad when he took his hands away from her waist and he held himself at bay.

"I'm sorry," she stammered, trying to find a way to apologize for having been there unannounced, yet having a purpose that she hoped to explain. "I didn't mean to disturb your sleep. But . . . I . . . need your help. . . ."

Her words trailed off when he showed no signs of having heard her. His eyes were focused solely on her cropped-off red hair.

She sucked in a wild breath when one of his powerful hands reached up and he ran his fingers through the soft, curly tendrils.

"Where is the rest of your hair?" Silver Wing blurted out, forking an eyebrow. "Why have you cut it? Is it because you are in mourning? If so, whose death do you mourn?"

Recognizing his voice as the Indian's who had done all of the talking in Father John's study, Audra was momentarily speechless. His voice was so deep and resonant. His dark gray eyes were so mesmerizing.

But finally she had the ability to speak again when she saw the others awaken and lean up to questionably look at her.

"My hair was cut off when I was brought to the convent after . . . after . . . my mother died," Audra said, her voice breaking. "My father brought me here. He left me as though I . . . I . . . was something useless to him. It is the policy of those in charge of the convent to cut the hair of those who have come to practice as nuns."

She swallowed hard. "I don't want to be here," she murmured. "I never aspired to be a nun. And I hate my hair. I want to let it grow as long as it was before I came here. Can you help me? Can you help me find a way to leave this place? I would forever be grateful."

"You ask something of we Nez Perce that is impossible," Silver Wing said, yet he understood she had been forced into a life that was not of her liking.

"Helping you in any way is not something the holy man would allow," he said thickly. "Should I try and take you away, he would find me *and* you, and I would be placed in a white man's jail for going against the wishes of the powerful man of God."

"Just sneak me away," Audra pleaded, her eyes filling with tears. "They would not realize it was you who helped me."

"Your name?" Silver Wing asked, his eyes searching hers, her loveliness making his heart come alive, his desires having died many moons ago when the woman he had loved drowned in the Columbia River after her canoe capsized in the rapids.

He wanted to help this beautiful woman, but knew he would chance losing his life, therefore robbing his people of their leader.

"Audra, Audra Fredericks is my name," she murmured, feeling dead inside over knowing that he was unable to help her.

She should have known not to ask something so foolish of him.

She should have known that the Nez Perce wouldn't risk such a thing when their own lives would be put in jeopardy.

And being so far from their home, there would be no one to come and rescue them.

"I am called Silver Wing," he said. "I am my band of Nez Perce's people's chief. As is your mother dead, mine is also. Her bones lie in mother earth in Oregon country."

Although she already knew why the Indians were in San Francisco, Audra would act innocent and ask him anyhow. She wanted to spend just a little more time with him before heading back to her room. How dreamlike to be face-to-face with an Indian, an Indian whose mere presence made her heart race.

She was disappointed that he could not help her flee the convent.

But she was more disappointed knowing she would never have the chance to see him again. Now that she had met him, heart-to-heart, he was a part of her world that she would not let go of. When she needed escape, at least she could allow herself to remember him.

"Why have you come here?" she asked innocently enough as she gazed up at the rectory, glad to see that there were still no lamps burning in any of the rooms. That had to mean that Father John was still asleep.

She shifted her eyes and looked at the sisters' quarters. She smiled when she saw that the lamps there also were still dark.

"I have traveled far to take back with me to my people the holy book in which are teachings of things my people do not yet know," Silver Wing said, then sighed. "But our travels have been somewhat in vain. Father John will not part with a Bible. He, instead, insists to bring it to my people himself, sometime later."

Although he wasn't able to help her, Audra wanted to help *him*. She started to tell him that she would sneak him a Bible, that he *would* have one to take back to his people.

She was tempted to ask him to find a way to sneak

her away with him in exchange for this Bible, but already knew that he couldn't do that.

However, she didn't get the words out before Father John was suddenly there carrying a lamp, which proved why no lamplight showed in his room. He had it with him!

"Audra, what is the meaning of this?" Father John gasped. "Why have you left your room and so . . . so . . . shamefully . . . so brazenly come to speak with the Indians at this late hour?"

As Audra rose slowly to her feet, her eyes wide with guilt, Father John's eyes swept over her.

Then as she stood up, trembling, Father John stepped closer and spoke into her face. "Why are you wearing that shameless dress?" he asked shallowly. "Where is your habit?"

"Please listen to me," Audra pleaded, tears filling her eyes. "Can't you see my desperation in how I *did* come to the Indians like this? I want to leave the convent, Father John. I . . . I . . . came and asked the Indians to help my escape. I'm old enough to be on my own now. And my father could care less should you give me permission to leave. He's probably so drunk he doesn't even know what goes on around him."

"Stop it, Audra," Father John said, taking her by an arm. "This is not the time to discuss such things. Not in the presence of strangers."

Still holding her by an arm, Father John turned to Silver Wing, who was now standing tall over the priest, his gray eyes assessing the situation at hand.

"You must excuse what has happened here tonight," Father John said, his voice drawn. "This 'wild thing' still hasn't learned the meaning of obedience. Please return to your peaceful sleep. Audra won't disturb you any longer."

As Father John walked off with Audra, still scolding her, Silver Wing watched them. His hands doubled into tight fists at his sides. He didn't like the way the holy man was treating the gentle, *say-quis-nix,* very beautiful woman. It made him look less than holy. For certain she was his captive.

Silver Wing wanted to rescue her from this place, but he couldn't chance jeopardizing his own life for a white woman who was a complete stranger to him. He must return to his people. He was their leader, and they always came first to him!

Yet there was something about that woman . . .

Although she was lovely, loneliness showed in her eyes and desperation emerged in her voice as she spoke of a father who had betrayed her.

She was as no other white woman he had ever met before.

She had spirit.

She had courage.

She was, oh, so beautiful!

And anyone who forced a woman to cut her lovely hair surely could not be all good!

Troubled, he returned to his blankets, but his eyes would not close, for before them always was the lovely face, the hair the color of the sunrise, and the despair in her large green eyes!

4

From the fixed place of heaven she saw
Time like a pulse shake fierce.
——DANTE GABRIEL ROSSETTI

As Father John forced Audra up the steep stairs to
the second story in the convent, where she would be
locked in her room, she tried to yank herself free of
his tight grip on her elbow.

"You are wrong to treat me like this," Audra cried,
no longer caring whom she would awaken. "Let go of
me! You are a holy man. Act like one! Can't you see
my anguish? Can't you feel it inside your heart? I
don't belong at the convent. I shouldn't have to stay
just because my drunken father said that I should!"

"My dear, I know how you feel, yet I am helpless
to your pleas," Father John said softly. "I am even
touched by your words, yet it is my duty to make you
conform to the rules of the convent. And no matter
how you talk of not belonging here, I promised your
father that I would care for you. And surely you know
that if I allowed you to leave, you would become the
victim of San Francisco's woman-hungry men. You
would beg to return to the convent."

"Never!" Audra cried as he forced her into her

room. She tried to keep him from shutting the door, but his strength doubled hers and soon he had the door shut and locked.

"You were shameful, Audra, for leaving the room tonight and going to the Indians," Father John spoke through the door. "It proved to me that you do not have the sense one needs to live off one's own intuitions. What you did tonight is the same as a whore going to saloons and lifting her skirt to men. The seduction would have been no less had the Indian taken advantage of you being there so late at night. Surely he saw you as a hussy who came to be with a man."

"That's not true," Audra cried, leaning against the door, her back slowly sliding down to the floor in her frustration. "You know that's not true."

Her voice weakened as she continued to speak, not even sure if she still had an audience on the other side of the door, for suddenly everything was quiet except for her voice.

"You know why I went there tonight," she sobbed. "I wanted the Indian to help me, not . . . not . . . seduce me. I want to be free. I want to be . . . my . . . own . . . person."

She wiped the tears from her eyes, and her back stiffened against the door as she heard his footsteps leaving down the corridor.

And then she heard the stone-still silence again.

She hung her head sadly.

5

Unhappy they, whom choice, or fate
Inclines to prize the bitter weed;
Perpetual source of female hate.
——Philip Freneau

Audra tried the latch on the door again to see if some-one might have unlocked it during the night.

Her heart sank when the click of the lock seemed to have sealed her fate.

Still in her plain cotton gown, she reached for her hairbrush and fluffed up her scarlet curls as she watched the ships at the riverfront. The convent sat close enough to the river for her to be able to see when Silver Wing boarded the ship that would take him away from her.

She had watched the ships as soon as the morning's dawn made them visible to her. Thus far she hadn't seen the entourage of Indians board any of the huge ships.

A knock on the door startled Audra. She jerked around and stared at the closed door.

When a soft voice spoke from the other side, saying that she had brought Audra her breakfast, Audra's heart sank again.

Not wanting to lose the chance to see Silver Wing

one last time, she turned and gazed quickly out the window to look at the ships and the cobbled stones that led to them.

When she still saw only white people coming and going from the ships, she placed the hairbrush on her dresser and hurried to the door.

"I'm ready for you to unlock the door," she said, clenching and unclenching her hands at her sides.

Oh, but if only she had the courage to rush past Sarah.

Could she get outside before someone stopped her?

Could she get as far as the ships?

But no, she knew such an attempt was futile. This time of day there were too many people doing their duties at the convent to get past them undetected. If only it was the nun's time to go for prayers at the church, where above them on the high ceilings were beautiful, serene paintings, only then could she even consider fleeing the convent without being caught.

Audra would never forget the first time she had seen the paintings. They had given her a moment of peace after having been forced inside the church as her father rode away in his dilapidated wagon. At that moment she had pretended she had been brought to heaven, and for a while thought she might enjoy being there.

"Audra, as soon as you take the food from me, please step back so that I can lock the door again," Sarah said through the locked door. "And, Audra, do not attempt talking with me. Sister Kathryn said that you are to continue your world of silence."

"Sarah, just open the door and leave the food, will

you?" Audra said, sighing. "I doubt that these few words will cast a dark spell over you."

"Audra, please don't say such things," Sarah said, gasping. "Now, step back from the door, Audra. I am going to unlock it. Then I will hand you the food, leave, and again lock the door."

"Just hurry up, will you?" Audra said, still ignoring that she wasn't supposed to say anything to Sarah.

She looked nervously toward the window. She didn't want to miss seeing Silver Wing. Oh, just one last look at him could last her a lifetime. Last night, her dreams had been filled with him.

He had even reached out and gently touched her face.

At that moment in her dream, she had felt as though she were floating.

Her pulse raced as she heard the lock snap undone.

Her throat became dry as Sarah slightly opened the door, yet still only enough for Audra to see Sarah's dark, wide eyes that were filled with questioning.

"Audra, if Sister Kathryn knew you were breaking your vow of silence, by saying these things to me, your time in your room would be doubled," Sarah said, going ahead and fully opening the door.

Sarah bent and took up the wooden tray of food, then handed it to Audra. "But I won't tell, Audra," she murmured. "Honest, I won't tell."

"I know you won't," Audra said softly, her friendship with Sarah going back to the very first day of Audra's confinement at the convent. They had bonded quickly, for they had both been put in the convent by parents who had no feelings for them.

"Audra, I miss you so," Sarah said, tears welling up in her eyes. "Please behave so that we can be together again. You are the only one I confide my deepest thoughts to."

"As are you mine," Audra said, laying the tray aside. She drew tiny Sarah into her arms, the slight bones of her friend cutting into the flesh of Audra's arms.

Audra stepped back from Sarah and gave her a troubled gaze. "Sarah, I worry about you," she said. "Please eat better. You are too thin."

"The food is horrid," Sarah said, visibly shivering.

She gazed deeply into Audra's eyes. "I really must go," she whispered. "I'm afraid Sister Kathryn might be timing how long it takes for me to give this to you. She knows we are best friends."

"Be careful, Sarah," Audra said, her eyes wavering. "You can't afford any ill treatment. You might . . . not . . . make it, should you be confined to your room, especially if you are denied food."

"Thank God they allowed you to eat today," Sarah said, turning and grabbing the door latch. She smiled at Audra. "I believe I had something to do with that. I begged mercy for you, Audra. Sister Kathryn listened."

"Thanks, Sarah," Audra said, tears burning in her eyes. "Remember what I said. Be careful."

She watched the door close and listened for the lock, cringing when it happened, the click like a nail being driven in her coffin.

She then took the time to stare down at the food on the tray.

"Oatmeal and toast," she whispered, shivering with distaste.

Then her eyes brightened when she found hot chocolate in a tin cup and smiled when she realized who was responsible for that goodie.

Sarah.

Surely Sarah had sneaked it onto the tray while no one watched.

Hungry, yet feeling that she had been away from the window already for too long, Audra set the tray on her dresser and hurried back to look at the riverfront.

Her heart skipped several beats when she saw Silver Wing walking up the gangplank to the ship called *Sunset*. Today he still wore only a breechclout and moccasins, a lone blanket draped over his left shoulder. The sleek, lithe muscles of his handsome body rippled with each of his steps, his powerful strength echoing with his long stride. His long black hair blew behind him, the feathers tied in his hair fluttering in the wind.

She watched him until he and his friends positioned themselves along the front rail facing San Francisco.

If only she could open the window and wave.

Would he see her?

Would he know that it was she saying a sad, final good-bye to him?

She watched the ship as it left the shore, and along with it Silver Wing. She could not stand to watch any longer. Sobbing, she turned her back to the window and hung her face in her hands.

Now she knew she had fallen in love with him that first moment she had seen him beneath the moonlight.

It broke her heart to know that it was a love that never could be.

6

This is the ship of pearl which, poets feign,
Sails the unshadowed main.
The venturous bark that flings,
On the sweet summer wind its purpled wings.
——Oliver Wendell Holmes

Silver Wing was intrigued even more by the large river vessel now that he was on it. He saw its strength as it left the shore without men having to use paddles to give it its power to move through the water.

He was in awe of how large it was and how many people it held. Also he had seen many boxed-up supplies carried below.

He had even seen some cattle brought aboard, which stood now at one far end within boundaries of ropes.

Yet even with all of this to marvel over, he could not help but be distracted by something on shore; the large convent, where the woman of his intrigue had been taken last night after she had daringly come and spoke with him beside the fire.

Now his full attention was on that woman who had visited his troubled dreams throughout the night. No one's hair could be as brilliantly red—or as short. He would never forget how she told of it being cropped so short against her will.

Guilt filled his very soul for not having a way to help Audra flee a life that had been forced upon her. He could not help but wonder what her fate would be now.

He wanted to dive overboard and swim back to shore and save her, but he knew that if he tried, he would be imprisoned behind bars with criminals and treated as no less than a criminal himself.

No, he could not do anything to help the woman.

But he would never forget how her skin looked as soft as corn silk to the touch, and how her lovely green eyes revealed to him the depths of her despair.

He even now felt the weariness of her spirit as she watched the boat leave San Francisco's shores.

And as the sun shifted enough to splash onto her face and he could see the loveliness again, he would cherish having had the chance to have at least met such a woman.

It surprised him to know that white people treated their women in such a way, whereas his people's women were cherished.

He forced himself to look away from Audra, but he knew that she was inside his heart forever. He had fallen in love with her the very moment he had seen her standing there so bewitching beneath the moonlight.

7

Moving about in worlds not realized,
High instincts before which our mortal nature
Did tremble like a guilty thing surprised.
——WILLIAM WORDSWORTH

Harry Weston smiled wickedly as he watched the ship carry the Nez Perce Indians away from the shore, the Oregon country its destination. He was already counting off the days when he would board a ship for the same destination.

And once there, ah, how his life would change. Finally he would have a reason *to* live. To be rich and own lots of land and horses *was* now within his reach.

"Thanks to the Nez Perce," he whispered to himself, chuckling. "I'm coming, Silver Wing. Ah, yes, I'm coming to your land. *I'll* bring you Bibles, all right." Again, he chuckled. "But I'll take from you twofold!"

As the ship went farther out into the bay, he watched the sails flutter open, one by one.

"Soon," he whispered throatily. "I'll be following soon, Chief Silver Wing."

8

In spite of all the learned have said,
I still my opinion keep.

——PHILIP TRENEAU

The weeks had dragged by since Audra last saw Silver
Wing, yet she remembered him so vividly it was as though
he were there, his dark gray eyes mesmerizing her.

No longer locked in her room and now back to
her normal activities, Audra was dusting the beautiful
statues close to Father John's study in the rectory.

Her memories returned to that day when she had listened to Father John and Chief Silver Wing discussing
why Silver Wing had traveled so far from his homeland.

She still couldn't understand why Father John
hadn't given him at least one Bible. It was beginning
to look as though Father John wasn't going to go to
Oregon country with a promise of Bibles, after all.
Too much time had elapsed. There had been no ru-
mors of Father John going anywhere.

She hated to think of how Silver Wing was feeling
deceived by the "holy man," the label he had given
Father John.

She wondered what Silver Wing might be thinking
at this very moment.

Was he possibly pursuing other means to get a Bible?

It had seemed very important to him, otherwise why would he have traveled so far to acquire one, even passing through his enemy Blackfoot country, chancing death?

Audra smoothed the soft feathers of the duster along an angelic figure, then stopped short and swallowed hard when she heard Father John's voice loud and angry through the closed door of his study.

When he spoke Silver Wing's name, Audra's eyebrows forked. This was the first time she had heard Father John refer to the Nez Perce chief in any respect since Silver Wing had left on the huge boat for his homeland.

She could not help but be curious as to why Father John now spoke of him, especially while in such an angry state.

Slyly looking from side to side, to see if anyone was approaching on either end of the long corridor, Audra tiptoed over to Father John's door and leaned her ear against it.

As Father John shouted and raved, her eyes grew wider and wider and her heart thumped wildly within her chest. She soaked it all up, her mind already busy conjuring up ways to finally leave this convent and see Silver Wing again!

As she continued to listen, she slowly smiled. . . .

"So that's where Harry Weston has disappeared to, is it?" Father John shouted, his face red with rage as he held a letter out before him, again poring over the words as his close friend Abraham listened, his hands clasped gently behind him.

"Abraham, listen to what this letter says," Father John said, holding it closer to the lantern's light. "It's from Dennis Bell. You know . . . an old acquaintance of mine since childhood. He's living in Oregon country now. He's employed at the Dalles Trading Post that sits on the shores of the Columbia River some miles from the Nez Perce village."

He paused, sighed, then began to read the letter out loud—

"Dear John,
   It was good to hear from you, and I'm glad that you are considering making a visit to Oregon country. But I think you need to know something that I saw only recently at the trading post. Harry Weston. I know him as your gardener. Remember? The last time I was in San Francisco, you pointed him out to me. He was pruning the rosebushes. After he was finished, you gave me some fresh starts for my garden here in Oregon. Well, John, what puzzles me is that Harry Weston was dressed as a priest. It didn't seem right to me, so I made myself scarce while he was at the trading post and then followed him. He went to the Nez Perce village. I since have learned that he is there teaching the Nez Perce the Bible and songs from hymnals. Was he converted before he came to Oregon country? Or is there something sinister behind him being here?
   I look forward to your visit, John. May God be with you on the voyage."

Audra placed a hand over her mouth, her eyes wide,

as she, too, became very puzzled by Harry Weston's behavior. Why on earth would he go to the Indian village and pretend to be a priest? He *had* to be up to something. But what?

She listened further to what Father John said to Father Abraham. "I must board the next ship for Oregon country. I must confront Harry," he said thickly. "I must stop whatever scheme he is up to, for you know, Abraham, what he is doing isn't sincerely done from the heart. He has surely stolen the Bibles and hymnals from our church. He probably even stole a black robe that he wears while pretending to be one of us."

"What could be his reasoning behind this?" Father Abraham said in his soft, gentle voice. "Perhaps he has good intentions, John. Perhaps he sincerely cares for the Nez Perce. If he is taking the time to teach them from the Bible and the hymnals, surely it *is* being done from the bottom of his heart."

"Nothing that man has ever done has been from his goodness," Father John grumbled, slouching down into a chair. "I only hired him as my gardener because I saw him as a man in need. I looked the other way when I saw him sneak a bottle of whiskey into his room. I even prayed for his soul when gossip came to me about frequenting brothels and lifting the skirts of those evil women. But this? I doubt I can find it within my heart to forgive this man if he has gone to the Nez Perce for the wrong reasons."

"What do you have in mind, John?" Father Abraham asked, sitting down on a plush leather chair opposite John. "I can tell you've given this serious thought. What do you think Harry Weston's up to?"

"I think he must have heard about the Indian's vast herd of horses and their land, which Silver Wing had described as paradise," John said, his voice drawn. "I imagine Harry eavesdropped when Chief Silver Wing and I were discussing the chief's country. Truly, that's all that makes sense here. I just know that Harry Weston could never be anything close to holy."

"Then, you will be leaving soon?"

"Like I said, on the very next boat to Oregon country. I will be leaving on the ship *Madrona* tomorrow at dawn."

That was all that Audra had to hear. She scurried away from Father John's door, rushed breathlessly from the rectory, and headed for the convent. Her head was spinning with plans. She was going to stow away on the *Madrona*!

Hopefully when Father John found her, it would be too late for him to send her back to the convent. He would have no choice but to allow her to stay on the boat.

She could hardly believe it, but just possibly she would see Chief Silver Wing again after having given up hope that it could ever be possible.

The thought of being with Silver Wing again, their eyes meeting and holding, sent a sensual thrill through her.

She ran into the convent and rushed down the narrow corridor toward the back stairs that would take her up to her room. She didn't have much to pack. Only the one dress, sleeping gown, a change in underwear, and the hairbrush that she hoped would soon be used on long, flowing red hair instead of the dreadful short hair that was kept cropped short every two weeks.

And she would slip from her room tonight, go to the kitchen, and steal some unperishable food that she could take with her on the ship.

She could hardly stand the excitement!

"Audra, stop. What's the hurry?"

A soft voice behind her made Audra stop with surprise. She turned slowly and watched Sarah hurrying toward her, her blue eyes wide with wonder.

"Audra, I can tell you're up to something," Sarah said, stopping to give Audra a quizzical stare. "Tell me. I promise not to tell anyone."

"Sarah, I can't tell anyone, not even you," Audra said, her voice loud enough for only Sarah to hear.

"Audra, I can tell you are trying to hide something," Sarah whispered back. She looked guardedly over her shoulder, then edged up closer to Audra. "Share the secret with me. I promise, *promise,* not to tell a soul."

Audra swallowed hard. She shuffled her feet nervously beneath her long black robe. She knew that Sarah wanted to leave the convent as badly as she did, but if two attempted it, it would jeopardize things for them both.

Yet it would be nice to have a companion on the long journey north.

Her eyes wavered as she gazed at Sarah's thin face. She wasn't sure if Sarah was strong enough for the voyage.

Yet it was certain that living at the convent hadn't agreed with her. Too many times Audra had watched Sarah scarcely touch her food at the dining table.

Audra had forced herself to eat to keep up her strength. She had told Sarah to do the same, yet Sarah still scarcely touched her food.

"I plan to leave this place," Audra suddenly blurted out. "I'm going to leave tomorrow. Sarah, do you want to come with me?"

Sarah gasped. Her face drained of color. "You're going to leave?" she murmured. "How, Audra? You know that is all but impossible."

"Since I've been behaving myself, of late, my door is no longer locked at night," Audra said. She took Sarah's frail hand and squeezed it affectionately. "Nor is yours. Sarah, just before dawn tomorrow, when everyone is asleep, you and I will flee this place and go and slip aboard the ship *Madrona*. Sarah, that ship will take us to Oregon country. I shall see Chief Silver Wing again!"

"How do you know about the ship and when it sails, and where it is going?" Sarah asked warily.

"I overheard Father John say he's going to leave on the *Madrona* tomorrow," Audra said excitedly. "He's going to Oregon country."

"If he's going to be on the ship, surely he will see us," Sarah said, swallowing hard. She then shook her head violently back and forth. "No, Audra. I won't go."

"I understand," Audra murmured. "But if you change your mind, come to my room just as you see it turning dawn."

Audra suddenly drew Sarah into her arms and gently hugged her. "I shall miss you if you don't go with me," she said, her voice ragged. "We have grown so close, you and I. You . . . you . . . are that sister I never had."

"I shall also miss you," Sarah said, now sobbing. "I truly wish I could go, but I'm too afraid."

"Think about it some more, Sarah," Audra said, easing away from her. She held Sarah's hands and gazed into her eyes. "If you go, I promise to keep you safe."

"I will think about it," Sarah said softly. Her eyes wavered as she gazed into Audra's. "Honest, I . . . will."

Sarah slipped her hands free and, with a swirl of black skirt, ran from Audra.

Audra suddenly felt ill at ease about having shared such a private thing with Sarah. If Sarah chose to tell the sisters, even Father John, about Audra's plans, wouldn't it put her in a better light with the convent? Wouldn't she be in line for favors?

Now not feeling so confident about things, Audra walked at a slower pace toward the stairs, then spun around and looked down the long corridor.

Her heart sank, and she got an instant sick feeling at the pit of her stomach when she saw Sarah go into Sister Kathryn's private study.

"Oh, Lord, if Sarah tells . . ." Audra said, her voice breaking.

9

I slept in the dark
In the silent night,
I murmur'd my fears
And I felt delight.
——WILLIAM BLAKE

Audra awakened to another day. The sounds around her were now quite familiar as the ship's crew and passengers milled around the deck.

Although Audra had been able to flee the convent without being caught, saying a silent thank-you to Sarah for not alerting the sisters or Father John to the plan, the next step had been riskier.

But even then she had managed to get aboard the ship without being caught. She had squirmed among the women and their long, full skirts going up the gangplank.

Once aboard the *Madrona*, she had crept away from the passengers and climbed into a lifeboat at the far back of the ship.

At sea for three days, she felt dirty from hiding in the small boat all scrunched down beneath a stinking cover of leather loosely slung over the top.

Audra scratched her face and then her arms. She grimaced as she smelled the unpleasantness of her sweat-soaked hair as well as her armpits.

So desiring a bath, and now low on food, since she hadn't been able to steal as much as she had wanted to from the convent's kitchen, Audra's plan today was to show herself to the ship's captain and take the punishment for being a stowaway.

For certain, they were too far out to sea for them to turn back over having found her.

And surely he would take pity on her and at least make her comfortable until they reached Oregon country.

Once there, she would deal with the captain's decision to hand her over to the authorities.

But if he chose to take her on to Canada, the ship's final destination before turning around and heading back to San Francisco again, her whole scheme of things would be ruined.

She would take things one step at a time. Now it was important to get a decent meal in her stomach and the stench washed off her body and hair.

The only thing she truly dreaded about coming out of hiding today was Father John. Each day she had been able to pick up Father John's voice from the others.

One day he had actually rested his back against the boat as he had talked with Abraham, one of his traveling companions.

Audra had been almost too afraid to breathe while he was there.

But that threat had passed and here she was ready to show herself to the world. She knew that the women on board this ship would be mortified by her appearance. Surely no one could look as disheveled.

And her hair! Although dirty, it would be its length that would mortify the women the most. In today's world long hair was almost worshiped as though it were a God. And here she was with hers cropped almost to its roots.

Her stomach ached with hunger, giving Audra the courage to unfasten the boat's cover and sling it aside.

The sun poured down onto her face as she raised her eyes to look around her.

She froze when she found herself eye to eye with Father John. He was just strolling past, a Bible clutched in one hand, a cane in another, which he used to keep him steadied against the slow side-by-side pitching of the ship.

Audra's heart seemed to actually stop beating as Father John's color drained from his face and his eyes almost popped from their sockets.

"Audra . . ." he then gasped, taking a quick step away from her as she still sat in the small boat, stunned into stone silence.

Father John quickly shook himself out of his shocked state. He frowned darkly and hurried to the small boat. He leaned down into Audra's face, then took a quick step away from her again, his head reeling with disgust when her unpleasant scent wafted up into his nostrils.

"Father John, please let me explain," Audra said, finally getting the strength and courage to stand up and climb over the side of the small boat.

She was very aware of being gawked at as people shimmied closer to get a look at the vagabond stowaway.

"I knew you were a reckless sort, but I would have never expected this," Father John said, sighing heavily. "Audra, what prompted you to do something this foolish?"

"Father John, you know why," Audra said, holding down the skirt of her cotton dress as the wind whipped against her. "I . . . I . . . have wanted to be free of the convent for so long. When I heard about this ship going to Oregon country, where all people are as free as the wind, I could not help but try my luck at freedom."

She swallowed hard. "But I could not stay hidden in that dreaded boat another minute," she then blurted out. She visibly shuddered. "I feel as though I have fleas in my hair." She scratched wildly at the flesh of her left arm. "I feel as though fleas are crawling all over me."

A large, gray-haired man dressed in a full black suit, with gold epaulets braided across the top of his coat, and with a captain's hat braced on his head against the wind, elbowed his way through the crowd. "What have we here?" he said in a friendly tone. "What is the cause of this commotion?"

When he finally made his way through the onlookers and he saw Audra, he stiffened, his pale blue eyes flickering quickly over her.

"Please, sir, take mercy on me and give me food and, Lordy be, please allow me a bath," Audra begged, her eyes pleading up at the tall, friendly faced man. "If you might also find someone who will lend me clean clothes, I shall always be grateful."

She lowered her eyes, swallowed hard, then looked

up at the captain again. "And I apologize for taking passage on your ship without paying for it," she murmured. "But . . . but . . . I have no money. What you see on me is all that I own." She looked over her shoulder, then grabbed her hairbrush. She clutched it to her breasts. "This, too, is mine."

Everyone still stood quietly watching.

Even the captain seemed at a loss of words.

Father John started to grab Audra by an arm, but stopped when a lovely, middle-aged lady stepped forward and reached her white-gloved hand out for Audra. She was dressed in maroon velvet, and her hair was hidden beneath a beautiful hat covered with fake flowers.

"My dear, I shall pay for your passage," Linda Shaughnessy said, her voice soft and filled with sympathy. "Come to my cabin. I shall see that you are well fed. I shall have warm water brought to the cabin for your bath. I will give you your choice of dresses from my trunks."

Stunned by the woman's generous offer, touched deeply by it, Audra started to fling herself into the arms of the lady but stopped when the wind wafted the smell of her armpits into her nostrils again, reminding her how badly she smelled and looked.

"Thank you so much, ma'am," Audra murmured, tears filling her eyes. "But how can I accept so much from you? I . . . I . . . shall never be able to repay you."

"No payment is needed," Linda said. She gently took Audra by an elbow. She nodded a thank-you to those who stepped back and allowed them to pass.

"Audra, we aren't through with discussing this," Father John said.

Audra gave Linda a soft, quiet, pleading look. "Please give me a moment with Father John?" she murmured, smiling at Linda as the woman gently removed her hand from her elbow. "Thank you."

Audra moved back through the crowd and stood before Father John. "Father John, please, *please* don't hate me for what I have done," she said, her voice breaking. "You know how imprisoned I felt at the convent. You know as well as I that I was there against my will." She reached up and ran her fingers through her hair. "You know how I hated having my hair cut so short. I despise it. I have hated everything my life became after father abandoned me. I beg you not to send me back to the convent."

Suddenly Father John drew her into his arms and hugged her. "Yes, I have always been aware of your unrest," he said thickly, gazing over her shoulder, quite aware of their audience. "When your father brought you to the convent, I felt it was the safest place for you."

He eased her away from him and gazed into her eyes. "But, Audra, you *will* return to San Francisco with me after my duties at the Nez Perce village are done," he said, his voice low and steady. "I promise I won't take you back to the convent."

Audra's heart raced with joy to think that finally he did understand!

Finally he was no longer going to dictate her world!

She was free!

And if Father John saw her as a free person, then

surely he would not deny her the choice to stay in Oregon country, for that was where she desired to be.

She wanted to meet with Chief Silver Wing again.

She had not been able to shake him from her mind. Her dreams had been filled with him.

Her hopes of thinking that Father John was going to allow her the freedom she wanted were dashed when he continued talking.

Slowly Audra stepped away from him, her heart sinking the more he talked. . . .

"No, once we return to San Francisco I won't take you back to the convent," Father John said, leaning his full weight against the cane when the ship rolled and dipped through a huge onslaught of waves. "But I will have to put you in an orphanage until you are old enough to go out on your own. I doubt that anyone will adopt someone of your age."

Audra was momentarily rendered speechless. She had been foolish to believe that he had changed that quickly. But she wouldn't allow him to dictate another second of her life. Once she arrived at the Nez Perce village with him, she would get Chief Silver Wing on her side. She understood why it had been impossible for him to speak up in her behalf while he was in San Francisco. He was on foreign soil among strangers who, for the most part, hated Indians.

But in Oregon country, he was on his own land among his own people.

He was chief!

He ruled!

She wouldn't even have to plead her case with him. He knew the meaning of freedom. He would understand her hunger for it. In her dreams they had met and loved. Outside the realm of a dream, couldn't it truly happen?

Unless she had misread Silver Wing's feelings for her?

What if, instead, he was married?

If so, what then would she do?

Where would she go?

Who . . . would . . . ever want her?

"Young lady, come along with me," Linda said, reaching a hand out for Audra. She frowned at Father John. "I think you've had enough badgering for one day. While in my care, you can do as you please, say what you wish to say, and go where you want to go."

Audra turned and stared with disbelief at the beautiful lady. Never had anyone offered her such kindness.

Of course, in his own way, Father John thought he had been kind to her. Girls came and went at his convent. Surely their faces became one blur to those who worked there.

"Thank you kindly, ma'am," Audra murmured, smiling widely as she hurried toward Linda. "You'll never know how much I appreciate what you are doing for me."

Once again, Linda gazed at Father John, then looked away. "I believe I know well enough," she said, placing a gentle arm around Audra's waist. "You see, I was placed in a convent when I was fifteen. I was one of the lucky ones. I was at the convent for only three years, and then I met a man who has given me the world."

"Your husband?" Audra asked, taking the narrow steps that led down to the ship's cabins.

"Yes, my darling husband, my Charles," Linda said, taking the last step. She lifted a kerosene lamp from where it hung with many others along the wall. She held it out before her and Audra. "He awaits my arrival in Canada. I left him only long enough to do some shopping for clothes in San Francisco."

"You live in Canada?" Audra asked, her eyes wide with excitement. "How does it differ from America? Is it beautiful?"

"It doesn't differ at all," Linda said, laughing softly. "Well, it *is* much colder. But beautiful? Yes, so much it takes your breath away."

"I'd like to go there someday," Audra said as they both stopped before one of the doors that led inside to her private suite.

"You can, if you wish, travel on with me to Canada," Linda said, placing a key in the lock. "You can stay with me and Charles for as long as you wish. We have a large enough home." Sullenly she gazed over at Audra. "And there are no children. It seems I am not capable of having them."

"I'm so sorry," Audra said softly. "That is, if you wanted children."

"Yes, many," Linda said. "But as it is, I just filled my home with pets. I have four dogs, three cats, and two sets of lovebirds."

"It sounds like a paradise," Audra said, her breath stolen when she stepped inside a cabin that was plush with velveteen furniture, drapes, and a bed so large she felt as though she would be lost if she climbed onto it.

"A paradise you can share with me and Charles, if you wish," Linda said, closing the door behind them. She smiled as Audra still took in everything with her eyes. "Audra, I shall leave now for a moment to order you a bath and get you a tray piled high with delicious food."

Linda handed Audra the lamp. "Would you wish to travel on to Canada with me?" she asked softly.

Audra looked quickly over at her. The offer was so tempting, it would be so easy to say "yes."

But then again, she had to see Silver Wing.

"Thank you so much," Audra murmured, not believing that she was going to turn down such a fine offer.

But in a sense, wouldn't living with the lady be almost the same as the convent? Wouldn't Audra feel as confined if she went and lived in a house that did not belong to her?

Somehow, someway, she wanted a place of her own.

She wanted a man to call her own.

She wanted Silver Wing!

"But I must decline the offer," Audra quickly answered, realizing while saying it that she still had Father John to deal with when the time came for him to return to San Francisco.

Hopefully by then Silver Wing would want her!

"Think it through more carefully," Linda said, gently patting Audra's arm. "We have several more days of travel ahead of us. It will give you time to become better acquainted with me. I would love for you to become that daughter I shall never have."

Being described as anyone's daughter was threatening to Audra. She *was* someone's daughter. She shivered at being someone else's!

"I'm so very hungry, ma'am," Audra said, quickly changing the subject.

"Linda," the lovely woman said. "Please call me Linda." She opened the door, then turned and faced Audra again. "I shan't be long." Her gaze swept quickly over Audra. "I shall have bathwater brought to the cabin."

Audra smiled weakly, then turned and stared all around her again at the lushness.

She looked through the small porthole and saw the vastness of the water in all directions. Hopefully these next several days would pass quickly.

She was actually going to see Silver Wing again!

No matter if he wanted her or not, she would stay in Oregon country.

She would find a way to make her home there, finally *free*.

10

His eye was dry; no tears could flow,
A hollow groan first spoke his woe.
———WILLIAM BLAKE

Harry Weston found it difficult teaching the Nez Perce
the Bible.

He learned that the Nez Perce were guided by
supernatural powers found in nature. Things such as
fish, birds, and heavenly bodies influenced them in
important ways.

Tired of pretending to appreciate their beliefs, and
loath to be around them, Harry had suffered through
each day as he wore the damnable black robe and
read from the Bible. He needed more time to steal
their Appaloosa horses and to study the land.

But today, the children asked too many questions,
and Harry could no longer hold his temper at bay.
When a young brave spoke up, asking him in a mock-
ing tone to prove his theories of how the world began,
Harry's face flooded with color.

The skirt of his black robe blowing in the breeze,
he rushed into the trees and snapped off a twig from
a low-hanging limb.

Huffing, his pulse racing, he went back to the group of wide-eyed children, who sat in a circle on blankets.

Throwing curse words into the air like bullets firing from a gun, Harry stood over the young brave who he saw as the most insolent of the group. Growling beneath his breath, he grabbed the young brave by the arm and yanked him up from the others.

Holding the young brave as he struggled to get free, Harry began switching his bare legs with the twig until bright, scarlet welts appeared on his copper flesh.

"I'll teach you to respect Father Harry!" Harry screamed. "You will *all* feel the weight of my displeasure should you continue questioning me."

Silver Wing was drawn from his longhouse by the loud cursing and threats being shouted at the young braves.

When he saw what Harry was doing, he became enraged. Of late he had witnessed too much that hadn't seemed right about this less than holy man. The white man dressed in the black robe with its white collar had even brought jugs of firewater into the village.

Silver Wing never expected a holy man to approve of firewater, for most white people who were familiar with the fiery liquid never willingly handed it over to redskins . . . unless they did it for devious reasons.

Silver Wing had confiscated the firewater before any of his warriors had consumed it, and had poured it out in the presence of the holy man.

Silver Wing had waited for the black-robed man's

reaction, ready to imprison him if even the slightest anger entered his eyes.

To Silver Wing's surprise, Father Harry Weston had done nothing but watch the ground absorb the alcohol like a hungry sponge, then had turned, expressionless, and had gone, alone, to his lodge.

But now, after witnessing the holy man's heartless outburst, Silver Wing had proof enough that this man no longer deserved to teach the children. Anyone who touched the Nez Perce children with such disrespect deserved no respect themselves.

His heart pounding with anger, his spine stiff, Silver Wing stamped over to the group of children until he reached Harry Weston.

Being absorbed in punishing the child and enjoying the young brave's wails of pain, Harry hadn't noticed Silver Wing's approach. As he continued to switch the legs of the child, his curse words stinging the ears of those watching horrified, he unknowingly disclosed his true person to the Nez Perce.

Silver Wing stepped up behind Harry, grabbed him by the nape of the neck, and lifted him away from the child.

"You, who came to my people, who were given lodging, food, and who was trusted, treat our children in such a manner?" Silver Wing shouted, ignoring Harry's cries of pain as Silver Wing dragged him by the neck away from the children.

"You, who call yourself holy, can treat the children in such a way?" Silver Wing continued heatedly. "How dare you curse in their presence. How dare you harm them! Your teaching days are over, white man.

I am going to burn the Bibles and hymnals. I am going to burn your black robe in the same fire as those books that I now deem as unholy!"

"Please have mercy!" Harry cried, reaching back, trying to dislodge Silver Wing's hand from his neck. "You're hurting me. Please stop! Forgive me. I did not know what I was doing. I . . . I . . . just lost my temper, that's all."

"Quiet, white man!" Silver Wing shouted. "You are wasting your time begging this Nez Perce chief."

"You're wrong to do this to me," Harry cried. "Do you hear me? You're wrong!"

Silver Wing ignored him. He took him to a windowless longhouse at the far end of the village and threw him inside, then slammed the door and slid the bolt lock in place.

"This is the equivalent to your white man's jail," Silver Wing said through small slits in the door. "It, and others like it, were built expressly for people like you. As for what will happen to you now that I see you for what you are? I will meet in council with my warriors and decide a proper punishment for you, a man who has brought nothing but disillusionment and uneasiness to my people, especially the innocent children."

Harry leaned close to the slits and peered out at Silver Wing. "God will strike all of your people dead if you keep me locked away like this!" he cried.

"Your God is powerless among my people," Silver Wing said sullenly. "My people's *Tah-mah-ne-weq,* Great Spirit, is the Nez Perce's true God, now and for always. I was wrong to go against our Great Spirit and allow the white man's book to be so important to me. I was wrong to ask for the white man's book to be brought among my people."

Desperate to get set free, afraid he would soon be killed by the Nez Perce once the council had made a decision about his fate, Harry pointed heavenward. "Look up there!" he cried. "See Jesus? See Jesus up there?" He then pointed at himself. "No matter how you try to deny there is a true God that rules the world, claiming only your Great Spirit as the almighty, there is Jesus! Silver Wing, I am Jesus' messenger. I have come to your people so that they might reach the land of a better life after death. The Bible is the only book that tells people how to escape the 'fire land' of the hereafter. Silver Wing, although you question the way I choose to do it, I *was* trying to change your people's lives to a better spirit life."

"White man, you are anything but holy," Silver Wing hissed as he leaned his face down so that he was looking directly into Harry's glinting eyes. "Keep quiet. I never want to hear another thing about the white man's Jesus. And hear me well. If you say one more word about the Bible and its teachings, I will not wait until I meet in council with my warriors to discuss your fate. I will kill you now!"

"I'll be quiet, all right," Harry growled. "I wasn't cut out to minister to 'heathens,' anyhow."

Although his knees were trembling, he tried to control his fear. When he didn't show up at the hideout tonight, his men would realize that he had been jailed like a criminal and find a way to come and release him.

Before coming to the Nez Perce village in the black robe and with his satchel full of the stolen Bibles and hymnals, Harry had established his hideout deep into the mountains with his friends.

After he had successfully convinced Silver Wing that he was there in Father John's place, he had secretly ridden to his hideout.

Many Appaloosa horses had already been stolen and placed in the hideout's corral.

They planned to raid the Nez Perce village prior to staking a claim on much of their land.

Puzzled by Harry's lack of fear, Silver Wing walked away from him, troubled. There was something more about this man that he hadn't discovered.

Would others like him follow?

Did Harry Weston know they would?

Was Father John going to come and join Father Harry?

If so, when? And what true sort of man was Father John?

Something told him that he had better prepare his people for the arrival of more holy men, and not to welcome them, as they had Father Harry.

None of them were ever to be trusted again!

He remembered now, as he had so often since he had returned from his voyage from San Francisco, the woman with the red hair. He should have known by the way she was treated by the holy man called John that he should never trust any Bible-toting white man.

Whenever he allowed his thoughts to stray to the woman, he felt guilty for not having helped her.

Something magical occurred between them in the short time they were together.

When he thought of her now, he hungered for her lips.

His arms ached to hold her!

But if he did ever have the opportunity to see her again, was *she* even to be trusted?

From then on, white people were to be regarded the enemy!

11

That God forbid that made me first your slave,
I should in thought control your times of Pleasure,
Or at your hand th' account of hours to crave,
Being your vassal, bound to stay your leisure.
                    ——WILLIAM SHAKESPEARE

JUNE—*Toose-te-ma-sa-tahl,* Season for digging roots.

Audra rode a palomino pony through the Oregon wilderness. She was thankful her father had taught her to ride before he succumbed to alcohol.

Father John rode effortlessly next to her, his black robe blending in with the horse.

She had questioned Father John about how he knew the art of riding horses so well. She could not even envision him being anything but a priest, his pale face proving that he scarcely left the church or convent.

He had told her that he had been raised in Kentucky with a family of nine brothers and sisters. They had all been skilled horsemen. Their parents even raced some of their finest horses at the large racetracks in Kentucky.

But when Father John had gotten the calling to give his life to the service of the Lord, he had left all of that behind and had entered a seminary.

San Francisco was his first place to practice as a priest at age twenty-five.

Now fifty, he was still in the same church.

As Audra rode onward with Father John and Dennis Bell, she found herself in awe of this beautiful, somewhat mysterious land. It was a stupendous place of unspoiled scenery. The forested highlands were overhung with fog, like lace draping over the trees.

She could hardly believe the beautiful maze of canyons, the silver threads of rushing rivers, and the towering barren hills.

She could now see why Silver Wing called this his "precious land." Black bears, mountain goats, bighorn sheep, and elk roamed the steep slopes and deep valleys. Fish were abundant in the streams and rivers.

Audra had heard about Indians going to the mountains to get spirited and physical sustenance and now understood why.

She thought back to when she had arrived at the Dalles Trading Post in Oregon country. She had almost decided to go on with Linda Shaughnessy to Canada. Yet how could she be sure about the fine life Linda offered?

Perhaps the beautiful middle-aged woman planned to take Audra to her home and turn her into a slave. Being a stranger in Canada, Audra wouldn't have had any choice but to do as she was told. For certain she would have no money to flee back to America.

And being this close to Silver Wing's home, she felt something hidden was beckoning her there.

For certain her heart ached to see Silver Wing again. If their time together could be as it was in her dreams, she would find happiness that until now eluded her.

She hoped that when she did arrive at Silver Wing's village that Harry Weston hadn't spoiled things for her. The Nez Perce would not trust white men if Harry had wronged them.

Why would Silver Wing trust her any more than Harry?

He didn't know her.

Audra gazed over at Dennis Bell. An old friend of Father John's, Dennis was a middle-aged, sandy-haired, freckle-faced thin man, with a white-toothed smile that never ended.

When the ship had first arrived at the Dalles Trading Post and Dennis Bell was there to greet Father John, the two men eagerly hugged, then talked at length of old times.

While they chatted and laughed, Audra had moved slowly around the trading post. She had never been in one before. It sat on the banks of the Columbia River a short distance from where the river narrowed and boiled between high basalt ledges before it approached the cascades.

At the Dalles she had seen Indians from another tribe other than the Nez Perce who had made their temporary camps around the post. Their camping ground had been boisterous with dogs and children, with the foul stench of decaying fish heads lining the rocky shore above the turbulent riverbank. Keel boats, canoes, and rafts lined the river.

She had thought at first they were of the Blackfoot tribe, the ardent enemy of the Nez Perce to be avoided at all cost, but then learned they were from Washington state, the tribe known as Suquamish.

Audra's thoughts were suddenly interrupted, and she pulled a tight rein to stop her horse. At once, the entourage were surrounded by many Indians on beautiful, proud Appaloosa steeds.

She knew the tribe. It was a party of Nez Perce, for Silver Wing eased his horse away from the others and rode up closer, then stopped only a few feet from Audra. His deep gray eyes were no longer friendly. His right hand clutched a club made from the hard, heavy *syriaga* found growing among the canyon streams.

Nearly an arm's length and tied to Silver Wing's wrist by a thong loop, the weapon was frightening. His many warriors carried powerful bows made from wild sheep horn.

Audra had heard Dennis Bell discussing these things with Father John as they made their way slowly through the wilderness. He had said that an arrow from such a bow could drive clear through a deer and that a good archer could launch a dozen arrows with their flaked-stone arrowheads while the opponent would be awkwardly reloading a muzzle loader.

As Audra's pulse raced at the mere sight of Silver Wing, having for so long dreamed of a time they might meet again, she did not want to feel threatened. When they had been together in San Francisco, she had found him warm and wonderful. Surely since then he hadn't changed.

In one quick glance she saw that he was not wearing a breechclout as he had when they had first met.

Today he wore a shirt of dressed skins, long leggings, knee-high moccasins, and a piece of otter skin about his neck. His hair, blacker than charcoal, hung long and loose down his straight back.

"White holy man, you were wrong to send the evil man who calls himself Father Harry to my village to preach your Bible to the Nez Perce," Silver Wing said, his mind more on Audra than the answers he sought from the white man.

He couldn't understand why this woman who was more beautiful than the skies was there with the holy man. Did the holy man trust her so little that he brought her with him to keep an eye on her?

Then he remembered something that Father John had said when they had been discussing the priest coming to Nez Perce land. Father John had said that he needed to bring people with him to see to his meals. Surely he had brought the woman with him to cook and clean his clothes for him.

If so, Audra was still no less free than when she had lived in San Francisco.

His heart pounded at the sight of her. His arms wanted to reach out and hold her. He wanted to tell her that he would change things for her.

Yet he had to keep remembering that she was white-skinned and could not be trusted.

Father John started to speak, but Silver Wing interrupted. "You were invited to my village," he said, his eyes now shifting to Father John. "Not that heartless man who mistreats children."

Audra placed a hand to her mouth at the mention of Harry Weston mistreating the Indian children, al-

ready abhorred by the fact he called himself "Father."
He was a liar and a cheat. He was like her father had
become after discovering his love of alcohol. Harry
Weston had been chided more than once by Father
John for bringing whiskey to his room at the convent.

"Silver Wing, I didn't send anyone to your village,"
Father John said as Silver Wing finally allowed him
to speak. He edged his horse closer to Silver Wing's,
hopefully to get his undivided attention. Father John
noticed how the chief's eyes feasted on Audra.

"Harry Weston is no priest," Father John said. "He
was my gardener. When you were at the rectory and
we were discussing my coming to your land to bring
Bibles, Harry must have overheard us. He devised this
plan to come ahead of me and pretend to be what he
is not. He has deceived not only you, but also me. I
put my trust in that man. I was wrong to."

"What reasons would this man have to come to my
village and pretend to be what he is not?" Silver Wing
asked dryly.

"I have an idea, yet I cannot be sure," Father John
said, hesitating to say more to Silver Wing until he
had talked to Harry. He could tell that Silver Wing
didn't trust him. Surely, because of Harry's devious-
ness, no white man would be believed now.

"Silver Wing, this is my friend, Dennis Bell," Father
John then said, motioning toward Dennis with a hand.
"I'm sure you know him from the Dalles Trading Post.
He wrote me. He told me that he saw Harry Weston
at the post wearing the robe of a priest. Dennis followed him. He saw him at your village pretending to
be a priest. I came as soon as I could to make things

right for your people. I will preach the true word of God to your people. As promised, I will teach them the true meaning of the Bible."

Silver Wing's gaze shifted to Dennis Bell, whom he had known from the trading post, a man until now he thought he could trust.

He turned to Father John.

Then, catching everyone off guard, Silver Wing rode up to Audra and grabbed her from her horse and rode away with her, his warriors bringing those who were now his prisoners behind him.

Audra was stunned speechless by Silver Wing singling her out in such a way. She was torn with how to feel. A part of her was now afraid of this powerful, muscled, angry chief.

Yet she was still in awe of him.

His eyes were fierce.

His breathing was sharp and harsh!

She was afraid to discover to what extent Harry had actually harmed the children. Surely it was terribly bad to have caused Silver Wing's fury to be so roused against whites.

When Silver Wing rode into the Indian settlement, Audra first noticed that it was protected by ridges and hills at the bottom of a steep, but open, valley with ample escape routes.

Then she saw two tall cedar poles resplendent with carvings. An eagle was on the top. Carvings of toads, bears, and blackfish decorated the side. What appeared to be spirit-guide symbols were at the base of the poles.

As Silver Wing rode farther into the village, Audra

looked slowly around her at the cluster of longhouses with their cedar-plank sidings nestled beneath lovely, tall trees. Their gabled roofs were made of split cedar shakes. Some houses looked to be at least one hundred feet in length. Others were smaller. Bark canoes leaned against the walls of all of the longhouses.

She noticed the carvings on the houses. She had read somewhere that this was how some Indians recorded the tales of past eras.

The smokehouse was a large building with broad double doors. Tantalizing aromas wafted from it as she envisioned venison hams, elk, moose, bison, ducks. . . .

She looked guardedly at the people as they came from their lodges, their eyes wide with wonder. Some of the men wore white buffalo robes or elk skins dressed with beads, while the women wore ankle-length goatskin dresses. Seashells and mother-of-pearl accented their long black hair, and hung down the front of their dresses.

When Silver Wing ignored his people and rode onward without addressing anyone, his anger still tightly held within him, Audra became afraid.

She turned to look for Father John and the others and saw they were no longer on horses. Instead they were ushered into a longhouse that had no windows. Shocked, she realized they were prisoners—and now she knew she would be, too.

She wondered where Silver Wing was taking her, glad she would not be imprisoned with the men.

When Silver Wing finally stopped before a longhouse, he dismounted and lifted Audra from the horse. Gently he led her inside, where a fire burned in the earthen floor in the center of the lodge, the smoke escaping through the opening in the roof along the ridgepoles.

Relieved, she saw this was obviously not a place of imprisonment. The house had windows. Surely he did not see her as the enemy.

However, her heart sank when she made out a woman in the large room.

Audra scarcely breathed as Silver Wing left her standing just inside the door and knelt beside the woman who lay on a bed of blankets on the far side of the fire.

Audra's heart sank even more when she realized the woman, who seemed to be Audra's age, was very pregnant.

Then Silver Wing drew the woman up in his arms, hugged her, and gently rocked her as he spoke in his Nez Perce language. Audra suddenly felt jealous, for surely this pregnant woman was Silver Wing's wife.

Tears filled her eyes, and she felt foolish to have allowed herself to dream these long months about a man who could never be anything to her. Audra turned her back to them and tried to focus on other things . . . on fine furs and skins of every description hanging on the far wall, as well as well-tanned buckskins, robes, deerskin bags, and fancy plumes.

The woman began talking to Silver Wing in a soft, weak voice. Audra turned and saw how frail she was, and her jealousy quickly turned to pity. The woman was dying.

Audra had just begun to relax when Silver Wing's

hand pulled her roughly to another longhouse close by.

Audra's spine stiffened, and she went cold inside when she saw it had no windows, only narrow slits at the door.

She concluded from this that Silver Wing had only stopped at the other longhouse to see how his wife was before bringing Audra to her place of captivity.

"Sit," Silver Wing said, shoving Audra down on a mat woven from cattail leaves on the earthen floor beside the cold ashes of the fire pit.

Audra sat stiffly on the mat and watched Silver Wing prepare a fire. Her fear mounted that he saw her as an enemy. Apparently she had never been anything to him. Those magical moments in the courtyard back in San Francisco she had only imagined.

The fire burning gently among the logs now, Silver Wing sat down beside Audra on another mat. "I do not know why you are with the white holy man," he said as he turned to Audra. "But I must tell you that I cannot allow any men who call themselves holy to intrude on my people's cherished land ever again. This land belongs solely to my people. With her free bounty of land and waters, the earth is my people's mother and nourishes them as any mother would her children. We Nez Perce live in a state of balance and harmony with our surroundings, almost a natural part of the country itself. The wicked, white holy man who mistreated our children and brought lies and deceit among my people has threatened this balance. I should have never agreed to let any Bible-toting man come here."

"But you must not let one white man's evil scheme make you distrust all holy men," Audra said, relaxing more now that she was able to talk *with* Silver Wing. She would make him understand.

"All Bible-toting people are bad," Silver Wing said, causing Audra's hopes to falter. "I will never believe in the white man's God. The inanimate objects, as well as the creatures that live, are bound like the Nez Perce people to the earth, and possess a spiritual being that is joined through a great, unseen world of powers to the spirit within an individual Indian. I do not see white people as a part of this scheme of things."

He rose to his feet, went to the door, and opened it. He stared past his village into the beauty of the forest. "I cannot allow white men to threaten my people's way of life ever again," he said thickly. "The Nez Perce are brothers to the animals and trees, to the grasses seared by the sun, to the insects on the rocks, to the brooks running through snowbanks in winter, and the rain dropping from the leaves of bushes."

He turned and glared down at Audra. "I was wrong to invite the white man and his book he calls holy among my people," he said. "Everything about the white man who calls himself Father Harry was bad."

Still wanting Silver Wing to understand about Harry Weston, Audra rose to her feet and went to him. She wanted to reach out and touch him, but knowing now that he had a wife, she kept her distance as she pleaded with her eyes.

"The man you call Father Harry was wrong to allow you to think that he was a priest," Audra murmured.

"He is a false prophet. He is not a man of God. He only pretended to be. I truly apologize for any wrong Harry might have done to your people, especially . . . especially . . . your children. I plead with you to believe me. I beg you to give Father John a chance. He came to you with the best of intentions."

She lowered her eyes. "So . . . did . . . I," she said, her voice breaking.

When she felt his hand lift her chin, his flesh so warm against hers, her face so close to his, Audra's knees grew weak with a new passion.

But she had to fight it. He was married. She was nothing to him . . . except now, his enemy.

Yet when he spoke to her, his voice soft and no longer filled with a cold, tight anger, his mystique lured her on.

She had heard of love at first sight, and was sure she loved Silver Wing. But he had a wife . . . a wife carrying his child!

"I cannot understand why you can speak so favorably of this man Father John who kept you against your will," Silver Wing said, his pulse racing with desires he had held at bay for too long now.

He wanted to draw her into his arms, this woman he had fallen in love with that first moment he saw her beneath the stars.

His hand left her chin and went to her hair. She shivered when he slowly ran his fingers through her soft red curls, her heart pounding so out of control she felt faint.

"How can you speak so favorably of Father John when he forced your hair to be cropped short?" he said, the touch of her hair like silk against his fingers. "It is such a beautiful color. It is the color of sunshine."

She wanted to scream at him to quit talking to her so kindly, to quit running his fingers through her hair, all of which was making her want him even more—yet she knew he belonged to someone else.

She held herself erect when he withdrew his hand from her hair and took her hand in his. He continued to talk, his eyes like hot coals branding her as she willed herself to stand her ground and not reveal her feelings to him.

"How is it that Father John has allowed your release and brought you with him to Oregon country?" he asked.

He was aware of her trembling hand and sensed her feelings for him, for there was no disguising passion. In Audra's green eyes he saw it and knew that she was trying to guard against it. Was he not the enemy now?

He himself was trying to guard against such feelings for her, until he knew she could be trusted.

"Father John did not allow my release from the convent," Audra said, fighting to keep her voice steady beneath his studious stare. "I ran away when I heard that Father John was coming to your land on a ship. I stowed away on that ship. When Father John became aware of my presence there, he had no choice but to allow me to travel here with him."

She lowered her eyes and swallowed hard. "But . . . but . . . Father John is going to take me back with him to San Francisco and . . . put . . . me in an orphanage," she said softly.

"An orphanage?" Silver Wing said, forking an eyebrow. "What is this thing called . . . orphanage?"

"An orphanage is a place where children are taken when . . . when . . . they have no parents," she said, her voice breaking. "I tried to tell Father John that I am too old to go there, but he still insists on it."

"You do not have to go to an orphanage," Silver Wing said, gently placing a hand on her cheek. "You can stay with my people. Once I see that you can be trusted, you will be a free woman. You can do as you please. You can come and go as you please."

Audra was rendered speechless by his kindness. And she knew that he meant what he said. Although she scarcely knew him, she knew that he must be a man of his word. A man chosen for a chief had to be a man of truth and trustworthiness.

Silver Wing eased his hand to his side. He bent to his haunches before the fire and slid another log into the flames. "It is a sad time for me," he said, his voice low and drawn. "My sister, Climbing Rose, is in a weakened condition because of her pregnancy. Prior to my arrival home from San Francisco her husband was killed by a Blackfoot Indian. He had strayed too far on Blackfoot land during a hunt. It is now my place to care for my sister. She weakens more each day. Before long she will be joining her husband in the sky. The unborn child will probably travel the same road with Climbing Rose."

Audra's breath caught as he spoke of his sister.

Was . . . that . . . his sister?

It wasn't his wife?

Her thoughts were interrupted when Silver Wing began to talk again in a sad tone.

Audra inched down on the mat beside him, her love for him growing with each spoken word.

"My heart suffers so," Silver Wing said, the agony there, so apparent in his voice. "I am going to lose my sister after having suffered the loss of my parents long ago, and then my wife. My wife was killed four winters ago by a bear during *kehm-mes,* camas harvesting season. She died before giving me a child."

He turned to Audra. "I can never have my sister, once she is gone, or my mother and father back, but I hope to have another wife soon, and then many children," he said thickly.

He wanted to tell Audra that he had thought of no one but her since they had met, and that he hungered to have her as his wife.

But he could not allow himself to trust her that quickly. He hoped that she would give him cause to trust her . . . and soon.

Audra's heart ached for him, for she could feel his despair. He had suffered even more in life than she. He had lost a wife and both his parents. He was about to lose a sister.

The woes of Audra's life now seemed trivial compared to his.

She wanted to tell him that she wished to be loved by him and to be allowed to openly love him, yet she was still afraid to reveal such feelings to him. At this moment she was no less his prisoner than Father John, Dennis Bell, and the other four priests.

And what of Harry Weston? Was he imprisoned somewhere among those longhouses with no windows?

If so, what was Silver Wing's plan for him? Would there soon be an execution at his village? How many lives would be taken?

"Please release Father John and the others," Audra suddenly blurted out. "Please release me."

Silver Wing gazed at her for a moment longer, then rose to his feet and left.

Audra cringed when she heard him lock the door from the outside. She wondered how he expected her to prove to him that she was trustworthy when he locked her inside the longhouse, helpless?

She did not want to believe that she had fled one stifled life to find herself stifled by another.

But surely it was not for long. If Silver Wing felt about her the way he seemed to, she would be released soon.

Surely he would tell her that she was that woman who could fill his empty heart with love and tenderness.

"I so badly want to be," she whispered, settling down on a mat beside the fire. "Please, oh, please, don't wait long, Silver Wing."

She looked around her at the drab interior of the longhouse, the dark shadows creeping in around her.

She hugged herself with her arms as chills rode her spine.

"I feel so trapped in this horrid place," she whispered, her voice broken with sobs.

12

I see the wrong that round me lies,
I feel the guilt within.
      ——JOHN GREENLEAF WHITTIER

It was midnight. Shadowy figures moved stealthily through the Nez Perce village. When the four men came to Harry Weston's longhouse, they pried the lock from the door and stepped inside into darkness.

"I didn't think you'd ever get here," Harry said, shaking first one man's hand, and then another. "Lord, how'd you manage it? Aren't there any Indian guards? You were just allowed to slip into the village and not be seen?"

"We were watching from a bluff when you were placed in this longhouse," Frank Bradley said, raking his fingers through his long red greasy hair. "We've waited until tonight to come for you to make sure no guards or sentries were watching you."

"I heard a commotion earlier today," Harry said, shaking off the black robe. He nodded a thank-you to Adam Decker when Adam gave him a change of clothes. "Did you see what caused it?"

"Yep, seems that Father John you told us about arrived today," Adam said, resting his hands on his holstered pistols. "Dennis Bell was with him, as well as four other black-robed men, and also a lady with short red hair."

"You don't say," Harry said, forking an eyebrow. "That description fits only one lady I know—Audra. I wonder why she came with them? It don't make much sense. Not after the effort it took for Father John to keep that pretty thing from leaving the convent." He chuckled. "She is all fire and brimstone, that one."

"Hurry, Harry," Fred Lucas said as he looked from the door, watching for any signs of movement outside. "I want to get outta here. I'd not want any savages catchin' me in their village. I'm not hankerin' for a scalpin'."

"I've got my clothes changed," Harry said, kicking the black robe aside. "Let's go."

"I'd sure like to take that redheaded wench with us," Adam said, chuckling. "I've been without a woman for too long. They say redheads are quite feisty in bed. Let's go and get her, Harry. What do you say?"

"I say you're as loony as they come if you think I'm going to be bothered with that bitch," Harry growled. "Come on. Let's go, gents."

They scampered behind the longhouses and soon found cover in the forest until they reached the tethered horses.

They swung themselves into their saddles and rode off.

Harry leaned low as his horse wound its way through the trees. He laughed to himself as he thought of how his antics had paved the way for a miserable life for Father John at the village. Father John and the others might even be beheaded by the savage heathens.

But one thing he couldn't laugh about was that his plans had gone awry. They had not come to full fruition before he lost his head and switched the damn little savage on the legs.

Because of his damn temper, he might have cost himself much of the land and many Appaloosa horses.

He had to find another way. He hadn't come this far to give up all that easily.

13

O! That my young life were a lasting dream!
My spirit not awakening till the beam
Of an eternity should bring the morrow.
                    ——EDGAR ALLAN POE

After taking a warm sponge bath, Audra sat beside the fire in her assigned longhouse. She was wearing a goatskin dress and soft moccasins that a woman had brought to her along with the bathwater.

As Silver Wing sat beside her, carving animals on a huge bow, which seemed new and never used, Audra ate ravenously, her appetite having not been disturbed by her present circumstances.

Plucking another piece of meat from the wooden tray, she cast Silver Wing another glance. Today he wore nothing in his hair, nor any ornaments around his neck or arms. His raven-black hair hung down to his waist and was still wet from what she assumed to have been a morning swim in the nearby river. His copper skin glistened beautifully beneath the light of the fire, as did his dark gray eyes when he caught her eye.

Not sure of what to say or to do now that he had locked her away like a fiendish criminal, Audra had decided not to say another thing to him until she knew her eventual fate.

Yes, he had said that once he knew that she could be trusted, she would be free to go.

But how was she to prove this trust if she wasn't allowed from the longhouse?

The only time she had left the lodge was when a Nez Perce woman had come for her and had taken her into the forest to take care of her private business in the weeds.

Embarrassed by having an "escort," she had hesitated at first.

While with the woman, Audra had not attempted to escape. Not only because the Nez Perce maiden had a knife sheathed at her waist, but because Audra wanted Silver Wing's trust.

Now, with Silver Wing so close to her, she could still feel his eyes on her even though she had looked quickly away from him.

Oh, how she wanted to get these tense moments behind her. And she hoped that, although she had had her troubled moments with Father John, she could speak in his behalf again and help achieve his release, as well as the other men.

"I see that you are enjoying your food," Silver Wing said, smiling as he watched Audra gulp down one piece of meat after another. "That is good. That proves that you do not feel all that threatened by those of my people who are not familiar to you. Soon, if all goes well and I feel that I can trust you, you will mingle with my people. They, as well as you, will become acquainted."

Comfortably full, Audra shoved the platter away from her. "I don't understand why you can't put your trust in me now," she murmured, seeing his eyes on her hair again, which made her doubly self-conscious of its hideous length.

"I wrongly put my trust in the white man who brought Bibles and songs to my people," Silver Wing said sullenly, his smile having gone with the very thought of Harry Weston.

Audra smoothed her hands down the front of the dress as she positioned her legs more comfortably beneath its soft folds. "Where *is* Harry?" she asked guardedly. "Is he also your prisoner?"

"He is locked away, *xoyim-xoyim*, alone, from the other white men," Silver Wing grumbled, his eyes on his work as his fingers were busy again carving a bear onto his bow. "His fate will be decided soon. A council will be held. Whatever is decided there will be done."

"His fate?" Audra gasped, her heart skipping a beat. "Do you mean . . . you . . . might decide that he will be put to death?"

Having said too much already, for council discussions were a private matter, Silver Wing's lips tightened.

And he had to fight his feelings for this beautiful woman. The more he looked at her, the more he wanted her. He felt foolish now for having come to sit with her as she ate, except that his whole night had been filled with images of her. He had hardly been able to wait until daybreak so that it would look all right for him to be with her again. It was normal for a warrior to work on a new bow in the presence of a lady.

It gave *him* a way to busy his hands when, in truth,

he wished to use them to touch and caress the woman of his intrigue.

When he felt that he could trust her, he would reveal his true feelings for her. Hopefully by then, she would share her feelings for him. He could tell by the way she looked at him that she wanted more than friendship.

"I enjoyed breakfast," Audra said, sensing that his silence meant that he no longer wished to discuss such things as prisoners, especially not their fates.

She wished to have a more lighthearted conversation with him so he could trust her enough to release her. It had been so long since she had been truly free.

Even the boat after she had fled the convent was no better than a prison, especially after Father John discovered her there. At that moment she became his "ward" again, who must do and behave as *he* wanted.

Yet dreaming so long of moments like this, made her feel alive again.

Silver Wing was so close, she could smell the manliness of him.

He was so close that if she dared to, she could touch him!

"The word breakfast," Silver Wing said, forking an eyebrow as he gazed at her again. "What is the meaning of that word?"

"Breakfast is how one describes the morning meal," Audra said, smiling at the innocence of him not knowing such a thing as that. "This morning I not only enjoyed the meat, but the vegetables as well. I'm surprised to know that your people grow potatoes. It seems a strange crop for Indians to grow, especially since your village is so far north. Surely your growing period doesn't last long."

"We are north, yet the weather is hardly threatening to us, year-round," Silver Wing said, slowly running his hands over the smoothness of his bow. "There are only a few times during the winter months when the temperatures drop to freezing. We are protected from the harshest winds by the soaring mountains."

He picked up his knife and resumed carving on his bow, his eyes carefully watching the bear taking shape in the wood. "Men who called themselves British came to our land sometime ago and introduced vegetables to my people and encouraged the Nez Perce to grow them for trade to the forts in the Northwest country," he said softly.

He looked up at her again. "My people accepted the vegetable plants but refused to get involved with trading—especially to the stingy and taciturn British who my people disliked, not because they were evil, but because they were overbearing in their ways," he said. "Back then, when the British presence was evident everywhere, other tribes along the waterfront not only grew vegetables to trade, but also cultivated shellfish beds for the profit they received from the British. The Nez Perce are a tribe who did not want any solid connection with the British that threatened to destroy our solitude."

"You feel the same about Americans, don't you?" Audra dared to ask. "Yet you went to San Francisco to get Bibles from Americans."

Silver Wing's brow furrowed as he was quickly to correct her. "The Nez Perce *are* Americans," he said dryly. "We are the *first* Americans of this land."

"Yes, I . . . I . . . know," Audra said, seeing the hurt in his eyes as he spoke of being the first Americans, so obviously thinking of always being described as savages instead of the true people they are.

"The bow is so beautiful," Audra said, quickly changing the subject. "It's brand-new, isn't it?"

"Yes, it is new. It is almost done and ready for use," Silver Wing said, laying his knife aside. He held the three-foot-long bow out toward Audra. "Is it not a fine piece of weaponry?"

The fact that he labeled it as a weapon made a chill ride Audra's spine. She was reminded again of how deadly such a bow with its arrows was. "Yes, very fine," she murmured.

"It was made from a section of the curled horn of a mountain sheep," he said proudly. "After straightening it by a patient process of steaming and stretching it, it was backed with deer sinew that was attached by a glue made from the scraped skin of a salmon. Some use the boiled and dried blood of a sturgeon caught in the Snake River to get the same results."

He gripped it more strongly with a hand and held it up in the air. His eyes glistened with pride. "This bow is handsome *and* powerful," he said. "With this bow I will whip an arrow as long as the bow itself clear through the body of running animals."

He laid the bow aside and slid another piece of wood into the fire. "I soon will provoke captured rattlesnakes into striking pieces of liver and then smear my arrowheads with the venom," he said. "Although the venom is not as poisonous when it dries, there is still enough to kill instantly whatever animal the arrow enters."

A voice outside the longhouse suddenly spoke Silver Wing's name.

"Enter," Silver Wing said.

Audra turned to watch the door and looked up when a tall, thin warrior came into the lodge wearing a goatskin shirt and breeches. His hair was drawn back from his face with a headband made of otter skin.

"The white man who called himself Father Harry has escaped," Tall Shadow said, his hands doubling into tight fists at his sides as his eyes met and held with his chief's. "Someone came in the night and pried the lock off the door. All that is left in the longhouse is the man's black robe."

"He escaped?" Silver Wing said, rushing to his feet. "Who would help him? He knows no one in the area! He is a stranger!"

"Perhaps his strength was enough to loosen the lock," Tall Shadow said dryly. "I could not find prints outside the lodge. The grass grows too thickly there."

Silver Wing shrugged and sat down again beside the fire. "Return to your morning duties," he said, sighing. "And do not waste our warriors' time by searching for this man. He is one man alone against a vast wilderness. The trading post is too far away for him to reach it on foot. And even if he does, no one at the trading post would be foolish enough to side with the man against the Nez Perce."

Tall Shadow nodded and left the lodge, then returned only moments later with news more threatening to the Nez Perce.

"One of the white men is ill," Tall Shadow said solemnly. "He has strange red spots all over his body."

The description of red spots sent a warning through Audra. "Are there blisters which accompany the red spots?" she asked guardedly, thinking that if there was, the man might have chicken pox.

If not, more than likely he had measles. She had been downed with both diseases and knew symptoms of both. She had gotten through the chicken pox unscathed except for a few tiny scars on her legs.

But when she had been sick with measles, she had thought she was going to die.

She was now immune to both terrible diseases.

"There are no sores, only redness," Tall Shadow said.

"Measles," Audra whispered, afraid of what this meant to the Nez Perce. She had read somewhere how Indians died much more easily from white man's diseases. If measles spread among Silver Wing's people, there would be many deaths.

"Let me go and see the man that's ill," Audra said, moving quickly to her feet. "I would like to see what's wrong with him."

She paused, cleared her throat, then said, "But it's best that neither you nor your people get near him until I see what's wrong."

"What could be so wrong?" Silver Wing asked, forking an eyebrow as he rose to stand before her.

"Some diseases are worse than others," Audra said, afraid to even say the word "contagious" to him, not wanting to alarm him just yet.

Silver Wing gazed over at Tall Shadow and questioned him silently with his eyes, then gazed down at Audra again. "You know diseases well?" he asked, torn with what to do. He had wanted to keep her alone, away from the others, until he was positive that she was nothing like the white man who spoke lies to his people.

Yet how could he not trust someone whose eyes revealed so much warmth?

"Yes, I am familiar with some," she murmured.

"You can go and see the white man," he said, gently taking her by an arm. "But I will go with you."

"You can trust that I won't try to run away if you let me go without you," Audra said, pleading up at him with her eyes. "Please believe me?"

"Go," Silver Wing said, easing his hand from her arm. "But return soon and tell me how you read the white man's disease."

"Thank you," Audra said, then rushed from the longhouse with Tall Shadow. She gazed up at him. "I know the longhouse. You don't need to accompany me there."

"I will escort you there," Tall Shadow said blandly. "I will wait outside while you go in and see the white man."

Realizing that this Indian trusted her less than Silver Wing, Audra slowly nodded, then walked onward.

When she reached the longhouse, Tall Shadow slid the bolt lock aside then opened the door and closed it behind Audra as she stepped inside into the shadows of the room. The glow in the fire pit was the only light.

"Audra?"

She heard Father John's voice, and as her eyes grew used to the semidarkness, she saw him coming toward her.

Then she looked around and saw Dennis Bell lying on a pallet of blankets on the floor. She couldn't see his skin well enough to determine what he was infected with.

"It's measles, Audra," Father John said as he took her gently by an elbow and led her over to Dennis.

Audra swallowed hard.

She bent to her knees beside Dennis.

She reached a hand to his brow and touched it, the heat of his flesh causing her to flinch.

"I . . . I . . . was exposed recently by someone at the trading post," Dennis said, his voice weak, his temperature soaring. He grabbed for Audra's arm. "You . . . must . . . keep this from Silver Wing. It will cause a panic among his people. I . . . I . . . might even be put to death to stop the spread of the disease."

"Silver Wing wouldn't do that," Audra said, paling. "And I must tell him that you have something dangerous and that Silver Wing should forbid any of his people to get near you."

"I advise against it," Dennis said, then turned his eyes away and fell into a feverish sleep.

"What should I do?" Audra asked as she rose and faced Father John. She looked away from him and gazed at the other men, then back at Father John.

"What you *must* do," Father John said, clasping his hands together behind him. "We must do what is civilized. We don't want this to spread among the Indians. It would be disastrous."

"Then, I have no choice but to tell Silver Wing," Audra said, hurrying to the door.

"None of us have had measles," Father John said, stopping Audra dead in her tracks. "Ask if we can be moved, Audra."

She swallowed hard, took one last look at Dennis, then looked at Father John and nodded.

She waited for Tall Shadow to lock the door again, then walked with him back to where Silver Wing waited for her in the longhouse.

When they arrived, Tall Shadow waited to see that she went inside, then turned and left.

Audra gazed down at Silver Wing as he sat peacefully beside the lodge fire. He was still carving on his bow.

"Silver Wing?"

He looked up at her with questioning eyes.

She fell to her knees before him. "It's not good," she murmured. "Dennis Bell has . . . has . . . something contagious. You must keep your people away from him. And . . . and . . . Silver Wing, please allow the other white men to go to another longhouse. None of them have had the disease."

She sighed heavily. "And, Silver Wing, you must allow me to go and take care of Dennis," she murmured. "Perhaps I can do something to help save him."

"If the disease is so bad, how can you trust not getting it yourself?" Silver Wing said thickly.

"I have already had it," Audra said softly. "I am immune to getting it again."

"Then, the disease does not always kill its victims?" Silver Wing said, a keen relief rushing through him.

"No, it doesn't always kill," Audra said. "I am proof of that."

"I will see that the white men who are not ill are moved to the longhouse where Harry Weston was imprisoned," Silver Wing said, laying his bow aside. "But know that I will have another lock placed on that door. They will be guarded. They will not be able to escape."

He went to her and gently touched her cheek. "And, yes," he said softly, "you can care for the ailing man for as long as you wish."

"Thank you," Audra murmured, her insides stirring sensually at the touch of his hand.

He dropped his hand from her cheek and led her from the longhouse.

She turned her eyes up at him. "Please don't go all of the way with me to their longhouse," she murmured. "I . . . I . . . don't want you to contract the horrid disease."

"You can go there alone and the door will no longer be locked, so that you can come and go as you please, especially when you need fresh air after caring for the ill," Silver Wing said softly. "I will send cloths and water to the longhouse. I will have them left outside for you. When you need something more, you know that I will see that you have it."

It took all of Audra's willpower not to fling herself into this man's arms. Tears filled her eyes as she smiled up at him.

Then she broke into a run and hurried toward the longhouse. She prayed to herself that Dennis Bell didn't die. No matter how kind and wonderful Silver Wing had just been to her, she was afraid of what his reaction might be if a white man died of a dreaded, contagious disease in his village.

14

O Holy Night! from thee I learn to bear
What man has borne before!
Thou layest thy finger on the lips of care,
And they complain no more.
——Henry Wadsworth Longfellow

A loud wailing outside the longhouse awakened Audra with a start. Grabbing a blanket around her shoulders, she went to the door and opened it.

Her eyes widened and her heartbeat quickened when she saw a crowd of wailing Nez Perze standing before Silver Wing's lodge.

Some were even now chanting as they gazed with a deep sadness at Silver Wing's longhouse.

Audra placed a hand at her throat. "Silver Wing?" she gasped, her heart sinking to think that he might be ill.

Then suddenly she realized who *was* ill in his lodge. His sister!

Audra remembered how his sister had looked as though she was at death's door when Audra had last seen her.

"Oh, but what of the child?" she whispered, overwhelmed with sadness, wondering if not only the woman, but also her unborn baby had died.

Audra started to leave to comfort Silver Wing, but then turned quickly when Dennis spoke her name.

Feeling ashamed for having forgotten to consider his welfare this morning, Audra peered down at him.

"Audra, I . . . I . . . am worse," Dennis whispered harshly. He reached a quivering hand out toward her. "Help . . . me . . ."

When she saw that not only his hand was trembling, but also his whole body, Audra hurried to him. His red face indicated that his temperature was surely a fiery inferno this morning.

"Dennis, I'm sorry you are feeling so badly," she murmured. She reached a hand to his brow and quickly drew it away when she felt just how hot his flesh was. "Oh, Dennis, your fever is so much worse today."

"But . . . I . . . am so cold," Dennis said, visibly shivering. "Do something, Audra. Oh, Lord, do something."

"Let me get the fire going stronger and then I shall bathe your body with cool water," Audra said, turning quickly to the fire pit in the floor.

Her own hands trembled as she placed wood into the glowing embers, then bent low and blew on the hotter coals.

She was relieved when the fire burst into flames along the bottom of the logs, and then began lapping in orange, velveteen streamers upward along the wood.

Then she pushed herself up from the floor and went outside.

She was glad when she found that through the people's grieving, someone had taken the time to place a fresh wooden basin of water just outside the door, as well as a wooden pitcher of water for drinking.

Audra stopped long enough to gaze once again at Silver Wing's lodge. She ached to be with him during his time of sorrow.

Instead she grabbed the basin of water and pitcher, and hurried back inside the longhouse.

As she sat beside Dennis, she held his head up enough for him to sip from the wooden cup.

Then, as he lay back down, his eyes closed, she gently bathed his feverish brow.

Only then did she realize what a beautiful day it was. Sunlight spiraled through the open door. Birds sang sweet melodies in the trees.

But nothing erased the sounds of mourning outside, nor Dennis's groans.

Lowering the blanket from Dennis, resting it at his waist, Audra gently bathed his bare chest, then turned him and bathed his back.

But still, no matter how much she tried to get his temperature lowered, it raged onward. Dennis's body was so hot the heat seemed to radiate away from his flesh.

"I've got to do something else," Audra whispered to herself. "I'm no help at all this morning. Surely . . ."

She looked quickly at the door.

Yes, surely someone in the village knew something about fevers and might have a way to get Dennis's lowered.

Slowly turning Dennis over to once again lay on his back, Audra gave him a wavering gaze. "Dennis, I'm going to see if someone in the village might know how to help you," she murmured as his glassy, bloodshot eyes opened and gazed up at her.

She smoothed the blanket up to rest beneath his chin, then snuggled it tightly around his body. "I hope not to be too long," she murmured.

"Those wails coming from outside," Dennis said thickly. "I know that the Indians wail when someone has died. Who died, Audra? Who . . . ?"

"I think it might be Silver Wing's sister," Audra said as she rose slowly to her feet. "I have only seen her once, but that was enough for me to know how weak and ill she was. And . . . and . . . she was pregnant. I am so afraid that the child might also have died with her."

"Audra, don't . . . bother . . . Silver Wing and his people at this time," Dennis murmured, swallowing hard. "It . . . wouldn't . . . be appropriate."

Stunned by this man's big heart, Audra placed a gentle hand to his cheek.

"In one's lifetime rarely does anyone have the opportunity to know someone like you, whose heart is so good toward others," Audra said, her voice breaking. "Dennis, I'm honored to have made your acquaintance. And . . . and . . . I *will* try to get you some help."

Dennis smiled weakly up at her, then closed his eyes and fell into another deep, fever-induced sleep.

Audra gazed at him a moment longer, then hurried from the longhouse.

She was not even slightly aware of how unkempt she looked this morning after having tossed fitfully through the night on the hard earthen floor that was only scarcely covered with blankets.

In her dreams she had been reaching out for Silver Wing, but had never been able to truly touch him. He would be just inches away from her, his own arms outstretched toward her, a deep, troubled look in his beautiful gray eyes.

When she had awakened in a cold sweat in the middle of the night, she had even felt as though Silver Wing had been there, standing over her.

She had gotten up and opened the door. The moon's glow gave off enough light for her to see the interior of the longhouse, and she saw no one but Dennis. Silver Wing had only been in her dreams. No one was there except for Dennis Bell, who moaned and groaned in his sleep.

Today she felt as though she had not had any sleep. Her footsteps were heavy as she gently pushed her way through the throng of wailing Nez Perce, sighing with relief when she finally reached Silver Wing's closed door.

Ignoring the frowns of his people, Audra spoke Silver Wing's name through his door.

As she waited for some kind of response, she hated having to disturb him. But she still felt that she had no choice—she needed his help. She did not know how to control a raging fever.

Her thoughts were stilled when the door suddenly opened and she found herself under the scrutiny of Silver Wing's sorrowful gray eyes.

For a moment she was speechless; never had she seen a man's eyes filled with such despair.

And she could tell that, although he was a powerful chief, he had been crying.

She started to speak to him, but suddenly he turned and walked away from her as though she wasn't there.

But what puzzled her the most was why he had left the door open if he wanted her to leave?

Could the open door be his silent way of asking her to go inside?

Audra lowered her eyes and started to walk away, but stopped when Silver Wing came again and stood at the door.

Slowly Audra raised her eyes to look at him, then took a shaky step backward when she found him holding a baby within his arms, a blanket wrapped loosely around it.

"Before my sister died she gave birth to a precious child . . . a daughter . . . my niece," Silver Wing said, his voice breaking. "Before my sister took her last breath of life, she named her child *Lap Lap,* in your language meaning Little Butterfly. My sister gave the child this name because of my sister's love of butterflies." He swallowed hard. "My sister now lives through her child."

At a loss of words, yet happy that a child had been born of this tragedy, tears filled Audra's eyes. She was touched deeply, to the very core of her being, at how gently Silver Wing held his niece and how he gazed down at the baby now with such a deep, sad longing.

He then looked up at Audra again and held the baby out for her. "You are my choice to be the child's mother," he said, his eyes pleading with her. "Hold her. Love her."

Stunned that he had asked her to be the child's mother, Audra took another slow step away from him.

But when he continued to hold the baby out for her, the wails and chants having ceased, Audra knew that Silver Wing was serious. He *did* want her to care for the child. Of all the people he could ask, especially knowing that anyone among his people would be honored to take the child as theirs, he had asked *her* to take Little Butterfly.

Did that also mean that he wanted her to be his wife? Did he now trust her?

Yes, that was surely a part of this choice for her to take the child.

Touched, she couldn't believe that he had openly shown his feelings for her in the presence of his people. And it seemed like a dream that he had, and that he truly did love her as she loved him.

"Do you not want to hold the child?" Silver Wing asked, his eyes wavering. "Do you not care enough for how I feel? Do you not see why I would single you out to be the child's mother?"

"Oh, Silver Wing, I am so sorry about your sister," Audra finally blurted out. "And, I am honored to have been chosen to care for her child. I . . . want to hold her. She is so very precious! But I shouldn't hold her now. I shouldn't even be near her. I might have germs of measles on my hands . . . on my clothes."

Afraid that he truly didn't believe her reason for backing away from his offer, Audra turned and ran back to the longhouse, where Dennis Bell still slept and moaned.

"Oh, what am I to do?" Audra cried, nervously

raking her fingers through her short red curls. "Now what will Silver Wing do? What will he think? Surely he doesn't understand!"

His heart aching, Silver Wing watched her until she ran into the longhouse, then he turned and placed his niece in a cradle that a close acquaintance had brought for the child.

He gazed at length at his sister, who still lay in repose, awaiting her burial.

Silver Wing knelt down beside his sister and ran a gentle hand over her soft brow. "I *will* make things right for Little Butterfly," he whispered. "The mother I have chosen for her *will* love her as I love her, for this woman's heart is true toward me. So will it be for the child."

He brushed a kiss across his sister's brow, then rushed from his longhouse just in time to see Audra run into the forest.

Hearing her crying and seeing how she ran blindly into the forest, Silver Wing could not help but believe that her tears were for him.

He knew now that he was right to allow his heart to feel so much for her.

The very moment they had met on white man's soil in San Francisco, their joined destinies had been written in the stars.

Soon he would take her as his wife.

When he caught up with her, he reached out and grabbed her gently by an arm and stopped her.

Swinging her around, his eyes met and held with hers. "You came to my lodge to help me in my time of sadness, yet when I ask for your help, you run away?" he said, questioning her with his eyes. "Why is that, my woman? Is it truly because you fear inflicting the white man's disease on the child? Or is it because you fear the responsibility of being a mother, and soon a wife?"

"I am so deeply saddened over your loss," Audra said, wiping the tears from her eyes with her free hand. "And no one has ever put such trust in me as you have. I . . . I . . . would adore being the child's mother. I am touched deeply by knowing you trust me enough now to even consider having me as your wife."

She couldn't bring herself to tell him the real reason she had come to his door today. Yes, she was sad over his loss, and she had wanted to, eventually, let him know her feelings. But she had gone to his longhouse to ask for help for Dennis! She was afraid that if someone didn't help him, *he* would die.

No, she couldn't tell him that was why she had come to his lodge.

"Then, you will come and be a part of my lodge? You will share my grieving over my sister? You will help me through my sister's burial ceremony by your mere presence at my side?" Silver Wing said, his pulse racing at knowing soon his dreams of having this woman would be true. "You will care for the child as though she is yours?"

"I do love you so, Silver Wing. And I want to do all of those things you ask of me, yet I am afraid that to do so now might endanger not only you, but also the child," Audra murmured. "Dennis Bell is quite ill. I . . . I . . . might be carrying his germs on my clothes and in my hair even now."

She eased her wrist from his hand and slowly backed away from him. "Please stay your distance," she murmured. "I would die if you came down with measles."

"You say Dennis Bell is worse?" Silver Wing asked softly.

"His temperature is so out of hand, I'm not sure if anything can be done for him," Audra said, her voice breaking. "Unless your people know about fevers and how to lower them."

"My people's shaman is powerful against all diseases," Silver Wing said. "Now that you are asking for help, *she* will go to the white man's lodge with her medicine. She has not gone there earlier because she has not been summoned."

"But she might get measles," Audra said, sighing nervously.

"My shaman's medicine keeps her protected from all diseases, even diseases that white men bring to our village," Silver Wing said flatly.

"I have never heard of women shaman," Audra said softly.

"The Nez Perce people can choose either a man or a woman as their shaman," Silver Wing said. "Our village shaman's name is Rainbow."

He nodded toward the river. "Go there and bathe the germs from your clothes and body," he said. "When you return to my lodge, my sister's body will have been taken to the large council house for her burial ceremony. When you return to my lodge, clothes will be there for you. The same maiden who has given you clothes to wear will bring you more today. Soon you will attend the burial rites with me for my sister. But before the burial, you will stand with me as I prepare my sister for her grave. While there, you will hold the child. She will be present at all times until her mother is taken on that long road to the hereafter."

He reached out for Audra, then stopped short of touching her again. "It is good that you will be my wife, and that you will be Little Butterfly's mother," he said thickly. "Our life as a family will be good."

In a daze, soon to be marrying the man of her dreams, mothering a lovely, orphaned child, and anything but a prisoner at the Nez Perce village now, Audra went to the river and bathed.

When she arrived back at Silver Wing's lodge, she saw that the people no longer openly mourned there. They were now outside the council house, which had to mean that his sister's body lay in state.

She looked at the people at length, wondering how they would react to their chief marrying a white woman. Not only that but their chief was going to hand over his sister's child to this woman. She could not help but be afraid of their reaction.

However, knowing that Silver Wing was their chief and their voice of authority assured her that things would be made right for her among his people.

Just as she stepped inside the longhouse, she saw a lovely doeskin dress awaiting her on the rush mats beside the lodge fire, as well as newly beaded moccasins.

The child also awaited her in the cradle, all sweet and pretty, wrapped in a soft doeskin blanket, her dark eyes gazing up at Audra as though she already knew and loved her.

Audra quickly dressed, then knelt down beside the cradle and smiled down at the child. "My daughter," she whispered, testing how that sounded as it passed across her lips.

When she heard soft footsteps behind her, she turned with a start, then found a pretty young maiden dressed in goatskin standing there.

"My chief beckons you to the council house," the woman said softly. "Bring the child."

A tremor of apprehension coursed through Audra's veins, for she knew what awaited her at the council house . . . a dead body waiting to be prepared for burial.

"Come now," the woman said, reaching out a hand for Audra.

Her heart pounding, Audra swept the wrapped child from its cradle.

Her knees somewhat weak, she left the longhouse and walked toward the council house, where her future husband and his dead sister awaited her. . . .

15

The airs that hover in the summer sky
Are all asleep tonight.
———WILLIAM CULLEN BRYANT

Dressed in a denim shirt and breeches, and wearing
fancy leather boots and a heavy gun belt with pearl-
handled pistols at his waist, Harry Weston crawled to
the edge of a butte that overlooked the Nez Perce
village.

He flopped down on his belly and gazed down at the
village. With Father John and others from the convent
there, he could not help but wonder how they had
been treated. He hoped they had been taken away
and put on a ship for San Francisco, for he did not
need them to get in the way of his plans.

Today he found the village in mourning, their wails
and chants proof that someone of importance had
died.

As his men came and nestled on their bellies on
each side of Harry, their eyes wide as they also
gawked down below at the milling crowd of Indians
outside the council house, Harry glanced quickly over
at Adam Decker, the best man of those he had chosen
to accompany him to the Oregon country. They had

known each other since they had been pups and had gotten into more scrapes than anyone Harry had ever known.

Harry had tried to turn over a new leaf when he began working at the convent—but was bored to tears with that quiet, sedate life. It had been good to say good-bye to San Francisco's shores.

"Adam, look down yonder," Harry said, nudging him in his side. "It's obvious someone's died. Don't you see the advantage that gives us? Today we can round up many of their Appaloosa without being caught. Surely everyone has joined the grieving at the village."

"I wonder who died?" Adam said, idly scratching his whiskered chin.

"It doesn't matter, now, does it?" Harry spat out. "Come on. Let's ride. Can't you just imagine how many horses we can round up today?"

"It's not wise to steal so many of the Injun's horses at once," Adam grumbled. "Thus far the few horses we've stolen each day has not been enough to alert the Nez Perce they're losin' some of their best steeds. They have so many, on such a widespread piece of land, how can they keep track?"

"Adam, I told you that time is running out," Harry said angrily. "You know that in time they will put two and two together and realize that I couldn't have left on my own. And that Dennis fellow might remember having seen me talking with you guys that one time at the trading post while buying supplies for our hide-out and conclude that *you* were the ones who might have helped me escape. If he tells the Nez Perce chief that, perhaps using it as a bargaining tool to get himself released, then we're dead, Adam. Dead!"

"I think you're worrying for nothin'," Adam grumbled as he again gazed down at the village. Then his eyes widened. "Look! It's Chief Silver Wing. See? He's walking with that redheaded dame. Damn it, Harry, she's as free as a bird. She's not locked away with the others."

Harry scooted on his belly closer to the edge of the butte, his jaw tightening when he also saw Audra with Silver Wing. "I guess the chief's hot for her," he said chuckling. "That's why he's being more lenient with her."

"I'd like to have a piece of her myself," one of the other men said, leering at Audra. "Ain't she a pretty one?"

"Well, at least we damn well know the chief isn't the one bein' mourned over," Adam said, inching a hand down to the pistol holstered at his right hip. "I'd like to plug him right now and see him squirm like a snake on the ground before he died."

"We aren't here to kill Indians," Harry reminded him. "I don't want no killin'. Just horses and land."

"You're as stupid as hell if you think we'll achieve those things without takin' lives doin' it," Adam said flatly. "When the time comes that the Indians know we exist, you know many a body'll have to fall. I'm goin' to make sure it ain't mine."

"Let's go and get us some horses," Harry said, taking one last look at Audra. "Maybe we'll find a way to get us a lady later."

"A redheaded one, I hope," Adam said huskily as

he scooted away from the butte with the others. "It's been too long since I've had my hands up a lady's skirt. I'm hungerin' for a feel."

"I'm hungerin' for more than a feel," one of the other men said, chuckling. "I want all of her."

They went to their horses, where they had left them tethered in a grove of cottonwoods. They led them farther away by foot, and then mounted their steeds and rode away in the direction of the Appaloosa's grazing land.

When they arrived, they saw horses reaching out so far across the beautiful green landscape it was impossible to see where they ended.

"What a beautiful sight," Harry said, drawing his mount to a quivering halt. He rested a hand on the pommel of his saddle, his eyes feasting on the horses.

"So far we've not run into any Nez Perce guarding the horses," Adam said, spitting over his shoulder. "But of course the horse herd's so large, how *could* the Indians expect to keep them all guarded. And, hell, the horses have been here for so long, they find it natural to graze there without being tended to. It sure makes it easy as hell to steal them."

"Come on, let's get started," Harry said, taking a rope from where it hung over his pommel. "I'll rope one of the horses. You guys get your own. We'll separate them from the herd, tie them where no one can see them, and keep on until we have several to chase back to our corral at the hideout."

Harry rode away from the others. He swung his rope in a circle over his head as he eyed the first horse he wanted to take.

He sank his boots into the flanks of his horse and rode at a hard gallop into the herd, the rope still circling overhead, his eyes still glued to the beautiful horse with the proud eyes and muscled flanks.

Then Harry drew his horse to a shuddering halt, and he stared at a body on the ground amid the horses. "What the hell?" he said, growing cold inside when he saw that the Indian's body had been riddled with arrows, the arrows looking grotesque where they were lodged into the Indian's back.

He shuddered when he saw that the man had been scalped, flies now buzzing and landing on the bloody remains.

Surely this man was a Nez Perce, he concluded. He had probably been there to check on the herd and had been ambushed.

He looked quickly up at the herd, his eyes slowly roving over them. There was no way to see if some of them had been stolen, yet why else would this man be killed in such a way, unless . . . unless . . . it was done by another tribe who hated the Nez Perce.

"The Blackfoot," Harry murmured, recalling having heard that the Blackfoot and Nez Perce were ardent enemies.

Fearful that the Blackfoot might still be near, yet curious to examine the scalped man, he dismounted to see the Indian closer.

His men did the same.

Together they knelt down around the Indian, their eyes taking in the bloody scalp, and then the arrows.

"I wonder if I know him?" Harry said, shuddering when he reached a hand over to the Indian, took him by an arm, and turned him on his side, enough to see his face.

What he discovered sent a warning through him that made him grow pale. He flinched as though he had been shot. "This man has measles!" he cried, yanking his hand away from the dead man. "This man has measles and, oh, Lord, we've all just been exposed, for this man's body is still warm!"

Scrambling to their feet, they ran to their horses and quickly rode away.

Harry's mind was a jumble of things to worry about.

Measles!

Bloodthirsty Blackfoot!

And now Silver Wing, for when this man's murder was discovered, Silver Wing and his warriors would be scanning the country for the murderers.

They would even take a count of the Appaloosa and realize that several had been stolen. Those that Harry and his men had stolen were hidden, but now he was afraid that they might not be hidden well enough.

Although it should be obvious to Silver Wing that no white man could be responsible for this murder, since it was done with arrows and by someone who also took scalps as a trophy, Harry knew that it wouldn't be safe for him or his companions to be anywhere except their hideout for the next several days, perhaps *weeks*.

If Silver Wing did come across them while searching for the murderers it would be easier to kill Harry rather than chance imprisoning him again.

And . . . Harry and his cohorts must now wait out

the incubation period to see if they got the damn, dreaded measles.

He saw the riches he had planned to gain here in the Northwest country float away in the wind. It did not seem that luck would ever be on his side. He had been born poor, and he would die poor!

"I just can't allow it to happen!" he cried, drawing the men's eyes quickly to him.

He smiled awkwardly at them and pressed his heels into the flanks of his horse. Breaking away, he rode quickly onward toward his hideout.

He now wished that he had never thought up such a scheme as this.

He should have known that no good would ever come of it, for nothing he had ever tried worked.

He seemed cursed from the moment he had taken his first breath of life.

He wiped tears from his eyes just as the men came and rode up next to him.

He avoided their questioning stares.

16

Thine eyes are springs in whose serene
And silent waters heaven is seen.
———WILLIAM CULLEN BRYANT

The moon had replaced the sun in the sky. Audra sat quietly on soft mats beside Silver Wing in the council house, the burial of his sister behind them.

Except for sweet Little Butterfly, who was sleeping in her cradle, everyone else had gone to their own longhouses.

Audra hadn't asked Silver Wing yet why he hadn't returned to his lodge, instead of having come to the council house after the burial. A fire burned low in the fire pit and platters lay empty beside it, the people having eaten their evening meal only moments ago.

Audra was still shaken from having helped Silver Wing prepare his sister for burial; not so much by the act itself, but more because it brought back troubled memories of her having done this for her own mother.

When her mother had died, Audra had placed her in her finest dress, which, in truth, was only made of cotton. She had brushed her mother's long red tresses until they had shone.

She had placed a touch of rouge on her mother's ashen cheeks and pale lips to give her some color.

Audra almost choked with remorse now as she recalled having folded her mother's hands gently together atop her abdomen.

She closed her eyes and tried to blot out how cold her mother's lips were when she had bent down into the pine casket and kissed her a final good-bye.

"You will come with me, will you not, to take a hot sulphur bath to cleanse my heart and soul of the taste and smell of death?"

Silver Wing's voice, after being silent for so long, startled Audra from her deep thoughts.

"What?" she murmured, gazing quickly over at him. She still found it hard to gaze at him with the black ash spread across his face. It made him look so distant from the man she loved, yet she knew that it had been placed there because of mourning.

"What did you say?" she continued. "I . . . I . . . was thinking of something. I . . . I . . . did not hear you."

Silver Wing reached over and stroked her cheek with a hand. "Today has been a burden none of us ever wishes for," he said. "Burials are the hardest part of living. Especially when it is someone who was as loved as my sister."

"Yes, I, too, have known such sorrow," she murmured, again brought back into moments of remembering her mother's burial. "My mother. I sometimes miss my mother so much, I can hardly bear it."

"And how did she die?" Silver Wing said, drawing his hand slowly away from her.

"Mostly from heartache," Audra said. She lowered

her eyes to keep him from seeing the shine of tears. "Father became a stranger to us both when he began drinking so heavily. He drank so much he lost his job. My mother's final years of life were . . . were . . . spent in poverty. She worked so hard. She was more a slave to her husband than a wife. I shall never forget seeing her struggling to lift her heavy tubs of water that she used for washing clothes. Father would just sit at the kitchen table watching her, his mind and eyes clouded with whiskey."

"Then, when she died, you were put in that place called a convent," Silver Wing said, drawing her eyes to him.

"Yes, and I guess I should be grateful that my life did not continue as it might have should my father have placed me in the role of my mother and made *me* do the scrubbing, the washing and ironing, and the cooking. I would have soon become old for my age . . . as . . . did my mother," she said softly. "I should not resent the convent as much as I do. But I lost my freedom the day I stepped across its threshold. And I am a person who loves the out-of-doors and . . . and . . . breathing the fresh air. Inside the convent I was kept from all of those things. I soon learned to hate it."

Silver Wing reached out and placed his hands at her waist. He drew her over next to him, his eyes searching hers. "But now it is different for you," he said hoarsely. "While with me, you will have all those things that were denied you while you were in the convent. Father John will no longer dictate your life to you."

"Father John," Audra gasped, paling. "I have absolutely forgotten about Father John." She glanced toward the closed door, then at Silver Wing again. "Are he and the others all right? Have any of them become ill with measles? And . . . how . . . is Dennis? Did your shaman help him? Is his fever lowered?"

"Father John and his friends are being seen to well enough," Silver Wing said, easing his hands away from her waist. He gazed into the slow, licking flames of the fire. "They are being fed well. Fresh water is taken to them often during the day for either bathing or drinking. And the door is opened often for them to have fresh air, although guarded so they cannot escape."

He gazed at her again. "As for the sick white man, only time will tell whether or not Rainbow has helped him," he said, his voice tight. "She gave him wild cherry bark tea. That is what she saw was best for measles. She also made a drink from the berries of red cedar for his headache, which came with his high fever."

He paused, then said, "My woman, the question I asked earlier that you did not hear is will you go with me where I must go and take a hot sulphur bath? I must cleanse my heart and soul of the taste and smell of death. I would rather not do this alone. Will you go with me?"

She wanted to question him about this sort of bath, never hearing of hot sulphur baths before, but knowing that she had delayed him enough already by having talked about other things, she nodded. "Yes, I will go with you," she murmured. "I want to do anything I can to help you through this troubled time."

Outside a voice called as Silver Wing went to the door and opened it. A Nez Perce lady who appeared to be perhaps in her mid-twenties came into the council house. Audra noticed right away how large her breasts were as her goatskin blouse fit so snugly over them.

Otherwise she was a petite lady with floor-length black hair and friendly gray eyes that squinted when she smiled.

"Drinks Water, whose breasts are heavy with milk from recently having a baby, will sit with Little Butterfly in our absence," Silver Wing said, going and taking the child from her crib. He carried her to Drinks Water and placed her gently in her arms.

Audra watched as Drinks Water adoringly held the child and eased down onto a mat before the fire.

The woman raised her blouse at one side to expose a healthy, plump breast, then placed Little Butterfly's lips to it.

Little Butterfly began to suckle, her tiny hands kneading the copper breast contentedly.

"Drinks Water is the woman who has fed Little Butterfly since her birth," Silver Wing said. He stepped next to Audra and affectionately slid an arm around her waist as he, too, watched his niece suckle. "She will feed my niece until the child is of weaning age."

Having never seen a child nurse before, Audra was mesmerized by it and longed for a child's lips at her own breasts.

She looked quickly up at Silver Wing and caught him gazing at her, in his eyes a look of knowing.

When he smiled at her, she knew that he understood her feelings. Obviously they matched his own.

Together they would have a child, perhaps many!

"Let us go now," Silver Wing said, ushering Audra from the council house.

One horse awaited them just outside the door. He helped her into the saddle of a beautiful Appaloosa, its white mane thick and beautiful, then swung himself up behind her.

He soon left the village behind them, and the sorrows that still hung over it like a dark, heavy cloud.

In silence they rode for a while, the horse going at a steady lope beneath the moon and the stars.

Audra was aware of Silver Wing's muscled arm holding her protectively around her waist, and of his hard-muscled body pressed against her back.

Silver Wing was very aware of Audra's body against his and of how long he had been without a woman, sexually. Not since his wife's death many moons ago had he taken a woman to his blankets. He had been this long in mourning for her, so much that he had not looked at a woman as a possible wife . . . not until he had seen Audra in San Francisco. Since then she had been the only woman he secretly desired!

But he would deny himself a woman's body for just a little while longer. It would not be right to take Audra to his blankets and make love to her so soon after placing his sister in the cold black earth of the Oregon country!

But it would be hard . . . this denial of something

that made his loins ache unmercifully every time he looked at this woman.

Silver Wing concentrated now on guiding his horse through a narrow gorge of rock, where its walls rose high above him on both sides. Then he carefully led his horse down a steep, rocky ravine where tall spruces towered on each side.

In the distance a coyote howled to the moon, its mate soon answering from a distant butte. Owls hooted. Crickets chirped. And somewhere in the night, where the huge herd of Appaloosa grazed beneath the moon, horses whinnied as though they sensed Silver Wing was near.

And then Silver Wing and Audra reached the hot springs.

Audra was in awe of this water that seemed to bubble to the surface from nowhere.

And there were beautiful flowers bending toward it as though they were worshiping it.

Silver Wing drew a tight rein and stopped his horse, then slid out of the saddle to the ground. His eyes on her, he helped Audra from the saddle.

When she was standing before him, her eyes holding with his, he reached a hand up and stroked his fingers through the short curls on her head.

"Come into the hot springs with me?" he said huskily, his eyes searching hers.

Knowing that meant she would have to undress in front of a man for the first time in her life, Audra quickly shook her head back and forth.

"No, I don't think so," she murmured, swallowing hard.

Disappointed, yet seeing her denial as that of a shy woman, Silver Wing felt that he must do something that would change that, for soon he wished more from her than a mere swim in hot water. If she was too shy now, what would her reaction be then?

Silver Wing stepped away from her. His eyes still holding with hers, he boldly removed his breechclout and moccasins in her presence.

Embarrassed and shy, she quickly turned around and placed her back to him.

She could not deny, though, how his nudity had affected her.

A thrill had grabbed at her heart.

A warmth had fully enveloped her.

She ached at the juncture at her thighs. It was painful, yet delicious.

Truly she was confused by these sorts of feelings, yet knew they came with her being a woman longing for a man.

She flinched when she heard the water splash behind her.

She so badly wished to at least place a toe in it to see what the difference was between it and normal water. She hadn't asked Silver Wing to actually explain what mineral water was, and why it was hot.

And how could it help him? There were too many other things on her mind, especially now when she waited for him to leave the water.

What *then* would he do?

Alone with him, she knew that he could do anything and she would be helpless—yet she wanted him as a woman wanted a man.

When the splashing stopped and he had left the water, her insides tightened because she knew how vulnerable she was with this naked, handsome man. She had seen the need in his eyes as he had watched her reaction when he had undressed in front of her.

Would he now satisfy his needs through her?

Should she try and fight him off so that she could look less forward in his eyes?

Or should she just let things happen and allow him to take her wherever he wished to take her—to paradise and back?

She scarcely breathed as she waited to see what his next move would be.

When a hand rested gently on her shoulder and he slowly turned her around, she expected Silver Wing to still be naked. She expected to be taken sexually.

Instead, not only was the ash washed from his face, but he was dressed!

She didn't know whether to be disappointed or glad. She let out a deep breath when he took her hand and led her to his horse.

Their eyes met and held for a moment, and then he lifted her in the saddle and swung himself up behind her.

There was a chill in the air now as he rode back toward his village.

His arm around her was warm and welcome.

His breath on her neck as he bent low to brush a kiss across her nape sent a sensual thrill through her.

She closed her eyes and tremored in ecstasy when he whispered to her how much he loved her . . . how much he wanted her.

She wanted to ask him why he hadn't made love to her, but she already knew why. It was too soon after his sister's burial. His respect for his sister was admired, as well as his self-control while he had been with Audra, alone, their bodies aching for each other.

She didn't dare return his sentiments verbally, for she knew that her voice would reveal her true hunger for him. If he knew how badly Audra wanted him, he might go against his respectful feelings for his sister tonight.

The thought of him undressing her, his eyes raking over her nakedness, made her feel wanton, yet more alive than she had ever felt before.

Patiently she would wait to come together as one, relishing the anticipation.

When they rode into his village, Audra gasped when she saw that Silver Wing's home had been dismantled.

He rode on past the empty space and stopped before another lodge at the far end of the village, its fresh lumber and roof covering proof that it had only recently been built.

Silver Wing drew a tight rein and slid off his horse, then lifted Audra from it. He could see the puzzlement in her eyes as she stared at the new lodge, and then at him.

"This lodge was purposely built for my use after my sister died," he said. "Tearing down the lodge in which my sister died is a way to help erase painful memories of those moments from my heart and mind of her fighting for her life."

Audra leaned into his embrace as he led her inside

the lodge, where Drinks Water was asleep on blankets on the floor beside Little Butterfly's cradle.

This longhouse was different from the others. A fireplace rather than a fire pit was built into the wall, and an actual floor was made of wood. Hand-hewed furniture provided comfort, and a glass chimney hurricane lamp on a table with a wax candle burned softly.

Twined storage bags hung on the wall. Rush mats, dyed and woven in symmetrical designs, were spread out before the softly burning fire in the fireplace.

What took her by surprise were French glass beads hanging in long streamers, which separated the lodge into two nice, comfortable rooms.

"I had planned to get you in San Francisco and bring you back to live with me as my wife," Silver Wing said, seeing her astonished look. "When I began planning this, I went to the trading post and bought these special things that would make my lodge an attractive home for you. I see it in your eyes that you are not disappointed."

"You . . . were planning . . . to come for me?" Audra asked, still stunned by what he had told her. "Actually? You were going to come and take me from the convent?"

"I was planning the journey just prior to Harry Weston's arrival at my village," Silver Wing said. "After his arrival I felt that I should stay and see if things went well enough between him and my people. When I saw that he as not as trustworthy as I would have thought, my journey to San Francisco was delayed."

"You would have traveled that distance again to get

me?" Audra said, now touched to know that he truly loved her!

"This time I would have come on a ship," Silver Wing said. "But my plans changed when Harry Weston mistreated our children. It was then that my doubts about all white people made me even doubt you."

"But now you don't," Audra murmured.

"No, and never shall I again," Silver Wing said softly.

In awe of him, of how much he did care for her, Audra stood beside the slow-burning embers of the fire as Silver Wing awakened Drinks Water and sent her to her lodge to be with her children again. Her husband, Red Bonnet, was taking his turn guarding the Appaloosa herd. He had been there for several days and would soon return to be with his family while another warrior went to take his turn.

Audra had become keenly aware of how the Nez Perce people shared everything, as though they were of one family.

And now that she was a part of them, she, too, felt the oneness.

It was a good feeling.

It was something she hadn't felt since before her mother had died . . . that wonderful sense of belonging.

Silver Wing bent over the cradle, gently picked up his niece, and took her to Audra.

Smiling, he held the child out for her.

Already loving the child as though she were her own, Audra took the little bundle of joy.

Silver Wing reached up and slowly pulled the corner of the blanket away from Little Butterfly so that he and Audra could see her face.

"She is so beautiful," Audra said softly, taking in the sweetness of the tiny copper-skinned child. Little Butterfly's eyes were closed, her lips moving occasionally as though she still might be suckling from a nipple.

When Silver Wing placed a finger to one of the child's hands, Little Butterfly circled her tiny fingers around it.

"We will bond with her and be the true family that was denied her," Silver Wing said, his voice breaking.

Audra could never love a man as much as she did at this moment when she saw the deep, emotional affection Silver Wing showed for the child.

Audra vowed to herself at that moment to be the mother that had been denied Little Butterfly.

She vowed to be the best wife for Silver Wing!

Yes, together they *would* bond as a family with the child.

Silver Wing gazed over at Audra and smiled, for in her eyes he could see her love for the child. Suddenly so much of the sadness he felt over the loss of his sister was gone.

"*I-ett*, my woman, I will soon show you the strength of my gratitude for what you have brought into my life," Silver Wing said hoarsely.

Audra glanced quickly up at him. The look in his eyes, the utter adoration, made her heart melt with love for him. "I am so grateful to you for so many things," she said, her voice breaking with emotion.

It took all of Silver Wing's willpower not to take

the child and place her back in her crib, then take Audra to his bed of blankets and prove his love to her tonight.

But his sister was only now beginning her journey to the stars.

Soon that would be behind him and then, ah, then. . . .

17

My love is a fever, longing still.
—WILLIAM SHAKESPEARE

Audra felt as though she were in a dream as she sat eating breakfast with Silver Wing.

Had Silver Wing actually said that he loved her?

Was she *truly* going to marry him?

And how she loved the baby. When she held Little Butterfly, she felt so wonderfully at peace.

How sad, though, that the child's true mother had died. Yet although an orphan, the child was with family. Audra knew how it felt to be abandoned, and even though she had a father, she, too, was an orphan.

But now Audra belonged. Silver Wing was offering her a life that seemed borne of a fantasy. Silver Wing was going to raise Little Butterfly as his daughter. She was going to be Audra's daughter.

"Your eyes speak so much this morning that you have not said aloud," Silver Wing suddenly said, drawing Audra's eyes quickly to him.

Sharing the food spread on a wooden platter that sat between them, Silver Wing sat beside Audra on a pallet of blankets. They each had cups filled with a sweet drink that Audra was not familiar with, yet truly enjoyed. Silver Wing was dressed only in a breech-clout.

Audra loved the dress she wore today. It was made of doeskin. It was so soft it felt like the petals of a rose against her skin.

It had been wonderful how Silver Wing had drawn her brush through her tight curls. She could hardly wait for it to grow to shoulder-length. She was tired of people staring at her boy-like hair.

"Yes, my thoughts are filled with wonderful things today," Audra said, smiling at him. "You just don't know how happy you've made me. When I stowed away on that ship, I knew the risk of you rejecting me. Had you, I . . . I . . . don't know what I would have done."

He reached for Audra and drew her over to him.

He lifted her on his lap so that she faced him.

"Do not linger your thoughts on what was or what might have been," he said hoarsely. "There is only now. There is only tomorrow. There is only *us* . . . you, me, and Little Butterfly."

"And there are your people who depend on your leadership," Audra said, twining her arms around his neck.

"Yes, there is always my people," Silver Wing said, his eyes mesmerizing Audra as he gazed so intensely into hers. "They are now also your people."

Audra shivered sensually when he placed a gentle hand at the nape of her neck and drew her lips to his, the kiss sending spirals of wondrous desire through her.

The pit of her stomach felt mushy and warm.

Her head was spinning with passion.

Her breath caught in her throat, and she felt dizzy with rapture when Silver Wing slid a hand down and cupped a breast through her dress. No man's hand had ever touched her in such a way. She had no idea that doing so could cause so many pleasurable sensations to soar through her. She tried not to show her disappointment when Little Butterfly began to cry from her cradle. The child had already had an early morning feeding, but it was time again to get her nourishment from Drinks Water's milk-filled breasts.

Audra eased away from Silver Wing and smiled at him. "Seems someone is hungry," she murmured.

He brushed a kiss across her lips, then rose and went to the cradle.

Audra sat there and watched the gentleness with which he took the child into his arms. She smiled to herself when she heard Silver Wing speaking quietly to the child as he softly rocked her back and forth in his arms, the child's cries fading into a quiet cooing sound.

When he came and sat down beside Audra and slid the child into her arms, love surged inside her. "I've never seen anything as beautiful," she murmured. "Oh, Silver Wing, look how she looks up at me. She is studying me so closely."

"This is the way children learn to bond with their parents," Silver Wing said. He reached over and took one of Little Butterfly's hands from inside the blanket. He laughed softly as the child's hand clasped onto his forefinger. "She is learning that you are her mother and that I am her father."

Suddenly Audra became aware of how quiet Silver Wing became.

She looked into his eyes and saw a deep sadness as he continued to gaze at the child.

She did not have to ask him what had changed his mood. It was sad for Audra, even, to think about the beautiful young woman lying in her grave, having too soon been robbed of *life.*

She then thought of her mother and felt a lump grow in her throat as she remembered how old her mother had looked when she had died. She, too, had been robbed of the joys in life. Audra felt blessed to have the chance to have a better life.

Tears misted her eyes as she continued to look at Silver Wing. She owed him so much. She would show him in many ways how thankful she was!

Then her thoughts skipped elsewhere . . . to Father John and the others, who were still locked away.

And Dennis. She had to go soon and see how he had fared through the night.

She would also check on Father John. She wished that she could tell him that he was to be released, yet she knew that Silver Wing had no plans to do that just yet.

She hoped that he would, and soon.

Until then, she would hope and pray that those who were locked up would be patient, for she did believe that Silver Wing would eventually release them. He was a kind man who would not want to place such a burden on anyone for long, especially since they hadn't done anything wrong. It wasn't fair that they were paying for what another man had done.

Yes, she did expect Silver Wing to come around soon and do what was right.

"I will take Little Butterfly to Drinks Water's long-house so that she can be fed," Silver Wing said, gently taking the child from Audra. He gazed at Audra, his eyes somewhat wavering. "And while I am doing that, feel free to check on Father John and Dennis Bell. I know that you wish to do so. You cannot help but worry and wonder about them, although Father John was something less than kind to you."

Audra pushed herself up from the blankets. She ran her hands down the front of her dress to smooth out the wrinkles, then walked outside with Silver Wing.

She inhaled the wonderful fragrance of the early morning and enjoyed the touch of the sun and breeze against her face.

"I was wrong not to trust you," Silver Wing said hoarsely. "I will not make the same mistake again."

She wanted to beg Father John's case, yet knew this was not the time. She walked with Silver Wing until he reached Drinks Water's longhouse. He reached a gentle hand to Audra's face, then walked on into the longhouse, leaving Audra to her own affairs.

Audra felt blessed that he trusted her this much. She would never *give* him cause to doubt her again.

First she went and checked on Dennis's welfare. When she entered the longhouse, she found him alone, a slow fire burning in the fire pit casting off a soft light around the room. She moved to her knees beside Dennis. She saw that he was asleep so did not disturb him.

He looked much better. His breathing was easier. His fever was all but gone. And some of the red spots were fading, which meant that he was finally on his road to recovery.

Satisfied that all was well, Audra left Dennis and went to the longhouse where Father John was being held. A stout warrior stood just outside the door, his muscled arms folded across his equally muscled bare chest. He gave Audra a wary look, then turned and unlocked the door so that she could enter.

She nodded a quiet thank-you to him, then went inside, glad that he didn't lock the door behind her. He needn't worry—no one would get past him.

"Audra, what's happening out there?" Father John rushed out as he rose from the mats, while the others sat gazing up at Audra with a quiet sort of contempt. "When are we going to be freed?"

"I hope soon," Audra murmured, uneasy as the four priests continued to stare at her in an accusing manner.

"You aren't telling me everything," Father John blurted out, his hands on his hips. "Do I even have to ask how it is that you are so free and we are still locked up? It's the chief, isn't it? You've had your eye on him since you shamelessly went and met with him in the convent's courtyard. It seems it has worked, Audra. It's got your release, whereas we're still locked up like criminals."

"It's not at all as it appears to be," Audra said, blushing, because she knew that he was probably thinking the worst about her behavior. "Yes, I have feelings for Silver Wing, as does he for me. But nothing indecent has happened between us. I would never use my body as a tool for anything, especially a release from imprisonment. What Silver Wing and I share is pure and wonderful." She lifted her chin proudly. "In fact, I am going to marry him."

Father John took a shaky step away from her, his face drained of color. "You are going to do what?" he said in a raspy gasp.

"I'm going to marry him," Audra said again. Then she explained to him about Silver Wing's sister, and then the child that Audra was going to help Silver Wing raise.

"I love the child as though she were mine," Audra said. "She has stolen my heart, Father John."

"Audra, you're wrong to let yourself get attached, not only to the child but also to Silver Wing," Father John said warily. "Soon Silver Wing will come to his senses and release me. We must all leave this place. And, yes, that includes you, Audra. It's apparent that Harry Weston ruined all chances of teaching Christianity to the Nez Perce. The Nez Perce won't be able to trust anyone again. You must realize that includes you, Audra. If you stay behind when I leave and you do something that looks suspicious to the Nez Perce, then they might turn on you."

Audra's heart skipped a beat at that thought, then just as quickly brushed it away, for she knew that Silver Wing's feelings for her ran too deep for him ever to do anything to hurt her. And she would never give the Nez Perce cause to turn on her. She was going to be a part of them, as one *with* them.

"I must go now," Audra said, turning to the door. She stopped with a start when Father John grabbed her by a wrist and turned her to face him.

"Be careful, Audra," he warned. "And find a way to get us out of here. I want to go home. I should have never come here in the first place."

"I shall do what I can to assure your release," Audra murmured. "But I can't promise anything. It's all up to Silver Wing."

Father John surprised Audra when he swept his arms around her and gave her a fierce hug, then as quickly stepped away from her and joined the others on the mats beside the fire.

"Audra, sinners go to hell," Father John said, giving her a heated frown. "Be wary of sinning with Silver Wing."

Audra gasped and stared at him for a moment longer, then turned and left the longhouse, her face hot with embarrassment over what he was implying.

It made her wonder if she truly *could* make love with Silver Wing before vows were spoken?

Yet she knew that Father John was trying to make her feel guilty so that she would reject Silver Wing's advances toward her.

He did this not only because he saw women as sinners who gave themselves to men in such a way, but also to ruin the contentment that she had finally found in her life after being so miserable for so long.

She now knew that Father John might try anything to get her back on that boat to San Francisco. He didn't like for anyone to get the best of him, which she had the moment she had fled from the convent without his permission.

"You aren't going to spoil anything for me ever again," she whispered to herself, doubling her hands to her sides. "I'm happy for the first time since my mother died. No one is going to take this from me!"

She hurried to Silver Wing's longhouse, disappointed that he wasn't there. She busied herself straightening his lodge and shaking dust from the mats.

And when this was all done, she hurried to the river and found an isolated place for her bath.

When she returned to the longhouse, smelling fresh of river water, she found Silver Wing there, kneeling beside the cradle, slowly rocking it as he sang a soft tune to the child.

Touched deeply by the sight, tears filled Audra's eyes.

Then she crept over and knelt down on her knees beside Silver Wing, their eyes meeting when he turned and found her there.

"I need you," she murmured, reaching a soft hand to his cheek. "I ache for you."

She wouldn't allow herself to feel brazen for openly offering herself to him. She hoped that he wouldn't see her as a loose woman for this behavior.

But she loved him so much she could hardly wait another moment to be held by him . . . to be kissed by him . . . to be taken to paradise in his arms.

When Father John's image appeared before her, she

brushed it away. She loved Silver Wing too much to think of anything now, but him.

When he reached for her, she floated into his arms. Their lips met in a frenzy as they both worked at disrobing the other.

When they stood nude facing each other, Silver Wing's gaze became hot with passion as he swept it over her silken nakedness.

His hands trembled as he ran them over Audra's breasts, and then across her flat belly, and then down to where she was throbbing with hungry need for him.

She closed her eyes. She held her head back and sighed when his fingers feathered through her tight, red tendrils of hair, beneath which lay her womanhood.

When his fingers began stroking her swollen nub, awakening in her feelings that were unfamiliar, yet delicious to her, Audra moaned throatily and knew that she would soon know the true mystery of being a woman.

She sighed from the strange, yet pleasurable sensations being awakened inside her.

She trembled as she became further alive beneath his caresses.

"Come with me," Silver Wing murmured, her eyes springing open to see where he was taking her, his hand in hers leading the way.

When they reached his bed of soft pelts and he laid her down, his body soon blanketing hers, Audra scarcely breathed, for she could feel his heat probing where his fingers had just been, arousing her to heights never known to her before.

"Spread your legs," Silver Wing said, gently placing his hands at her thighs, softly urging them wider apart.

She smiled weakly up at him as she felt herself opening to him like a sunflower opens to the sun. She sucked in a wild breath of pain when he thrust into her, bursting past that layer of skin that proved her virginity to her lover.

And then as he held her endearingly in his arms and his lips kissed her sweetly, she closed her eyes and felt herself melting away into a warmth that spread further within her with each of his thrusts.

She clung to him.

She lifted her hips and met his every plunge, his manhood deeply, magnificently filling her.

Her head rolled as a cry of sweet agony escaped from between her lips, his lips now at a breast, sucking the nipple between his teeth, his tongue lapping wetly at it.

Silver Wing's body felt fluid with fire as the passion spread within him.

He sculpted himself to her moist body, molding perfectly into the curved hollow of her hips.

He placed his hands beneath her buttocks and held her in place against his thrusting loins, her body moving with his as he pressed endlessly deeper.

"*En-ha-wettsa*, I love you," he whispered.

Again, he kissed her.

His fingers stroked through her short hair.

His tongue flickered in and out of her mouth.

The passion grew now to a bursting point.

He held her tightly against him as he made another deep thrust into her, then groaned against her throat as a great shuddering began in his loins and he sent his seed deeply into her.

Startled by the intensity of the pleasure she received as their bodies jolted and quivered, Audra's gasps became soft, long whimpers.

And then they lay side by side, breathing hard, their bodies gleaming with pearls of sweat.

Audra turned on her side and gazed at Silver Wing. She was amazed at how making love made one feel inside . . . so at peace . . . so blissfully wonderful.

And making love with him had seemed so right . . . so natural!

She would cherish forever the remembrance of these moments of bliss with Silver Wing. It seemed a miracle that she was there, and that his love for her was so real.

Silver Wing reached over and drew her against him, his hand moving gently over her flesh, stroking her. "Tomorrow I will take you to a place that will be like heaven on earth for you," he said huskily.

"How can any place be better than where I am at this moment with you?" Audra said, sighing.

"I shall show you tomorrow," Silver Wing said, smiling at her. "It is a place where one can dream and truly believe that dreams can come true."

"My dreams have already come true," Audra said, snuggling closer to him. "Nothing could ever make me happier than I am at this very moment."

Then she sighed heavily and turned her eyes up at him. "But I must admit, Silver Wing, I feel guilty to be this free . . . to be this loved . . . while Dennis Bell is still so ill . . . and while Father John and the others are still imprisoned."

"Father John and his friends will be released tomorrow," Silver Wing said, surprising Audra into silence. "They will be free to leave or to stay for a while among my people, but only if Father John promises not to preach Christianity to the Nez Perce. My people no longer want to hear it."

Audra gave him a big hug. "You have nothing to worry about," she said, laughing softly. "Father John will honor your request. I doubt that he will stay any longer than he has to. I imagine, though, he might want to stay until Dennis Bell is well. They are dear friends from long ago."

When Little Butterfly began whimpering and stirring in the cradle, Silver Wing pulled on his breechclout, got the child, and brought her back to Audra.

"Sweet thing, one day I hope to give you a brother or sister," Audra murmured as she slowly rocked Little Butterfly back and forth in her arms.

She glanced up at Silver Wing, saw the quiet gleam in his eyes, and knew that what she had said had pleased him.

He reached over and placed a hand at the nape of her neck and brought her lips to his. As Little Butterfly cooed, they kissed.

For a moment Audra felt apprehensive of all of this . . . her contentment . . . being loved . . . and feeling so quickly as though she belonged.

She recalled Father John's warning about not getting too attached.

She already was!

She prayed that she was not wrong to relax with this new life, whereas only a few days ago she felt so alone, so unloved.

When Silver Wing wrapped his arms around her, which also included the child, Audra knew that this was all right . . . and that nothing would take it away from her!

Yet the harsh lessons of life had taught her long ago how things could change in less time than a heartbeat!

18

The moment of desire!
The moment of desire!
The virgin that pines for man
should awaken her womb to enormous joys!
——WILLIAM BLAKE

Proudly Audra rode on a lofty Appaloosa horse. Its color intrigued Audra—white over the loin and hips with dark egg-shaped spots that dominated the hips.

When Silver Wing had brought her this horse for their outing today, he had told her that all true Appaloosas were distinguished by four features—their spots, their eyes encircled by white, similar to the human eye, and the skin beneath the coat having a muddy, mottled pink and gray speckling that was most readily detected around its nostrils.

He had further explained that part of their hooves had vertical black-and-white striping.

He had said that the dual coloration of these horses were produced by hereditary-spotted genes. Their coat color patterns might combine white with any other solid color, which was frequently roan.

But not only was she thrilled to ride such a steed as this, feeling strangely bonded to it as it sometimes gave her a quick glance with its dark, beautiful eyes, she felt free as the wind while she rode with Silver

Wing to a place he had not yet explained. All that he had told her was that he was taking her to a place where one was made to believe that all dreams could come true.

And so much had already come true for her. The sun shone down on her from a sea-blue sky, and the breeze whipped gently across her face. Surrounded by mountains, and wide meadows suddenly turning into deep valleys, all of which were dotted with beautiful late-spring flowers, she seemed distant to that person she was only a few weeks . . . even a few days ago.

The way she dressed was no longer dictated to her.

She was free to do and say as she pleased, when she wished to say it.

The freedom she had sought for so long enveloped her today like a soft caress.

And she would soon marry the man who made her heart soar.

Not only that. She had a child who already seemed hers. She had never thought that holding a child could give one such inner peace . . . such joy!

But Little Butterfly made all of this happen.

She had even hesitated leaving her today, yet knew that she was in good hands with Drinks Water. Little Butterfly would be surrounded by the laughter of Drinks Water's own three children.

Audra glanced over at Silver Wing as he rode tall and straight in his saddle, remembering him saying that his sister still lived through her child. This man, who was the embodiment of man and who had been a fierce warrior on the battlefield against his enemy Blackfoot, was the gentlest man she had ever met.

When he held her, it was with such endearing love.

When he made love to her, it was with such ease and understanding, and he always made sure that she received as much pleasure as he through the love-making.

For certain he had given her a renewed life.

Suddenly a monarch butterfly came and settled on her hand holding the reins. Its loveliness, its softness, its body bearing no weight against her flesh, caused Audra's breath to catch.

And even though the horse was going at a steady lope, the butterfly continued to sit on Audra's hand, its feelers going over her flesh, as though testing her to see if her hand might have pollen to offer.

Silver Wing saw the butterfly land. He smiled and edged his horse closer to Audra's. "Your sweetness has drawn the butterfly to you," he said. "Do you like butterflies?"

"They, as well as fireflies, have always intrigued me," Audra murmured, not taking her eyes off the butterfly as it now slowly crept up her arm. "And see how it clings even though the breeze threatens it?"

"Like you, it has a strong will," Silver Wing said, his coal-black hair and breechclout fluttering in the wind.

He silently admired how graceful a rider Audra was, even somewhat daring. He enjoyed learning everything new about her.

Audra watched the butterfly suddenly take wing and soar away into the huge field of wildflowers.

Then she looked over at Silver Wing. "There are so many things to thank you for," she said. "Today you set Father John and the other priests free. You've given Dennis Bell your permission to leave as soon as he is well enough to travel. You've made me feel worthwhile and wanted again. My darling, how can I ever thank you?"

"You being with me, you promising to marry me, is all the thanks I need," he said hoarsely. "You have brought sunshine into my life again. For so long, since the death of my beloved wife, and then knowing I would soon lose my sister, I felt as though dark clouds were enveloping me. You have even helped me leave my mourning for both behind me. If not for you, I would be swallowed whole with self-pity."

"I want to make you *and* Little Butterfly happy forever and ever," Audra murmured.

"As do we, you," Silver Wing said, then frowned. "I do wish that the white men could leave soon, but no ship will arrive on the Columbia for a while."

"Thank you for giving them permission to stay at your village until the ship comes that will take them back to San Francisco," Audra said softly. "Under the wing of your protection, I believe they have more of a chance than should they have to find lodging elsewhere. You have mentioned the Blackfoot as your enemy. Surely they are the enemy of whites, as well."

"I cannot speak for the Blackfoot in that respect," Silver Wing answered. "But I *will* allow the whites to stay. If they begin preaching to my people again, I will have no choice but to send them away."

"I'm sure they won't do anything they know will anger you," Audra said. "And as for Dennis Bell, I'm so glad that his fever has broken and he is on the road to recovery. He is a very kind white man, Silver Wing. His heart is good toward your people."

"I knew him before he came to my village with Father John," Silver Wing said. "I know the good he is, yet I could not see past Harry Weston and trust even Dennis Bell, whom I had always seen as good-hearted."

"You even doubted my trustworthiness," Audra murmured, then gasped with delight when another butterfly landed on her hand, and then another and another.

Her eyes widened when she saw where they were coming from. While talking, she had not been aware of where she and Silver Wing were going. They had entered a mountain valley that was filled with more lush and fragrant wildflowers, more beautiful than she could have ever imagined possible.

All kinds of butterflies fluttered around everywhere. She could hardly tell where the butterflies ended and the flowers started.

"Silver Wing, would you look at that?" Audra cried, drawing a tight rein to stop her horse. She swept Silver Wing a quick glance, then looked at the wonder of the butterflies again, four of them still on her arms, as though they were extensions of them.

"I have brought you to 'Butterfly Valley,' " Silver Wing said, drawing rein beside her. He reached over and coaxed one of the butterflies from her arm, to the palm of his hand. "This was my sister's favorite place. It was because of this place and her love of butterflies that she named her daughter *Lap Lap,* Little Butterfly."

"I now see why you would say that place makes one feel as though all dreams could come true," Audra said, feeling drawn into the mystique of the surroundings. "I have never seen anything as beautiful. It's as though God is here, smiling."

"I have come here often and studied the butterflies," Silver Wing said. "The Queen Anne's lace is a nectar treat for swallowtails, while snow-on-the-mountain's delicate striped leaves are a feast for monarchs."

He watched the butterfly soar away from his hand, as did those fly away from Audra's arm. He slid from his saddle, then went and reached for Audra. "Butterflies also love bright colors," he said, glancing up at her hair. "I am surprised they were not drawn to your hair."

He brushed a kiss across her brow, then watched her run amidst the flowers, laughing as butterflies landed on her and fluttered around her. She giggled when one of them landed on the tip of her nose.

Then she ran to Silver Wing and grabbed him by a hand. "Run with me," she cried, her eyes pleading with him. "It's such a paradise, Silver Wing. Enjoy it to the fullest with me."

Careful not to trample butterflies in their wake, Silver Wing and Audra laughed and played among the flowers, then fell to the ground on their backs, panting.

"I doubt anything can ever compare with this,"

Audra said, turning on her side to gaze with enduring love at Silver Wing. "Let's come often to this place."

"There is only one season for such a number of butterflies," Silver Wing said. "Soon they will move on. But they will return this same time next year. We shall return and enjoy them again.

"Being here with you is what makes it so truly special," Silver Wing then said, turning on his side, drawing her into his embrace. His lips brushed across her brow, her cheeks, her closed eyes, and then he crushed her lips beneath his with a passionate, stirring kiss.

Audra gave herself up to the rapture as one of Silver Wing's hands lifted the skirt of her doeskin dress and slid her undergarment down her legs and away from her.

She sucked in a wild breath of pleasure against his lips and surrendered herself to him as his fingers began to stroke her, flaming her passions, her needs, her desires.

She reached a trembling hand between them and felt him hard and ready beneath his breechclout.

All shyness foreign to her now, Audra slid her hand down the front of his breechclout and wove her fingers around his manhood.

She heard his quick intake of breath as she began moving her hand on him, amazed at how he still seemed to grow within her fingers, hot and throbbing.

"Remove my breechclout," Silver Wing whispered huskily against her lips.

Doing his bidding, Audra slid his breechclout down past his thighs.

He then reached down and scooted it on down his legs himself, then kicked it away.

Moving over Audra, her dress hiked up to her waist, Silver Wing's gaze was flamed with passion as in one thrust he buried himself deeply inside her.

Kissing her hungrily, his kisses inflaming her heart, his hands swept beneath her hips and brought her body more tightly against him, moaning as she moved her body with his, her legs now wrapped around his waist.

Happiness bubbled from within Audra as she felt the bliss spreading like warm rays of sunshine through her. His groans of pleasure fired her passions.

Their tongues met.

Their bodies swayed and quivered.

The world melted away for both of them when the quiet explosion of their love reached the peak.

Audra groaned as she clung to him, their lips trembling together, as he still drove into her, then sighed with contentment after their peak was found.

His heart pounding, Silver Wing rolled away from her and stretched out on his back beside her.

Her own pulse racing, her face beaded with sweat, Audra laid on her back beside Silver Wing.

As Silver Wing gazed up at the sky, everything wonderfully peaceful, he reached over and twined his fingers through Audra's. "My happiness could never be as complete as it is now," he murmured, closing his eyes in ecstasy as Audra turned to her side and with her free hand cupped his shrunken manhood.

He sucked in a wild breath of pleasure as she began

moving her hand on him again, the wonders of her touch causing his manhood to grow again.

"I don't want today to end," Audra whispered, bending low, flicking her tongue across the tip of his tight, long shaft. "I . . . love . . . you so."

His eyes closed, enjoying being made love to by his woman in this way, Silver Wing spread his legs and stiffened them to his toes as she moved her mouth over him.

He placed his hands to her head, leading her in how and where to do this thing with her mouth and tongue.

And soon too near to exploding, the pleasure so intense he could hardly bear it, he urged her away from him, then rolled her beneath him and plunged into her, his thrusts eager and quick.

Twining her arms around Silver Wing's neck, Audra drew his lips to hers. As they kissed, she moved her body with his and soon again felt the wonders of their togetherness spilling over inside her, filling her with warmth and completeness.

Again, they rolled away from one another, spent.

Audra lowered her dress and reached for her undergarment. Having seen a stream as they entered this lovely valley, she pushed herself to her feet and went to it.

Kneeling beside it, she filled her hands with water. As she splashed water and cleansed herself, Silver Wing came to the stream and walked into it. He, too, bathed himself while watching Audra.

With her legs so spread out as she washed herself, he saw it as seductive and erotic and wanted her again, but brushed such thoughts aside, for twice already today was enough for any hot-blooded soul. They still had tonight to find pleasure in the darkness of his longhouse.

"You are looking at me so wickedly," Audra said, laughing softly, heat rushing to her face as she realized exactly where he was looking.

Silver Wing walked dripping from the water. He knelt down beside Audra and swept a hand between her thighs. He watched her eyes become clouded over with passion as he stroked her.

And when her eyes closed and her body trembled, he knew that he had taken her to paradise again.

There was no denying himself the same pleasure, For when Audra came out of her blissful trance, her hand went to him and stroked him until he came again in torrents, his seeds spilling into her hands.

"And so this is what makes babies," Audra murmured, studying the milky substance in her outstretched hand. "No one ever explained anything of life to me."

She gazed over at Silver Wing. "All mothers should tell their daughters about how men and women come together and what to expect of it," she said softly. "But I imagine most mothers are too busy with their daily activities to even think about the importance of such teachings."

He took her hand and held it down into the water, swishing it around as he cleansed it.

"I shall be your teacher," he said huskily, smiling over at her. "And I have only just begun."

"I adore my teacher," Audra murmured, lowering her dress, then drawing him over to her. She ran her fingers over his bare, powerful chest, then touched his lips with a forefinger. "Do you realize what wonderful lips you have? They were made for kissing."

As he chuckled beneath his breath and she giggled, she kissed him.

As Silver Wing slid his breechclout on, Audra's gaze was drawn past him. She was flooded with her past when she saw several hollyhock spires that were mingled with the wildflowers.

Many spires of hollyhocks that stretched skyward had grown beside her mother's porch. Those precious moments with her mother, though few they were, sent Audra to her feet and to the hollyhocks.

As she plucked a bright red blossom to take back to Silver Wing, she recalled how at night at her childhood home the lamplight from her bedroom window had streamed out onto the hollyhock spires. She smiled as she recalled. . . .

"And so you also enjoy looking at such delicate, beautiful flowers as this," Silver Wing said, stepping up beside her.

He, too, plucked a flower and laid it in the palm of his hand and gazed at it. "When my sister and I were small, I would pluck these blossoms and make hollyhock dolls for her. I would sometimes choose pink for the skirt and yellow for the bodice."

Audra was in awe of what he was saying, and that he also had made hollyhock dolls. And to have done it for his sister was surely as sweet a memory as Audra's was, for when she and her mother made such dolls, they twirled them on toothpicks as though they were dancing ballerinas.

She shared all of this with Silver Wing, then watched him pick up two thin twigs and make her a doll with a crimson skirt and bodice.

"I so love it," she murmured as he gave it to her and she held it gently in her hand.

He took her free hand and led her down on the grass, where they again stretched out on their backs among the flowers and butterflies and gazed heavenward.

"I do want to know everything about your people," she murmured. The horses neighed, drawing her eyes to them. "I can hardly wait to see your great herd of Appaloosa horses. Will you take me soon to see them?"

"Before we go home today I will take you there," Silver Wing said, then twined his fingers through hers and brought her hand over to rest on his abdomen. "Already in 1805 when Lewis and Clark came to my people, the Nez Perce had been horse Indians for more than a century," he said softly. "We were even breeding Appaloosa war ponies."

He sat up, then drew her up onto his lap to face him. "The white man's name for our war ponies came from the Palouse valley of the Palouse River," he said. "These horses descended from wild mustangs that in turn descended from Spanish horses brought in by explorers. Where our herds are kept, they are protected by the high mountain valley, where they profit more from better forage than is available on the plains. The horses are excellent racers. They are active and durable. The Nez Perce are proud that they belong to them. In order to keep our breed of horses pure, we breed only the best of the best. All other tribes are interested only in the number, rather than the quality."

"Does anyone ever steal them from you?" Audra asked softly.

"The herd is so widespread, reaching over so much land, yes, some are stolen, and rarely found again," Silver Wing said sullenly. "In the most strategic places we have sentries standing guard. My warriors take turns. They take enough food to last for a week and stay without returning home. When that warrior does come home, another one leaves and takes his place. It is something my warriors take pride in . . . watching the herd. The herd is too large, though, to watch them all every minute of the day and night."

"Red Bonnet is there now, isn't he?" Audra asked softly.

"Yes, but soon he will return to his family for several weeks before returning to the herd," Silver Wing said. He eased Audra from his lap, rose to his full height, then took her hand as they walked toward their horses. "Come. We will go now and see the herd and see how Red Bonnet is faring."

Audra hated letting go of her hollyhock doll, but had no place to put it as she rode the horse, so lay it on the ground. She laughed softly when a butterfly fluttered onto it.

"I always saw the hollyhocks as dolls of summer," she murmured.

"My sister and I enjoyed eating the seeds," Silver Wing said. "They were a treat to enjoy on summer days."

"I'm sure Drinks Water will be so happy to have

Red Bonnet home with her again," Audra said as she swung herself up into her saddle. "She has told me how much she misses him. The children also miss him so much."

Silver Wing mounted his steed. "Let us now go and introduce you to Red Bonnet *and* the horses," he said.

Smiling, Audra rode away with him. She looked back over her shoulder at the butterflies fluttering everywhere. Just like a fantasy, yet it was real . . . for she had been a part of it.

19

Let not my love be called idolatry,
Nor my beloved as an idol show,
Since all alike my songs and praises be
To one, of one, still such, and ever so.
——WILLIAM SHAKESPEARE

The longer they rode, the more Audra became in awe of this Northwest Country. Pine, hemlock, and spruce trees were everywhere. Deep rivers, bluish-green, flowed between high bluffs, and at points turned into dangerous rapids.

"Not far from where we are riding is where the woman's camas harvest is done," Silver Wing said, frowning as he looked into the distance. "Bears frequent the area. That is how my wife died. A bear came out of the brush so suddenly no one could do anything to stop him before he mauled my wife to death."

"That's so horrible," Audra said, visibly shuddering. "Do the women still go there even though there is such danger in doing so?"

"No bear, no man, nothing will stop our women's camas harvest," Silver Wing growled. "It is valuable to our people. Soon the women will be harvesting the camas again."

Audra swallowed hard. She could not help but wonder if she would be required to attend the harvest, since she was now a part of his village women.

She gave Silver Wing a wavering stare, but did not question him about this. She didn't want to look afraid. Thus far he saw her as courageous and brave for having fled the convent and boarded a ship alone.

She never wanted to disappoint him. If the harvest was required of her, so be it!

They rode onward through tall grass bending in the wind.

Overhead an eagle soared, casting its large shadow along the ground.

Audra followed alongside Silver Wing. When they topped a rise and she saw the huge herd of Appaloosa grazing in the lush green grass, her breath was stolen away.

"I couldn't have ever imagined there would be so many horses," she said, looking quickly over at Silver Wing. He seemed to have not heard her.

And she puzzled over how he looked suddenly so tense and angry as he stared ahead of them, his knuckles rendered white as he gripped harder to the horse's reins.

"What's wrong?" Audra asked, now following the line of his vision, still seeing nothing amiss that she could tell.

"The herd that is kept here is less than it should be," Silver Wing uttered angrily. "I know this herd well. I can visibly count their heads. Today many of those heads are gone!"

"You mean that someone stole them?" Audra asked, suddenly afraid. She looked quickly around her, to see if there were any signs of anyone lurking in the shadows of the tall butte that towered over the grazing horses. She was relieved when no one seemed to be anywhere near.

Yet she still felt threatened because Silver Wing's attitude was less than reassuring.

She flinched when he sank his heels into the flanks of his horse and rode away from her in a hard gallop.

She soon followed, then drew a tight rein when he suddenly stopped, his gaze locked on the ground.

As some of the Appaloosa parted and she, too, saw what lay there, the color drained from her face, and she felt suddenly faint.

She swallowed back the urge to vomit as her gaze stayed transfixed on the man's body that had been riddled with arrows, and on how he had been scalped. Blood had dried on him and on the ground. Flies buzzed hungrily over him.

Sickened by the gruesome sight, she started to ride away, but she stopped when she saw something else on the man's body just as Silver Wing leapt from his horse and knelt down over him. The man's body was covered with a red rash.

She realized the man had been suffering with measles on the day he had been murdered.

"Stop!" Audra shouted at Silver Wing as he snapped the last arrow in two so that he could at least remove that part of the shaft that extended away from the dead Indian's body.

But she was too late. Silver Wing was now lifting the dead man into his arms. Mournfully he wailed the dead man's name, and Audra knew that it was Red

Bonnet—Silver Wing's friend and Drinks Water's husband.

"Put him down!" Audra cried. "Silver Wing, please put him down!"

Her shouts drew Silver Wing's wails to a halt. He gave her a questioning look.

"Red Bonnet has measles," Audra said, swallowing hard. "Silver Wing, I'm not sure if someone can contract measles from a dead man, but if so, you have just been exposed."

In his sorrow, he hadn't even noticed the red blotches on Red Bonnet's face and body. "How could Red Bonnet have gotten them?" he said, his voice drawn. "He has been with the horses, tending to them, the entire time the white man with the disease has been at our village."

"He must have come in contact with the same person that Dennis came in contact with, surely at the trading post," Audra said. "Silver Wing, I know how distraught you are to find your friend killed in such a fiendish manner. I know you want to take him home for his family, and for a proper burial. But you can't go to your village just yet. Nor can you take Red Bonnet there. You must go into quarantine so that none of your other people will get the disease. Lord, Silver Wing, you wouldn't want to expose Little Butterfly."

"For how long is this quarantine?" Silver Wing said, lowering Red Bonnet's body back to the ground. He sat on his haunches over him, his heart aching over having lost such a friend who was devoted to his people and his family.

"Oh, Silver Wing, I'm not even sure if it's necessary, since I don't know if you can get measles from someone who is dead," Audra said, her voice breaking. "But to be safe, I think you should stay away from home for at least a full week."

"I will stay with the herd as these days pass," he said thickly. "Tall Shadow was to come today and replace Red Bonnet with the herd. Go to him. Tell him it is not necessary . . . that I will be here with them."

He reached a gentle hand to Red Bonnet's shoulder. "I will bury my friend," he said, swallowing hard. "Once my quarantine period is over, the village can come and mourn over the grave."

"Oh, how I dread breaking the news to Drinks Water," Audra said, tears filling her eyes as she stared again at the gruesome way this man had died.

"She is a strong woman," Silver Wing said. "And she is a mother who must stay strong in the eyes of her children. And . . . and . . . she knows the importance of keeping herself under control, emotionally, because she feeds not only her baby from her breast, but also Little Butterfly. Emotions are felt by a child. She will guard against it."

"I will return soon with food and blankets for you," Audra murmured. "I will bring you a change of clothes and your pipe and tobacco."

Silver Wing hung his head. "There are always too many graves to dig," he said hoarsely. "There are always pieces of my heart being torn away. My woman, I suddenly feel like an old man. Oh, so old and weary."

Audra slid from her saddle and went to him. She avoided looking at Red Bonnet as she twined her arms around Silver Wing's neck and drew his head down to rest against her breast. "I will do what I can to help you get through this latest loss," she murmured, gently stroking her fingers through his long hair. "I love you so, Silver Wing. I hate seeing you tortured like this."

"My sister has just been buried and I now, so soon, must bury my best friend?" he said thickly. "What in life is fair?"

"Our love, Silver Wing," Audra whispered, framing his face between her hands, drawing his eyes up to meet with hers. "We have each other."

"But you, also, will be taken from me," Silver Wing said, feeling like a child now in the eyes of his woman, instead of a strong man who had fought the fiercest of battles against the Blackfoot.

"No, I won't," Audra said, raising her chin. "I'm going to be here for as long as you want me."

"That is forever, my love," Silver Wing said, enveloping her within his muscled arms.

He kissed her, then leaned away from her and gazed at Red Bonnet again. He frowned darkly. "Go now and tell my people why I cannot return home just yet," he said thickly. "Also tell them about Red Bonnet's death and how he died . . . by arrows! Tell my warriors that the arrows are not Blackfoot. Even the scalp was not taken by a red man. It is all the work of white men who wished to make the Nez Perce believe a red man did this atrocity against another red man so that it would send we Nez Perce to the wrong people for vengeance."

"But who . . . ?" Audra asked, suddenly afraid to ride back to the village alone.

Yet she wouldn't voice this fear aloud to Silver Wing. He needed her to carry the message to his people about the warrior's death.

And she wanted to bring him supplies that would last him until he could return home again.

"Tell my warriors to search for the stolen horses, and when they find the horses they will, in turn, find the ones who are responsible for Red Bonnet's death," Silver Wing grumbled.

Audra flung herself into his arms again. "Hold me before I go," she murmured. "Please . . . hold . . . me."

Again, he held her within his strong arms. Their eyes met and held, and then he kissed her.

Wanting to get the journey to the village behind her, the threat of being alone causing a chill to ride her spine, Audra eased from Silver Wing's arms. "I'll be back as soon as I can," she murmured.

"Bring an escort," Silver Wing said hoarsely. "It is enough that you will be traveling *to* the village alone. It is not necessary for you to return under the same sort of threat."

"I will," Audra said, moving to her feet. She went to her horse and swung herself into the saddle. "But whoever comes with me will have to keep his distance from you. We must remember not to expose anyone else to measles."

"I will be glad when these strained times are behind us," Silver Wing said, again staring down at Red Bonnet's lifeless body. "But when they are, there will be something else to sadden my heart. It never fails that just when I find a small measure of happiness, something bad happens to take it away."

"The happiness we have between us has not been taken away by this ordeal, only strengthened," Audra murmured. "I could never love you more than now."

Wondering gray eyes stared at her.

She blew him a kiss, then wheeled the Appaloosa around and rode in a hard gallop across land that until only moments ago had seemed magical.

Now it was dirtied by spilled blood!

20

Thy step is as the wind, that weaves
Its play way among the leaves.
                    —WILLIAM CULLEN BRYANT

Audra silently watched the Nez Perce after she had
told them about Silver Wing, and about what had happened to Red Bonnet.

Her heart went out, especially, to Drinks Water, for
she had lost a husband.

But Audra was amazed at the woman's strength.
Instead of wailing and visibly showing her remorse,
she had gathered her children around her, giving them
comfort, since they had lost their beloved father.

Audra's heart melted when Drinks Water came to
her and placed a gentle hand on her arm.

"Go and be with Silver Wing in his time of sorrow,"
Drinks Water said softly. "I lost a husband, but Silver
Wing has lost a dear, loyal friend. I will care for Little
Butterfly until you return. And I will keep my grieving
from her. I would not want to do anything that would
erase her sweet, happy smile."

With tears Audra hugged Drinks Water, then
turned quickly when she heard another soft voice behind her.

She turned to see several women with parfleche bags filled with food and blankets for Silver Wing. Now she knew why Silver Wing was so proud and protective of his tribe. They were a special people whose hearts were good.

Audra wanted to embrace them one by one, but she was anxious to get back to Silver Wing. He was vulnerable out there all alone.

After thanking the women, and watching them hang the bags and blankets at the back of her horse, Audra went to the warriors assembled to search for the murderers and horse thieves.

"I think several of you should come and place sentries close to where Silver Wing will be making camp," she said, her eyes searching theirs for approval of a white woman suggesting things to them. "I'm worried that he is in danger out there all alone."

When no one answered, just gave each other questioning looks, she stepped closer to them and spoke again. "Some of you could do as Silver Wing asked you to do," she murmured. "Go and search for the murderers. But some of you could also go and guard your chief. You would not have to get close enough to be exposed to measles yet close enough to be there should he need you."

Black Fox, one of the tallest and thinnest of the warriors, stepped away from the others as their spokesperson. "We will do as you suggest," he said quietly. "It is good that you care this much for Silver Wing."

"Thank you," she said, sighing heavily.

She turned just as Father John came up behind her.

"You are taking risks leaving the village," he said, clutching a Bible at his right side. "Let the warriors go. They can take Silver Wing his supplies."

"I want to be with him," Audra murmured, trying to look past the look of shock that came into Father John's eyes. She knew already how he felt about her staying with Silver Wing in his lodge.

Father John glared at her for a moment longer, then turned with a flutter of black robe and walked away.

Audra glanced down at the Bible in Father John's hand. A sudden warning rushed through her, then she rushed to him and grabbed him by an arm.

She flinched when he gave her a look of utter annoyance for having stopped him in such an abrupt manner.

"Father John, I hope you won't take advantage of Silver Wing's long absence," she said. She tried to keep her voice steady, while in truth she found herself feeling as she had as a child when she had first entered the convent . . . small and frail beneath the scrutiny of the powerful man of God.

She forced herself to say the rest of what she was thinking. "I hope you will stay true to your promise to Silver Wing," she murmured. "That you won't preach the Bible to his people."

"A promise in the face of God is a promise, and I am appalled that you would think that I would even think of breaking one," Father John said, a true hurt in his eyes. "Audra, I will stay my distance from his people. And I will leave as soon as I know the ship has arrived. One of Silver Wing's warriors went to the Dalles Trading Post and asked them to send word when the ship is seen coming up the Columbia. Hopefully, it will be soon."

He eased his way away from Audra's hand and resumed his slow walk toward Dennis's longhouse.

Audra heaved a deep sigh of relief, then rushed to her horse. She rode off, with the warriors who had chosen to guard Silver Wing riding behind her.

She smiled when she recalled Silver Wing telling her to arrive with an escort. He would be surprised to see so many!

When she finally arrived where Silver Wing had made camp, she dismounted and went to him. On one side was a tall wall of rock, the butte high overhead, and bushes reached out on two other sides, which would give good cover.

They didn't embrace, for Silver Wing gazed at his men. They were dismounting in various strategic places just beyond where the herd began its grazing.

When Black Fox waved to him, he understood they did not want him to end up the same as Red Bonnet.

"I asked them to come," Audra murmured, drawing Silver Wing's eyes quickly to her.

She reached a hand to his face and slowly ran her fingers over his copper flesh. Her eyes searched for signs of measles.

When she saw nothing even close to a red rash, she flung herself into his arms and hugged him. "If anything happened to you, I would die," she said, a sob lodging in her throat. "I don't know how I got so lucky to have you care for me, but I thank God every day for blessing me in such a way."

"I am the one who is blessed," Silver Wing said,

then took her hand and began walking away from his campsite.

"Where are we going?" she asked, giving him a questioning glance.

He said nothing, only continued to walk.

When he stopped and stood over a mound of rock, Audra gazed down at it and knew that it was Red Bonnet's grave.

"Red Bonnet is protected now from predators of the night," Silver Wing said. "When you return to the village, tell Drinks Water that her husband has a safe haven until she comes later for his burial rites."

"I shall tell her," Audra said, swallowing hard. "She is a woman of much courage and strength. She thought first of the children, second of herself. She was there for them."

"I know Drinks Water well," Silver Wing said softly. "I know that Little Butterfly is still being well taken care of."

"Yes, very," Audra said, turning with him and walking back to his campsite. She helped him unload her horse, then sat down on a blanket with him beside a campfire. "I shall stay the night, then return tomorrow, at least for a while, to see Little Butterfly. Several of your warriors, under the leadership of Tall Shadow, are searching for those who came and took so much from you and your people."

"Is Father John still keeping his promise not to talk of his Christianity to my people?" Silver Wing asked, frowning over at Audra.

"I already spoke to him about that," Audra murmured. "He has promised to . . . to . . . behave."

"It will be good when he is gone," Silver Wing grumbled. "It will be good when the ship arrives and takes him away."

"I'll feel much better, too, when he is gone," Audra said, not able to feel guilty for wanting to rid her life of the priest.

If she allowed herself to think about how her life could have been, she *did* see that she owed so much to Father John. But he had made her feel so confined. She would be glad when he was out of her life.

She laid her head on Silver Wing's shoulder and tried to forget the past.

"I wish so badly to make love with you," Silver Wing said huskily. He drew her into his embrace, his gaze moving past her shoulder to his men, who were preparing a camp.

"And I, you," Audra said, her pulse racing. She eased from his arms and snuggled down beside him, her eyes following the line of his vision, also seeing the warriors, who were there and able to see their every move.

"But there is a time and place for everything," she said, smiling up at him. "For now, we are at least together."

"Yes, together . . ." Silver Wing said, trying hard not to think about the grave and his friend he had known since they were small braves, learning ways of warriors.

He thought of the long hunts he and Red Bonnet had gone on, challenging each other for that first kill of the season. He thought of them riding together into battle against the Blackfoot, and how they worked together to keep each other alive.

"What are you thinking about?" Audra asked, aware of his body tightening and tensing, and sometimes even flinching as though someone had slammed a fist into his gut.

"Of things long past," Silver Wing said, not ashamed for the tears that were streaming down his cheeks.

Audra saw his grieving and understood. She turned and held him as though he were the child, she the mother.

"It's going to be all right," she whispered, stroking a hand across his muscled, tight back. "In time, this grieving for a friend will, too, pass."

"He will always be there in my heart," Silver Wing said, swallowing hard.

"Yes, as is my beloved mother still in mine," Audra said, recalling those few times her mother sat Audra on her lap and read books to her.

Yes, those times were cherished, but were so few.

"Together we will forget many things that have hurt our hearts," she said, then brushed a soft kiss across his lips.

He drew her into his arms and gently hugged her, yet his mind could not help but stray to his warriors who were hunting the murderers. He so craved to be there doing his duty as chief.

21

Whither, midst falling dew,
While glow the heavens
With the last steps of day.
                    —WILLIAM CULLEN BRYANT

Having made a wide circle around the Appaloosa herd
near Silver Wing's campsite, Tall Shadow had found
tracks that led him to a deep canyon.

His rifle now drawn from its gun boot, with his warriors following, he rode slowly into the canyon.

They found part of the stolen herd grazing in a corral made of rope, then rode farther to find another
corral filled with more. They knew they had found not
only the horses, but surely the men responsible for
Red Bonnet's death.

Tall Shadow drew a tight rein and turned toward
the warriors behind him. "We will dismount and go
the rest of the way on foot as we search for the
thieves' hideout," he said, his eyes narrowed angrily.
"We must not allow them to hear our approach. We
will surprise them this early morning hour as they
sleep."

Following his lead, their horses' reins tied to tree
limbs, the Nez Perce moved stealthily along the tall
wall of rock until a slight rise in the land brought them

where they wanted to be. A cabin sat nestled beneath a canopy of cottonwoods, only a tiny spiraling of smoke rising from its stone chimney.

Tall Shadow's eyes moved quickly from the cabin to many horses in a smaller corral just behind the cabin. None of them were Appaloosa. They must have been the thieves' personal steeds.

Seething, Tall Shadow turned and nodded toward his men. "We still must move quietly enough not to awaken those who are in dreamland," he growled. "When we reach their cabin, rush inside. Do not chance any of them grabbing a weapon. It is enough that we have lost one valiant warrior. We need no more deaths today."

The warriors nodded.

They moved across scrub grass and rock until they reached the cabin. Several surrounded it, their rifles aimed at the cabin door.

Several other warriors went with Tall Shadow and stood by as he suddenly kicked the door open.

Shouting the war cry, they rushed inside and soon had all of the men on their bellies on the floor.

Tall Shadow singled Harry Weston out from the men and grabbed him first, slamming him to the floor.

"Have mercy!" Harry cried, looking wildly up at Tall Shadow as Tall Shadow held him in place on the floor with his foot grinding painfully into his abdomen. "Tall Shadow, you know me. I'm your friend! I brought Bibles to your people. I taught the children songs!"

"All was done with falseness!" Tall Shadow shouted, his eyes lit with fire. "And how can you plead for mercy when you are guilty of not having only been a false prophet to my people, but also have stolen horses from them . . . and killed one of their most honored warriors?"

"I didn't kill anyone," Harry cried, trying to dislodge the foot from his abdomen as he pulled and yanked at it with his trembling hands.

When Tall Shadow only ground his foot more deeply into his flesh, Harry cried out with pain and almost blacked out.

"You lie!" Tall Shadow hissed. He fell to his knees and placed the barrel of his rifle across Harry's throat. He shoved it into his flesh, almost cutting off all of his breath. He smiled cunningly as Harry's face grew red and he clawed at the rifle.

"Give . . . me . . . air," Harry gasped. "Please have mercy!"

"There is no mercy for a man who kills and scalps one of our people's favored warriors," Tall Shadow growled. "Confess everything to me now!"

"My friends and I found the Indian," Harry gulped. "He was already dead. There were arrows in his body. Some . . . some . . . one even scalped him. We got outta there. We . . . we . . . didn't want to be blamed for killing and scalping *any* Indian."

"You lie so easily," Tall Shadow said, tightening the rifle against Harry's throat. "Now, start all over again, and this time tell me the truth."

Harry gripped the rifle and again tried to move it, but still Tall Shadow held it in place.

"How . . . can . . . you . . . expect me to tell . . .

you anything else . . . if you continue to cut off my wind?" he managed to whisper, his eyes bulging.

Tall Shadow removed the rifle and smiled as Harry gasped and choked and rubbed his neck where the rifle had left an imprint in his flesh.

"All right," Harry then said, gratefully taking deep breaths. "You saw the horses. You know we stole them. But they weren't stolen today. They've been stolen slowly from the herd for weeks. Today when we came upon the dead Indian, we hightailed it outta there. It looks as though you might have other horse thieves on your hands. The Blackfoot. Surely it was the Blackfoot who stole horses after they killed your warrior friend. Don't the arrows prove it was Indians who killed him? Do you see any bows and arrows in this cabin?"

"Bows and quivers of arrows can easily be discarded to throw away a man's guilt," Tall Shadow said. He grabbed Harry by an arm and jerked him up from the floor. He nodded to a coil of rope hanging on the wall beside the door. "Get the rope. Come outside with me."

"A rope?" Harry gulped, his eyes wide. "Oh, Lord, you're going to hang us, aren't you? You're going to hang us!"

Tall Shadow enjoyed seeing the man groveling and afraid. He ignored his pleas and looked at the other warriors and their captives. "Bring them outside, also," he said, a deep respect for him in the eyes of the warriors as they nodded and followed him outside.

"Please don't hang us!" Harry cried. "Let us *go.*

We'll be on the next boat that leaves down the Columbia. You'll never see or hear of us again."

Tall Shadow still ignored Harry's frightened ramblings. He shoved him against a horse. "Get on," he said, his voice lacking emotion.

"No!" Harry cried, believing he was going to be led beneath a tree on the horse and hanged on the spot. "Please don't hang me."

Tall Shadow gave him another shove. "Get on the horse and be quiet," he said flatly.

Tears filling his eyes, trembling so hard he could hardly grab hold of the saddle's pommel, Harry gave Tall Shadow a soft pleading look, then finally got himself in the saddle.

As others now stood with rifles aimed at Harry, Tall Shadow laid his rifle on the ground long enough to tie Harry onto the horse. He looped the rope around Harry's neck, then around his wrists, and swung the rope around the horse's body, and then again around Harry's.

"If you try to get free, you will hang yourself by the rope that is around your neck," Tall Shadow said, tying a fast knot in the rope.

Harry sat stiffly as the other men were roped on their horses in the same way.

Tall Shadow went and placed his hands on the shoulders of two of his warriors. "Release the stolen horses and lead them back to their grazing grounds," he ordered.

His men mounted their steeds, went back to the stolen Appaloosa, and cut the rope corrals with their sharp knives.

Tall Shadow then commanded others to take the men on to the village and lock them up.

Then Tall Shadow and several others rode off and stopped when they found the sentries guarding Silver Wing.

Quickly Tall Shadow explained to the sentries what they had done, and then shouted to Silver Wing.

Silver Wing and Audra awakened with a start. Audra quickly dressed. Silver Wing threw a blanket around his shoulders and stepped away from his camp to see Tall Shadow sitting on his horse a short distance away.

"We found the stolen horses and the men who stole them," Tall Shadow relayed to Silver Wing, glancing over at Audra as she came and stood beside him.

"Then, you found the men responsible for killing Red Bonnet!" Silver Wing said, his spine stiffening. "Who, Tall Shadow? Who did this thing against our people?"

"Harry Weston is the leader of a gang who is now on their way to be imprisoned at our village," Tall Shadow answered. "Of course they all deny having killed Red Bonnet."

"How can they deny this when the proof is in them having our horses?" Silver Wing said, circling his hands into tight fists at his sides. "They will pay."

Audra found it hard to believe that Harry could be this devious and reckless.

Yes, she could see him stealing horses.

But murder?

And with arrows?

And she couldn't believe that he could do such a fiendish act as scalping a man.

No, she doubted that he was responsible, yet he and his men had been caught red-handed with the horses.

Something else concerned her, though.

She was afraid that Harry's irresponsible behavior might endanger Father John's continued freedom. Seeing Harry and his men as so evil, Silver Wing might believe that all white men are evil schemers.

And might he even reconsider trusting her, since she was white?

"Harry Weston and his men might not be responsible for Red Bonnet's death," Tall Shadow said thickly. "Harry Weston does not seem the sort to have the spine to kill and scalp in such a way. To me he is a spineless weasel."

"Then, who do you think is responsible?" Silver Wing said sullenly.

"You saw the arrows yourself and the way he was scalped," Tall Shadow said. "Were they the work of red men?"

"No, the scalping was done wrong and the arrows are those I am unfamiliar with. They were not the Blackfoot's," Silver Wing said, narrowing his eyes as he tried to blot out the image of his dead friend.

"I believe there are others out there who are responsible for the murder and scalping of our friend," Tall Shadow uttered. "I believe we have more horse thieves than Harry Weston and his cohorts."

"Then I urge you to begin searching for those responsible," Silver Wing said. "But it *is* proved that Harry Weston *is* a horse thief. Wait until I can return to our village to pass true judgment on him. I wish to be a part of the council that condemns him."

Tall Shadow glanced at Audra again, their eyes holding momentarily, then he looked at Silver Wing. "Whatever you say will be done," he said tightly. "And as for the white woman. Your trust in her is still as strong as before?"

Audra went pale at the warrior's words.

Silver Wing glowered at Tall Shadow. "This white woman is going to be my wife," he answered gruffly. "Never include her in talks when we are talking of enemies!"

Tall Shadow nodded, then wheeled his horse around and rode away, the others following.

Silver Wing turned soft, apologetic eyes at Audra. "It is only natural they will doubt all whites at this moment," he said softly. He placed a gentle hand to her cheek. "Do not be afraid of those who see you as wrong for their chief. I *am* chief. My word is final among my people. No one dares question it, not even my choice of women."

Audra moved into his arms and felt protected, at least for now. But she knew that he couldn't be with her every minute of her life.

Especially not now.

She *must* return to the village and be there for Little Butterfly.

Then she would return again tonight to be with Silver Wing.

Those moments of travel between the village and his temporary camping place were dangerous for her, yet she did not like the idea of having an Indian escort. *She* had seen the silent loathing and distrust in Tall Shadow's eyes when he had looked at her. She wasn't sure how far those feelings went among the other warriors.

Could one of Silver Wing's men believe they were doing their chief a service if they plotted against her to get her out of their chief's life?

No, right now she felt that the only person she could trust was Silver Wing . . . and he was isolated for several more days.

And she feared those days alone.

22

I cry! Love! Love! Love!
Happy love!
Free, as the mountain wind!
—WILLIAM BLAKE

Audra had stayed the night with Silver Wing, and he persuaded her to leave at daybreak for the village. He thought that would be the safest time to travel without an escort.

She had felt awkward having an escort traveling to and from the village so often.

It would be a bother for those who were asked to be with her.

And she still felt the warriors' resentment now that she was such a big part of their chief's life.

She was not sure how deep those grudges against her might go. For certain, she was keeping an eye over her shoulder when she traveled alone.

Audra sat comfortably beside the fireplace in Silver Wing's longhouse now. The fire was gently lapping at the logs, giving off comfort and light. Little Butterfly was peacefully asleep in Audra's arms.

But Audra felt a deep sadness over Drinks Water's loss.

She was thankful that Drinks Water had not seen

her husband and the vicious way he had died. That sight plagued Audra often these days as she could still hear the flies buzzing over his bloody remains.

"Please, Lord, keep Silver Wing safe," she whispered to herself.

Audra gazed down at Little Butterfly and watched her sleep.

Never had she seen such a beautiful child as *Lap Lap*.

Her copper skin was so soft and smooth.

Her long eyelashes fanned out over her cheeks like silken black veils, her tiny nose, and her perfectly shaped lips proved just how beautiful she would be as a woman.

All men would want to court her—or even battle over her!

"Sweet thing, I am going to enjoy watching you grow up," Audra whispered. "And I will always be there for you when you question life and its mysteries. I, for certain, will prepare you for womanhood. I will tell you everything my mother never told me."

Growing closer and closer to the child each day, bonding with her, Audra began to slowly rock her back and forth in her arms.

She began to sing a hymn she had learned many years ago.

" 'God be with you till we meet again,' " Audra sang, her voice carrying from the longhouse. " 'By His counsels guide, uphold you, With His sheep securely fold you; God be with you till we meet again. Till we meet . . . till we meet. Till we meet at Jesus' feet. Till we meet . . . till we meet. God be with you till we meet again.' "

Audra became suddenly aware that she was no longer alone with Little Butterfly. One by one, children had filed into the longhouse and stood behind her.

Her eyes widened as one by one they crept around and sat down around the fire, their eyes upon her.

"I know that song," one of the children said as she came and sat down beside Audra.

Audra recognized the child. Her name was Rose Bud. She was the six-year-old child Audra had shown Little Butterfly to more than once.

"Would you like to hear that song sung in the Nez Perce language?" Rose Bud asked, her dark eyes bright as she smiled at Audra.

"You know this song?" Audra said, forking an eyebrow.

"Yes, I know it very well in both my language and yours," Rose Bud said, nodding. "Father Harry taught me and my friends this song. He taught us other songs, too. Do you wish for me to sing the one you were just singing?"

The child's eyes shifted down to Little Butterfly. She reached over and gently touched Little Butterfly on the cheek. "I will sing it to *Lap Lap*," she murmured.

A warning rushed through Audra. The song the child offered to sing, the one Audra had sang was of a religious nature.

Silver Wing didn't want anything religious taught to his people.

She hadn't realized that her voice would carry it farther than this lodge.

But it had, and now she wasn't sure what to do. It was obvious that the children enjoyed the song. Surely they even wanted to hear more.

Not only would Silver Wing resent this, but also these children's parents.

She started to reach out and take one of Rose Bud's hands, to explain why they shouldn't sing any more hymns. She didn't get one word of objection out of her mouth before Rose Bud began singing, the other children soon joining her.

Audra's insides melted as she listened to them sing the hymn in their language. Their voices were so soft and sweet, and innocent. How could she stop them now that they had begun, especially since she could see the joy singing was bringing them?

She sighed heavily, held Little Butterfly closer as she rocked her, and smiled at each child as they continued to sing "God Be With You Till We Meet Again" in their Nez Perce language. . . .

" '*Godki pewakunyu hanaka, epinimpa piamktanu, sheepnim suhailakinwaspa, Godki pewaukunyu, hanak. Pewaukunyu; pewaukunyu; Jesusnim ahwapu nun, pewaukunyu, pewaukunyu, Godki pewaukunyu hanaka. Godki pewaukunyu hanaka, kaih kaihki waptaski hihikataku, palahaipa hinakniku, Godki pewaukunyu hanaka.*' "

Rose Bud's eyes were twinkling when they were through singing. She moved to her knees and smiled again at Audra. "Did you like it?" she asked softly. "Do we sing beautiful?"

Audra reached out and stroked the child's copper cheek. "Yes, oh, yes, you sing so very beautifully," she murmured. "I don't think I've ever heard a song sung so beautifully and sweet as you children sang it."

"The mean 'Bible' man taught us the song in his language, then we sang it back to him in ours," Rose Bud said softly.

Audra's smile faded. "What . . . do . . . you mean by referring to the Bible man being mean?" she asked guardedly. "Are you speaking of the man who called himself Father Harry?"

Rose Bud's smile faded. "Yes, that one," she said, frowning. "He is nothing like Father John, who I think is so nice. Father John does not speak of his religion. He just smiles and pats our heads, sometimes even hugs us. It was Father Harry." She lowered her eyes. "Father Harry was mean to me . . . and others."

Audra's eyes wavered as her heart skipped a beat. "What did he do to you?" she asked, almost afraid to hear the answer. She wasn't sure what Harry Weston was capable of doing. She knew that he had switched a child's legs. Had he done worse?

Rose Bud sat down and pulled up the hem of her goatskin dress. She pointed to scars on her legs. "He did this to me," she murmured. "He switched my legs when I did not do as he told me."

Although the sight of the scars tore at Audra's heart, she could not help but be relieved that Harry had not gone farther in his abuse.

"I'm so sorry," Audra said, reaching over and drawing Rose Bud into her arms. "But he'll not hurt you again, nor any of the other children."

"I hope not," Rose Bud said, tears filling her eyes. She eased from Audra's arms and again moved to her knees facing her. "He was a mean and angry man. He was not holy. We thought that he was supposed to be holy. Why wasn't he?"

"He was certainly nothing he pretended to be," Audra said softly. "He came to take *from* your people . . . not to give."

"But he did give to us," Rose Bud said, her eyes innocently wide. "He gave song books and Bibles to my people."

"It was all a ploy," Audra tried to explain. "It was done to wrongfully pull the Nez Perce into trusting him, while all along he was stealing your horses."

"Yes, I *did* trust him," Rose Bud said. "Is it wrong to trust so easily?"

Again, Audra reached out and placed a gentle hand on Rose Bud's cheek. "Sweetie, I wish that it could be that way, but no, it is best not to trust all that easily."

"I trust you," Rose Bud said, again smiling. "As do my people trust you. You are nice. Everyone believes your niceness is true, not false."

"I'm glad you and your people feel that way about me," Audra said.

She was truly relieved, for she wasn't quite sure what they felt.

Yet she had to remember that this was only a child's view. Perhaps the adults of the village held a deep-seated resentment toward her.

"When will Silver Wing be able to come back to us?" Rose Bud asked, a sadness creeping into her voice. "We all miss him."

"It shouldn't be too long before he can return home again," Audra murmured. "But we must make sure none of you children are exposed to measles. That is the only reason he stays away from you. He was exposed to the measles."

"How was he?" Rose Bud asked, cocking her head sideways.

Audra was taken aback by this question. She hadn't expected it.

And she certainly didn't want to tell the child exactly how Silver Wing *had* been exposed to the measles.

The details were too hideous.

She felt trapped.

Then she recalled having thought about how Red Bonnet had been exposed to the measles. She could tell the child that Silver Wing was exposed at the trading post.

"It seems, Rose Bud, that someone was at the Dalles Trading Post who had measles," Audra softly explained. "That man exposed Dennis Bell, and I am sure many others. Silver Wing might have been exposed by the same man."

"If our chief gets measles, will he die?" Rose Bud asked, her eyes sad.

"He is a strong man, so, no, I doubt anything as trivial as measles will kill him," Audra said, smiling reassuringly at the child.

She hid the fact that if Silver Wing got the disease, his immune system was no less weak than others of his tribe.

"If Silver Wing can survive skirmishes with the

Blackfoot, I am certain he can fight off such a thing as measles," Audra quickly added.

"He is such a strong, brave man," Rose Bud said, rising to her feet when the other children got to their feet and stood around her. "We will go now. Thank you for singing to us."

Rose Bud hesitated as the others went outside. "Can I kiss *Lap Lap* good-bye on the cheek?" she asked, her eyes begging.

"You certainly can," Audra said, smoothing the blanket aside to make way for the child's lips.

She watched Rose Bud give the baby a gentle kiss, then laughed softly as the child rushed on outside in a skipping fashion.

"So innocent," she murmured. "So sweet."

Her thoughts went to Silver Wing. She hungered to be with him, as never before. The Nez Perce children, their sweetness, made her think about having children herself. Hopefully they would look more like Silver Wing than herself. The Nez Perce children had captured her, heart and soul.

Little Butterfly began to stir in Audra's arms, then began a soft sobbing.

"You're hungry, aren't you?" Audra whispered, looking down at Little Butterfly, whose eyes were open and studying her. "I'll take you to Drinks Water, and then I'm going to go and be with your daddy."

A sensual thrill soared through Audra at the thought of making love again with Silver Wing. His skills at making love overwhelmed her so much she could almost feel his hands on her even now, stroking her.

She blushed as she actually felt a gnawing sort of pleasure at the juncture of her thighs.

Then she laughed softly to herself. "I'd best hurry to him," she whispered to Little Butterfly as she rose to her feet and left the longhouse.

23

She burnt with Love
As straw with fire flameth.
—WILLIAM SHAKESPEARE

The sun rose with all its splendor in the new light of
day, casting spirals of soft light through the spaces
in the wigwam covering overhead. "*Tots-mayee,* good
morning, my *I-ett,* woman," Silver Wing said huskily.

"There couldn't be a more wonderful way to awaken
in the morning than this," Audra murmured as Silver
Wing's hands fluttered across her naked body, touching and stroking all of her sensitive spots.

She stretched out on his pallet of pelts and blankets,
their privacy complete now since he had made a more
substantial dwelling than the lean-to he had built.

Audra had returned to him before dark last night
after having seen that Little Butterfly was content with
Drinks Water. Audra had felt pulled between two
loves and needs . . . to be with Silver Wing, and to
stay with Little Butterfly.

Knowing that Silver Wing must feel so alone while
apart from those he loved, she had opted to go to him.

When she had arrived and they had made love, she
had known she had made the right decision. Little

Butterfly was content no matter in whose arms she lay . . . Audra's or Drinks Water's.

Only Audra could give Silver Wing what he needed at this time.

"My hunger for you is never ending," Silver Wing said huskily as he slid over Audra, blanketing her with his nude, aroused body. "I need you more by the moment. *En-ha-wettsa, Tee-men-a, En-ha-wettsa.* I love you, Audra. I love you."

"I understand now how you say you love me in your language, but you said something else I haven't heard before," Audra murmured. "What else did you say?"

"*Tee-men-a,* means Spirit Woman," he said, framing her face between his hands. "It is a name that fits you well. You came to me in my life as a guardian spirit comes to fill one's life with comfort and love."

"*Tee-men-a,*" Audra said. "Spirit Woman." She giggled. "It makes me feel like a mystical being."

"You are anything but mystical," he said huskily. "You are *very* real."

His lips came to hers in a sweet, tremoring kiss as she opened her legs to him and sighed with pleasure as he thrust his thick shaft into her where she was hot, wet, and ready for him.

As he began his rhythmic strokes, his fingers continued to caress her swollen nub, each touch sending bursts of flames through her, fueling the desires already ignited within her.

His tongue swept into her mouth.

She flicked hers against his, then moaned with pleasure when he slid his mouth down away from hers and licked wetly around one of her nipples, and then the other.

Arching her body to meet his thrusts, moving with him, floating, her mind soaring with pleasure, Audra twined her arms around his neck and led his lips back to hers.

As they kissed again, his hands swept between them and cupped both her breasts, his thumbs tweaking the nipples until pain turned to pleasure.

Then he rose away from her and placed his hands at her waist. As he started to turn her, she questioned him with her eyes.

"This way is also good for the soul," he whispered, his voice deep with rising passion. "Get on your hands and knees."

Her heart pounding, feeling that this was a forbidden way to make love, yet desiring to experience anything he knew to teach her, Audra moved to her knees.

She then sighed with pleasure as he moved over her from behind and leaned his throbbing shaft within her again and began his thrusts, this time going more deeply, touching pleasure points she had not known existed within her.

His hands swept around her body.

He filled them with her breasts.

He kneaded.

He stroked.

His lips moved to the nape of her neck where he nibbled on her flesh, then licked his way around to her mouth as she turned her lips to him.

Again, they kissed, Silver Wing plunging over and over again within her.

Her buttocks strained into him, their naked flesh fusing in gentle pressure.

Aflame with longing, and feeling the wonders of their togetherness rising within her, Audra reached behind her and touched him as he momentarily slid himself from within her.

"*Tee-men-a,* move your hand on me," Silver Wing whispered, his pulse racing as she did as he asked of her.

He gritted his teeth as the pleasure spread like molten lava through his veins.

He tremored and groaned as he felt himself getting closer to that peak he had been seeking.

His heart thudding hard within his chest, Silver Wing reached down and grabbed Audra's hand away from him just in time, or he would have not been able to control himself any longer. He would have gone over the edge into total ecstasy.

And he didn't want to do that unless he was inside her and she felt the same sort of pleasure at that same moment.

Again, he placed his hands to her waist and turned her.

Again, she lay on her back, her eyes misty with pleasure.

Holding her arms out for him, he came to her and spread himself over her again.

When Silver Wing plunged inside her, Audra moaned with intense pleasure. She closed her eyes and held her head back as rapture gripped her insides and she was momentarily lost to everything but the warmth that spread through her entire body.

She could tell that he was receiving the same sort of pleasure, for she was familiar now with how his body behaved during those moments of ecstasy.

His body first stiffened, and then he would lunge deeply into her in one hard, long thrust.

His body would quake and shiver.

He would hold her as though in a vise.

His teeth would tighten together as his eyes closed and he moaned throatily.

Spent, yet still feeling the aftermath of pleasure, Silver Wing rolled away from Audra and stretched out on his back. "Each time it is better," he said lightly.

He reached for her and took one of her hands. He placed it on his shrinking member. He led her fingers around him, groaning as again he felt lusty waves of ecstasy enveloping him.

Understanding that she was giving him pleasure again, so enjoying giving it as well as receiving it, Audra moved to her knees and softly kissed his lips as his body shuddered and again he reached that peak of passion within her hand.

Reaching for a parfleche bag of water, Audra brought it over and gently poured some of it from the spout over her hand and over his manhood. She washed her hands, and then washed him until he again smelled fresh and clean as river water.

Setting the bag inside, she snuggled next to him, then jumped with a start when she heard a faint sound of voices outside the small wigwam.

Her eyebrows forked when she realized that the

voices she heard weren't those of his warriors who were standing guard. The wind was bringing to her the sound of women's voices.

"I hear them also," Silver Wing said as he sat up and slid his breechclout on. "It is the women of my village coming in this direction. It is the time of their camas harvest. Their fields are not that far from here."

"Yes, I remember seeing them," Audra said, quickly dressing. She tremored with ecstasy when he moved behind her, reached around, and cupped her breasts within his hands. Dropping them away from her, he picked up her brush and began pulling it through her short red curls.

"I think you should go with them," Silver Wing said, gazing intensely into Audra's eyes as she turned with a start and stared at him.

"You told me that your wife died during a camas harvest," she said, swallowing hard. "Yet you still think I should go with the women?"

"It is good that you learn everything about my people, especially those things of our women," Silver Wing said, laying the brush aside. "And one does not run from fear. They face it head on."

"I'm not actually afraid," Audra said, her eyes searching his. "I . . . I . . . just can't forget how you said she died."

"With you being my woman, who will soon be my wife, it is necessary you know the art of everything the Nez Perce women have learned from their mothers," he said seriously. "My wife was the only woman ever to die like she did during the harvest. I am certain that it will never happen again in such a way."

"I do want to go," Audra said. "I do want to learn."

She giggled when her stomach growled.

Silver Wing reached for his parfleche bag of food. From it he pulled some pemmican, that which was made from dried meat and vegetables. "Take this," he said, placing it in her hand. "Eat this. It will take away your hunger. The women will carry water for drinking."

The voices were no longer as audible. "They've gone on past," Audra said, going to the goatskin entrance flap, holding it aside. She turned and smiled at Silver Wing. "They aren't far. I'll hurry and join them."

He went to her and grabbed her around the waist. He drew her around, yanked her against his hard body, and gave her a quivering kiss. Reluctantly, he released her and watched her leave the lodge.

Frowning, he sat down beside the simmering coals of his lodge fire. Slowly he slid wood into the fire pit. He had encouraged Audra to go join the women, yet he could not deny being afraid for her. She had to learn camas harvesting in order to be a Nez Perce wife, even though the bears *were* always too close to the fields.

"*Wey-ya-kin,* Guardian Spirit, let her return home to me safe," he whispered as he cast his eyes heavenward. "Without her my life would have no true meaning."

24

True worth is in *being,* not *seeming*—
In doing, each day that goes by,
Some little good—not in dreaming of
Great things to do by and by.
—ALICE CARY

It was midday, nearly halfway through *Hillal,* the season of melting snow and rising rivers. Audra soon caught up with the women. She was welcomed among them. She joined the laughter and talking, yet she could not help but look guardedly around her for signs of bears.

But seeing the loveliness and peacefulness of the land made her fear lessen. Spring had warmed the plateaus of the mountains. The snow at the peaks and along the sides of the mountains were melting. Where the grass had poked through the snow on the slopes, it was thick, tall, green.

When they reached the taller, grassier slopes, Audra labored to keep up with the women, who were used to the climb.

She was glad when they finally reached the favored root-gathering grounds, where the camas wild lily bulbs' delicate flowers carpeted the prairie with a bluish sheen. She smiled a thank-you when one of the women handed her a sharpened digging stick.

She watched, then soon knew how to poke in the muddy ground and through patches of melting snow to turn up corm-like roots called *Kouse,* which, upon arriving home, would be boiled into a mealy mush or cooked and shaped into small cakes to be saved for later use.

She had seen the Nez Perce's stored foods. They were in grass-lined cache pits, called *We-kas,* found on the hillsides close to their village.

Audra quickly noticed how the camas bulbs resembled small onions but was told that when they were eaten, cooked or raw, they were agreeably sweet.

Her back aching, Audra continued to poke the soft earth with her sharp stick, turning over the fat, fleshy tubers one by one until the bag that she had been given was heavy with the harvest, as were the other women's.

Tired, sore, her face burning from the sun, Audra was glad when they began their trek home. Knowing that Silver Wing would want her to, she continued on past his temporary dwelling place, and went toward the village with the women, for she still had much to learn about the camas plant. She wanted to learn as much as she could.

Each step now an effort, the calves of her legs aching unmercifully, and sweat pouring from her brow, Audra continued onward with the women.

But when they went over a rise of land and Audra could see the village below them, she panicked when she saw smoke billowing upward into the sky.

The other women quickly noticed and realized that their village was on fire!

The bags filled with their harvest were dropped.

Screaming and wailing, the women ran toward the village, not sure yet how far spread the fire was, or whether or not their loved ones were dead or alive.

Audra's thoughts went instantly to Little Butterfly. Her heart sank with an instant despair to believe that anything might have happened to her. . . .

She looked over her shoulder, wondering if Silver Wing might have noticed the smoke filling the sky in billows of black.

25

O, wasn't thou with me, dearest, then,
While I rose up against my doom?
And yearn'd to burst the folded gloom,
To bare the eternal heavens again.
 —ALFRED, LORD TENNYSON

Audra's footsteps faltered when she got close enough to the Nez Perce village to see the extent of the fire damage. Half of the lodges had been destroyed by the fire.

Her heart skipped a beat and she went pale when she thought of Little Butterfly and others she had grown close to—especially Drinks Water and her children. Drinks Water had already lost someone special to her. Should some of her children have not escaped, Audra would be heartbroken.

She broke into a mad run again, forgetting how bone-weary and tired she had been only moments ago.

She looked in the direction of Silver Wing again. *Had* he seen the smoke? Would it draw him to the village to check on the welfare of his people? Would he forget the danger in mingling with them? If he broke out in measles while among them, many would die.

Her wonder about everything was drawn to a quick halt when she saw the despair among the Nez Perce. She was choked with sobs when she saw that many of them had burns on their flesh.

She soon found out that, thankfully, no one had died.

She ran and grabbed Little Butterfly into her arms as Drinks Water brought the child to her.

"Are you and your children all right?" Audra asked, not able to see any of her children.

"They are all right, and I have sent those who were old enough to walk away from the scene of destruction and pain," Drinks Water said. She wiped tears from her eyes with the back of her hands that were black with smoke. "I got them from our lodge just in time. The flames soon fully engulfed it. My baby is asleep in a blanket amid thick grass. Little Butterfly was there until she began crying."

Audra followed Drinks Water's gaze as the woman turned and looked at the remains of her longhouse. It lay in complete ruin, fire still consuming the last of the wood that had fallen away from the other main fire.

"I'm so sorry," Audra whimpered. She held Little Butterfly even more closely when she thought of what could have happened.

"The lodge can be rebuilt," Drinks Water said, turning to Audra. "The children's lives could not have been. The *Tah-mah-ne-weq*, Great Spirit took today, but also gave. He gave my children and your child more years to live that might have been stolen from them had he not alerted me to the fire soon enough."

Audra was touched that Drinks Water referred to Little Butterfly as Audra's child. For a brief moment the pains of the disaster lifted.

But the commotion, the wails, the shouts of the men who were still carrying water to extinguish the rest of the flames was nightmarish. "Who could have done this?" she asked, her voice breaking.

"It is the work of Harry Weston," Drinks Water said, her voice tight with anger. "When he and his men were locked up, there were outsiders who had allied themselves with them. They came today out from the shadows of the forest and not only wreaked havoc on our village, but also released the criminals and then set fire to the lodge holding them."

Audra's breath caught in her throat when she thought of Harry being loose again. Now she knew that Harry *did* have more friends than the ones incarcerated with him.

How foolish to have believed Harry when he had said that neither he nor his men were responsible for Red Bonnet's death. He was surely the one who gave the orders to kill him!

She just hadn't wanted to believe that a man who had been trusted back in San Francisco enough to work at the convent could be this far removed from God that he would kill, steal, and destroy!

And the fire *had* surely been set in the village to distract the Nez Perce while Harry and his men were being released.

Audra sighed heavily when she recalled having told little Rose Bud that it was not good to trust all that easily. Now she had been taken in by Harry's lies!

From now on she would practice what she preached. She would be more careful in whom she put her trust!

Again, those who had burned and destroyed today were white. She was white.

But another thought came to her: Would the Nez Perce continue to trust her?

Father John!

Father John and the other four priests.

Even Dennis Bell!

Where were they?

Had they died in the fire?

She looked frantically around her, then sighed with relief when she found them at the far side of the village. While some were helping the Nez Perce throw water onto the burning rubble, Father John was gently gathering children around him and ushering them away, to stand in small, clinging clusters at the edge of the village. She could tell that Father John had helped put out the fires, for his face was black from smoke, his robe torn and hanging in shreds from his small, lean body.

She looked quickly over at the longhouse in which they had been staying. Father John's lodge had been spared, and along with it his Bibles. It was as though the hand of God had reached down from the heavens and blessed that longhouse, sparing the holy word in the process.

Audra's eyes went quickly to Little Butterfly when she started to whimper. Audra smoothed a corner of the blanket away from the child's face and found her awake, her eyes wide as she gazed back at Audra.

Then Little Butterfly began to cry in earnest, her face pinched into a frown.

"Let me take her and feed her," Drinks Water said softly as she held her arms out for the child. "It is time, also, for my daughter to be fed. I will go to the children. They can sit around and watch as the babies feed. That will give them something to take their mind off the tragedy. My children are in awe of the way the babies feed." She managed a soft laugh. "They do not remember their own moments at my breasts."

Smiling, Audra handed the baby to Drinks Water. She felt empty inside as Drinks Water carried Little Butterfly away, soon lost to her sight as she walked through the throng of Nez Perce. They were now carrying the charred wood away and placing it in a pile at one side of the village.

Audra gazed around her and found the burned victims lying on blankets in the shade as Rainbow worked her magic. She was taking a concoction from a small vial, and smearing it gently on the injured.

The sound of approaching horses drew Audra quickly around.

She swallowed hard when she saw Silver Wing riding with his warriors. Silver Wing had forgotten the dangers of coming and mingling with his people. After having surely seen the smoke, his alarm had become too great to even consider the harm he might be bringing to his people.

But it was too late. His people were rushing to him. He was off his horse now and embracing them, one by one, his eyes now on Audra as he found her standing there watching him.

Knowing it would do no good to remind him about why he had been away from his people, Audra ran to him.

She wanted to be pulled into his embrace, wanted his solace.

But his arms were too filled with his beloved people. She stood back, for they needed his reassurance . . . his love.

She prayed that it was safe for him to be with his tribe.

As Silver Wing continued to embrace his people, one by one, Audra saw him silently mouth something to her. She could tell that it was a question. She watched his lips more carefully when he mouthed the question again, this time able to make out the name Little Butterfly.

Audra smiled reassuringly at him—Little Butterfly was all right. She nodded toward Drinks Water, whom Audra could now see sitting beneath a tall oak tree at one end of the village, the children sitting around her watching her feed the babies, one at each breast.

She saw the relief that flooded Silver Wing's eyes.

"Daughter," Audra whispered to herself. Yes, Little Butterfly *was* his daughter now. As was she Audra's.

That alone lifted her spirits.

The people had proved to be resilient.

They would rebuild. And those who were injured today would soon be well.

Scarred, perhaps, but well.

Finally Silver Wing came to Audra. He quickly drew her into his arms. "It was a nightmare to think that you or Little Butterfly might have been harmed in the fire," he said, relieved. "I had seen you and the women walking toward the village with bags filled from the camas harvest. Later, when I saw the smoke in the sky, I knew you could have been harmed. . . ."

His words trailed off when she gave him a reassuring hug. "I am fine and so is Little Butterfly," she murmured. She gazed up at him. Their eyes met and held. "But so many were burned. I . . . I . . . am so sorry."

"It is not of your doing," Silver Wing said, holding her away from him, his hands gently on her shoulders. "Do not blame yourself for what others do to my people. Those white men who came and destroyed today are not of the same mold as you. They are fiends. And fiends eventually pay for what they do wrongly to others."

Audra stepped away from Silver Wing when several warriors came and stood before him. "My warriors, I see the need of vengeance in your eyes," he said hoarsely. "I, too, need this the same as you. But it will have to come later. There is too much to do at our village. We must rebuild our lodges so that our women and children are sheltered from the weather and so that our people can resume their normal lives."

Audra noticed how his fingers circled into tight fists at his sides as he paused and took a deep, shuddering breath.

She shivered when she heard the hate in his voice as he continued through clenched teeth, the words coming out in a low hiss.

"*Then* we will find Harry Weston and his men. They will wish they had never been born!" He tightened his jaw. "Until now those thieves who were not jailed with Harry Weston eluded us. But I vow now to find them if I have to search until my dying day!"

The war cries and the shouts of hate as the men waved their fists above them made goose bumps ride

Audra's spine. Harry would surely die a slow, unmerciful death.

She glanced over at Silver Wing.

Would he eventually see *her* as the enemy because her skin was white?

That thought made her feel ill at ease, suddenly a foreigner to the man she adored.

She walked quickly away from him and pushed her way through the children sitting around Drinks Water.

She was glad to see that Little Butterfly was through eating.

She eagerly took the child and held her close.

Rocking her, she tried to feel that everything was going to be all right.

The child had bonded to her.

Surely nothing would sever that bond.

Nor hers to Silver Wing!

If she had to, she would fight to keep them!

26

O thou bright jewel in my aim I strive
To comprehend thee.
Thine own words declare
Wisdom is higher than a fool can reach.
—PHYLLIS WHEATLEY

Having learned to adapt well to changes inflicted not
only by white people but also by the Blackfoot, the
Nez Perce had worked steadily for days until once
again their village was rebuilt.

Although many warriors had gone to search for
Harry Weston and his men, they had not found any
signs of them. They seemed to have disappeared from
the face of the earth!

Tonight even that was forgotten as the Nez Perce
celebrated the rebirth of their village and the fact that
those who had gotten burned were now healing
quickly.

Audra sat beside Silver Wing on blankets, his people sitting in a wide circle around a huge fire. They
left enough room between themselves and the fire for
dancing and games.

As the fire reflected onto Silver Wing's face, Audra
turned to him and studied it. She was thankful that
he had not contracted measles. She doubted now that
he would.

She looked past him and smiled at Father John and his four friends, as well as Dennis Bell, who sat on blankets somewhat away from the Nez Perce. They were there, but not actually joining the celebration. They were observing, as well as enjoying the food that had been prepared for the feast.

She was happy for Father John. After he had saved so many children, and then cared for them while their parents were rebuilding their lodges, the children had grown to adore him.

Even Audra felt herself growing close to him. When she smiled at him it was genuine and with affection.

He returned the smile with the same affection.

Audra again looked around the crowd of Nez Perce. She sighed, thinking, yes, everything was as it should be. The laughter and the joy in the Nez Perce's eyes were proof that they once again found hope and happiness with the birth of each new day.

Most of the horses that had been stolen were once again with the large herd.

The land was bright with wildflowers.

Animals roamed the mountainsides, proud and beautiful.

The Nez Perce children were vibrant and full of life.

Earlier in the day they had joined the festivities by chanting and acting out a legend called "The Witch and Her Four Sons," a legend that was popular among young Nez Perce dancers.

Thinking of children brought Little Butterfly to Audra's mind. She looked over at Drinks Water's longhouse. Drinks Water had been the only one who had not joined the celebration. She had chosen to stay inside her lodge with not only her baby, but also Little Butterfly. Although she had proven to be strong after the death of her husband, she still grieved in her silent way.

"I must leave you for a while," Silver Wing said, drawing Audra's questioning eyes quickly to him. "I will join other warriors in the Nez Perce's sacred 'Feather Dance.'"

Audra smiled and nodded. She understood the feather dance. Silver Wing had explained it to her before the celebration. In this dance the warriors told of their war experiences and deeds of heroism. It was only performed by warriors of prestige.

Audra sat straight-backed, her legs tucked beneath her, and watched closely as the performances began. There were at least twenty warriors who would participate today. They stood back as Rainbow placed a feather on the ground.

The warriors then gathered around the feather in a circular manner. The tribal drummers began pounding their drums and singing a song that was special for the occasion. Silver Wing had told Audra earlier that this song was known as the "warrior's song."

Everyone watched, and Audra was caught in a trance as Silver Wing knelt before the lone feather. The beat of the song, accompanied by the drums, picked up his pace. Silver Wing stood up and began dancing around the feather that was being honored. He pointed to the feather as if he wished to grab it, but left it lying there, where it would stay until all warriors had danced around it.

Still dancing, Silver Wing moved back and watched

as the other warriors took their turns dancing around the feather, each one pointing to it as though wishing to have it as their own.

Then suddenly the singing and drumbeats stopped.

One by one the warriors took turns telling of a war experience, or deed of heroism, each one as intriguing as the last for Audra. She smiled when one of the experiences was about a warrior saving one of his brethren, then shuddered when another tale was of him killing his enemy, their scalp hanging even now on a scalp pole inside the warrior's lodge.

Then it was Silver Wing's turn to step before everyone and relay his tale. His was a story of heroism.

"As you all know, Tall Shadow and Red Bonnet have always been my two closest, dearest *latawah,* friends, since childhood," Silver Wing said, his voice thick with melancholy. "After we became braves old enough to wander without the escorts of warriors, we left often at night to seek the great wolf, to watch them, to try and understand them, since wolves hold great magic and possess the power of the night, the healing power of the spirits, and wisdom to instill courage. We felt that if we could find the wolves and roam with them, we might become as one with them and gain their same magic and powers."

He paused, looked to the ground, then turned to Drinks Water's lodge. He thought that this tale he was relaying to his people might reach her ears and draw her outside. He had tried in vain to persuade her to join the fun tonight. Although it pained him so to talk of Red Bonnet, since his loss was still like a knife stabbing his heart, he felt it was necessary. He did not like seeing Drinks Water folding into herself in her grief instead of being with others who could help her.

When she gave him a soft smile and nod, and she started walking toward him, he knew that it was right to have chosen this tale tonight.

He waited until she entered the wide circle and sat down beside Audra.

His gaze went to Audra when he saw her reach over and take Drinks Water's hand. He wanted to hug her, his emotions so strong.

But he had a story to finish. Their time together would come later tonight. It would be a private time, when both could ride the waves of wonder again as they made enduring love.

"Red Bonnet and I rode our Appaloosa ponies this one night alone without Tall Shadow because Tall Shadow was not feeling well. The moon was bright and high overhead," he said thickly. "We could hear the wolves. Some were barking. Some were baying. We followed their sounds, our hearts beating with excitement the closer we came to their den. We had looked for several nights without success in finding them. But that night we knew we would finally find their home. We could hide and observe them. We would soon know their magic!"

As Silver Wing paused to take a deep, heaving breath, Audra noticed that things had become so quiet among the Nez Perce, the only sounds that could be heard was the popping and crackling of the huge outdoor fire. Everyone's eyes were on Silver Wing, an anxiousness in them.

Suddenly several bloodcurdling howls from several

wolves cut through the night like a knife as though the wolves knew they were a part of an Indian's tale tonight.

Audra swallowed hard when she saw Silver Wing's head jerk to one side and saw how his eyes misted over as he stared at something standing before him. She shivered as she felt a presence.

Was it the spirit of dead wolves?

Or might it be Red Bonnet's spirit having come to join his friend during his tale of heroism?

Audra turned and looked farther than the village. Something grabbed at the pit of her stomach when she saw several wolves illuminated by the moon. They were on a high butte, yet far enough away not to be any danger.

She looked quickly away from them, swallowed hard, then slid her hand free of Drinks Water's and gazed intensely at Silver Wing again as he proceeded with his story.

"We found the wolves that night," Silver Wing said, his voice drawn, once again looking at his people. "But we soon discovered it was the wrong time to be near them. Suddenly we were surrounded by a *pack* of wolves, and not far from them was a fresh kill. We had unknowingly come upon the wolves shortly after they had killed one of our Appaloosa horses. The wolves' sharp white teeth, stained with the horse's blood, shone out from under their thick, white-furred jowls, as their silver-blue eyes turned up to me and Red Bonnet. We knew the danger we were in. There were only two of us and our two bows and quivers of arrows."

He inhaled a shaky breath, then continued. "We stood our ground," he said. "Soon the wolves saw us as no threat to their meal. They slinked away and returned to feasting upon the horse's flesh. Red Bonnet and I slowly backed our steeds up until there was a great distance between us and the wolves, then wheeled our horses around and rode off in a hard gallop."

He paused and gazed at Drinks Water, who knew what was coming next. She smiled, knowing this was the moment of heroism that had saved the young brave who grew up into a great warrior and then became her husband.

"We did not get far before Red Bonnet's horse's hoof tripped in a gopher hole," Silver Wing continued. "Red Bonnet was thrown. For a moment he was unconscious. Just as I slid from my saddle to go to him, one of the wolves, already fat from having eaten enough horse meat, appeared from what seemed out of nowhere. It seemed not to notice me. But it saw Red Bonnet. Its teeth bared, and growling, it paused for a moment, then lunged onto Red Bonnet just as Red Bonnet awakened and saw what was happening."

He paused and swallowed hard as if that day was being re-created before him.

"But Red Bonnet was helpless beneath the weight of the wolf and his bow had fallen from his shoulder during the fall," he then said. "I notched an arrow quickly on my bow and shot the wolf. But even that did not down him. He started to bite Red Bonnet's neck. I always carried a knife my father gave me when I was old enough for the hunt. I grabbed it from its sheath, jumped from the horse, and plunged it into the wolf's throat, stopping it just before it sank its teeth deeply into my friend's flesh. The wolf went lifeless and fell away from Red Bonnet. My . . . friend . . . lived."

A burst of applause and shouts of wonder filled the night air, silencing the wolves' howls on the butte and sending them running with fear into the cover of darkness.

Then everything became quiet again. Tall Shadow stepped away from the other warriors and pointed to the feather. "You have earned the feather, my friend," he said hoarsely. "You have proven tonight to be the bravest of our warriors."

Smiling and proud, yet aching inside over not having Red Bonnet there this time to hear the story about two friends who would die for one another, Silver Wing knelt to his haunches and gently, meditatingly, lifted the honored feather from the ground.

As he stood up again, he turned slowly before his people so each of them could see him place the feather in a coil of hair at the back of his head.

The sacred feather dance was now completed. Everyone relaxed, and the drums began their steady beat again as songs filled the air.

Silver Wing sat down beside Audra. He slid an arm around her waist and smiled at her.

"It was so beautiful," Audra murmured.

Drinks Water reached around Audra and clasped onto Silver Wing's arm. "You bring so much into my life when you speak of my late husband so endearingly," she said, tears streaming from her eyes.

"Never could friends be as close as Red Bonnet and I were toward one another, especially after the wolf attack," Silver Wing said, then turned his head with a jerk when a child's voice broke into song . . . a song forbidden to her, for it was a white man's hymn.

Everything and everyone were silenced by it!

When Silver Wing rose quickly to his feet, his hands in tight, angry knots at his sides, Audra felt afraid. Her spine stiff, she watched Silver Wing stamp over to Rose Bud, whose voice had been stilled by her people's reaction to it.

Rose Bud looked up at Silver Wing as he stopped and stood over her. "You do not like my singing?" she asked innocently enough. "My . . . singing . . . angers you?"

"It is not your singing that angers me," Silver Wing said, his voice hollow with hate. "It is the song you are singing."

Audra went pale when Rose Bud looked quickly over at her, then again looked wide-eyed up at her chief. "But your lady friend liked it," she murmured. "I sang it for her, and she liked it. I sang it to her in her language as well as ours."

When Silver Wing turned on a heel and stared accusingly at Audra, his eyes so cold and unfriendly, Audra rose to her feet and backed slowly away from him. Her future as she had seen it only moments ago now seemed bleak.

Yes, she knew now that she shouldn't have even been singing religious songs to Little Butterfly.

"I can explain," Audra murmured, hating it when

her voice quavered as though she was frightened of the man she would die for.

"No explanations can make right what is wrong here," Silver Wing said, his voice a tight hiss.

"Please let me at least try," Audra pleaded.

When he said nothing, and only stood there glaring at her, she felt her world slowly slipping away from her.

27

I prize thy love more than whole mines of gold,
Or all the riches that the Eastdoth hold.
—ANNE BRADSTREET

Audra's heart lurched when Silver Wing grabbed her by the hand and led her from the others. He did not stop until they were in the privacy of his longhouse.

The door closed, only simmering embers in the fireplace. Silver Wing released Audra's hand, then placed his hands gently on her shoulders as he stood facing her.

"I do not understand a woman who seems to want what her man wants, yet still goes against him in ways she knows will upset him," Silver Wing said, his voice drawn, his gray eyes intensely holding with hers. "You know that I only allowed Father John and the others to stay among my people if they promised not to spread the word among them about their God. You know that meant you, as well."

The blood rushed from Audra's face. She had thought that his love for her was true and that he wanted her at the village because he wanted her . . . and that he now trusted her judgment on all things. But now he implied that she was still there on particular conditions.

She recalled Father John's warnings . . . that if she did anything that displeased the Nez Perce, she could be as quickly condemned in their eyes. She knew that banishment could be the final ruling as a result of their council about her.

"How can you be something I did not think *you* were?" Audra blurted out. "How can you condemn me so quickly about something you only believe, but don't actually know? I didn't teach the children anything that you did not want them to be taught. It all happened by sheer accident."

She swallowed. Her eyes wavered. "You know that I would have never done anything that I knew you deplored," she murmured. "I love you so much. I want to make you happy. Don't you want the same for me?"

"Except for my loyalty to my people and *Lap Lap,* everything else I do now is based on my love for you," Silver Wing said, slowly dropping his hands to his sides. "But you know my feelings about the white man's religion."

He frustratedly swiped a hand across his brow, then clasped his hands behind him. "I will never forget that day when I found Father Harry switching the young brave's legs," he said, his voice drawn. "How can a man speak to my people with a soft voice about his God, and then the next mistreat innocent children?"

"Because the man who did this was *not* a man of God, but instead a fraud," Audra said, her voice lilting. "Oh, Silver Wing, I have explained this to you time and again."

"Nothing about this Harry man is important," Silver

Wing mumbled. "What *is*, is how you allowed Rose Bud to sing a white man's hymn, and not only in the English language, but also her own. The minute she began singing was the minute you should have stopped her."

"It was all done so innocently," Audra said, heaving another deep sigh. She nervously slid her hands over the fabric of her buckskin dress. "I was singing to Little Butterfly. The children of the village heard. They came inside your lodge and listened, as well."

"You . . . were . . . singing hymns to our child?" Silver Wing said, his voice low and measured, his eyes lit with fire.

As Audra recalled the moment, singing softly to Little Butterfly had seemed the right thing to do, for she would always recall how her mother had rocked and held her and sang hymns to her when she was a small child.

Audra had wanted to give Little Butterfly the same pleasure, the same peace that Audra had always received from her mother's voice.

"I'm sorry," she blurted out, truly wishing that she had thought before she had acted. Although she had enjoyed the songs, she knew they were forbidden, but for that moment, had forgotten that they were. "I didn't realize what I was doing. I . . . I . . . was just singing to Little Butterfly. I didn't think about the sort of song I was singing to her."

"You, who will be my niece's teacher of all things, you who are now her *mother*, must guard well your teachings," Silver Wing said solemnly.

"Silver Wing, I do want to do what is right, but I

wish you would let me explain to you about the religion I was taught as a child," Audra said, carefully making him realize that he had his religion and she had been taught her own.

When he didn't say anything, or tell her not to speak of her religion, she continued.

"Silver Wing, the white man's religion only seems bad because bad men sometimes use it for their own selfish, greedy purposes, such as Harry Weston used it," she murmured. "Otherwise, it can be as beautiful and wonderful as your own.

"You might even consider giving Father John a chance," she said softly. "Let him teach in the way *he* teaches. Father John's lessons are filled with love, joy, and kindness. Even the children at your village see him now as someone kind and special."

Silver Wing's eyebrows forked. "You fled the holy man's house, yet you now speak good of it?" he said, his voice drawn. "If his religion is good and innocent, why did you have such a desperate need to flee it?"

"It was not the religion that I fled from," she said. "Like I have told you before. Being at the convent made me unhappy. I was raised as a Baptist in Kansas City. I could wear what I wanted to wear. I was not confined there. And I didn't have to cut my hair. So you can see why being there was so hard to accept, especially since I was there without family."

She paused, then said, "But don't get me wrong, either, about the convent," she murmured. "Most who are there are there because they want to be. They have given their entire way of life up to work for the Lord. It is a calling, something someone wishes to do.

I was placed there, in a sense, for protection after my mother died."

"You are now here for protection, also you are here for *love*," Silver Wing said, gently placing a hand to her cheek. "*Tee-men-a*, you know how much *en-ha-wettsa*, I love you."

"Yes, I know," Audra murmured, leaning her face into his hand, relishing this moment of tenderness between them, when only moments ago she had thought that she had lost him forever.

"I still have things to work out in my mind," Silver Wing said, his eyes locking with hers.

Then, to her surprise, he spun around and left the longhouse, their moment of tenderness so brief, it seemed not to have happened at all.

Her lips parted in a gasp, Audra stood there for a moment, then rushed from the lodge.

She expected to see Silver Wing join his people again, but was stunned when she heard a horse riding away and she saw that Silver Wing was on it.

She grew pale when she realized that everyone else had seen his flight also, for suddenly there was a total silence behind her. All eyes shifted from their fleeing chief to her.

Torn, Audra ran back into the lodge and closed the door behind her.

Sobbing, she sank down on her knees before the fireplace.

She couldn't believe that Silver Wing did not accept her reasons for singing the hymn to Little Butterfly. She most certainly couldn't help it if Harry Weston had already taught the children the hymns and that

Rose Bud had remembered them so well she had joined in today to sing one of them before her people.

The creaking of the door drew Audra's attention.

She wiped the tears from her eyes and gazed at Drinks Water as she came into the lodge carrying Little Butterfly.

"The child will ease your loneliness while Silver Wing is away," Drinks Water said as she knelt down beside Audra and gently placed Little Butterfly in her outstretched arms.

"Drinks Water, I'm sorry for having caused problems, especially today when everyone was so happy about having their lives back again," Audra said, gently rocking Little Butterfly back and forth in her arms. "I . . . I . . . don't know where Silver Wing has gone, and not even truly why."

"He goes to pray to *Tah-mah-ne-weq,* our Great Spirit, for what disturbs him," Drinks Water said, sitting down beside Audra on the blanket. "I will stay awhile. We can talk."

"Thank you," Audra said, swallowing hard. "Your friendship . . . and . . . understanding . . . means so much to me."

"Silver Wing will return soon, and then you will see that things will be good again between you," Drinks Water said, reaching a hand over to gently touch Audra's hair. "Your hair is growing some. One day it will be the same length as mine."

"Yes, I can hardly wait," Audra said, looking past Drinks Water at the door. She loved having Drinks Water with her and was so thankful that the woman cared enough to be there for her in her time of trouble, yet Audra's heart ached for Silver Wing to be there. She tried to understand his need to flee, yet it was hard to understand why he could misjudge her so quickly if he loved her as much as he confessed to.

She gazed down at Little Butterfly, who began to whine restlessly. She smiled over at Drinks Water as the woman slid a breast free for nursing.

Audra handed Little Butterfly to Drinks Water and was content at least for the moment as she watched the child nurse.

Yet she couldn't quit glancing at the door, hoping that at any moment Silver Wing would return.

She worried about him being alone while killers still roamed freely.

28

His rising radiance drives the shades away—
But, oh! I feel his fervid beams too strong,
And scarce begun, concludes th' abortive song.
                              —PHYLLIS WHEATLEY

When night fell and Silver Wing hadn't arrived home, Audra imagined all kinds of worrisome scenes.

What if Harry and his men *had* seen Silver Wing riding alone?

What if they had abducted him . . . even killed him?

Pacing, Audra glanced down at the cradle where Little Butterfly was peacefully sleeping, then gazed at the door again.

If only it would open!

If only Silver Wing would step into the longhouse!

If only he would take her quickly into his arms and tell her that he was sorry for having not understood why she had so innocently sang a hymn to Little Butterfly!

"There are too many *if's*," she whispered to herself.

She hugged herself and stopped pacing when she heard a wolf howling in the far distance. Memories of Silver Wing's tale about the wolves haunted her. Tonight Silver Wing was alone! Should the wolves attack him suddenly from out of nowhere, surely he would not be able to defend himself without help!

Audra leaned over the crib, her heart warming at the sight of Little Butterfly lying on her side in a fetal position, sleeping. "You are so beautiful," she whispered, reaching a hand to stroke her soft, copper cheek. "If anything happens to Silver Wing, I promise I'll take care of you."

She turned with a start and ran her fingers through her hair. "What am I saying?" she cried. "Nothing is going to happen to him. He'll walk through that door any minute now."

She stood before the fireplace and watched the flames lapping slowly around the logs. In the flames she caught a vision . . . a face . . . a smile.

Realizing it was Silver Wing's smile, Audra took a shaky step backward.

Is it an omen? she wondered, her heart pounding. Is he trying to reach out for me and tell me something?

Surely the smile meant he was all right.

"I must go and find him," she said, a sob lodging in her throat. "I just can't stand by and wait any longer. I'm going to go and search for him."

She knew that it was too late to take the baby to Drinks Water. Surely it would awaken her children. And Drinks Water needed her rest. The trauma of having lost her husband was slowly eating away at her, although she still tried to appear strong and undaunted.

"Father John," Audra whispered, looking quickly toward the door. "He has proven to love little children. Surely *he* will come and sit with Little Butterfly."

Not thinking about the danger she placed herself in,

Audra ran from the longhouse and went to Father John.

Not hesitating, she knocked on the door.

When Father John came and opened it, sleepy and somewhat disoriented, wearing a simple white cotton sleeping gown, Audra was taken aback by his appearance. Never before had she seen him as just an ordinary man who needed sleep as much as the next person. Nor had she seen him void of his black, white-collared robe, his hair combed smoothly, his face shining and clean.

"Audra?" Father John said, stepping out into the moonlight, his gaze studying her. "Why are you here at this time of night? Surely it's past midnight."

"Yes, and that's exactly why I have come to you, to ask a favor of you," Audra murmured, nervously clasping and unclasping her hands before her.

She was aware of how Father John's eyes shifted to her hands, seeing her nervousness.

She slid her hands quickly to her back and resumed clasping and unclasping them. "Silver Wing hasn't arrived home," she said. "I want to go and search for him."

"You *what*?" Father John said, his eyes widening as he gazed intensely at her again. "What sort of foolishness is this? You get back to your house. Go to bed. In the morning you will be able to think things through more clearly."

"I don't need to go to bed to rationalize things inside my head," Audra said, her jaw tightening. "Father John, I need your help. Please? Please come and sit with Little Butterfly? I must find Silver Wing."

"Child, let his warriors do that," Father John said, gently placing a hand on her arm. "Now, do as I say, Audra. Go on back to your bed."

Audra yanked herself away from him. "Father John, I am no longer the child you saw me as when I was at the convent," she said, her voice tight. "I am a woman, and I can take care of myself."

"Audra, you are showing disrespect by talking to me in such a manner," Father John said, taking a shaky step away from her.

"I'm sorry," Audra said, sighing. "But I so badly want your help tonight. Please, please for a while, at least, forget that you promised my father to see after me. I am no longer the child that I was when Father brought me to the convent. I am . . . now . . . a woman."

Father John's face flooded with color.

"You care deeply for that man," he then said, clearing his throat nervously.

"Yes, and I must find him," Audra said, nervously shuffling her feet.

"Again, I say to you to go and have the warriors search for Silver Wing," Father John murmured.

"Earlier, when I first began worrying about Silver Wing, I went to the warriors and voiced my concern," Audra said softly. "I asked why they hadn't gone to look for Silver Wing. They told me that their chief was a wise man who made wise decisions. They said that if Silver Wing had a need to ride alone, possibly to go and commune with the Great Spirit, it was his right. They said they were not in their right to go and search for him."

"Then, you should respect their wishes," Father John said dryly.

"I guess I will have to take the baby with me," Audra said despairingly, "if that is the only way I can leave tonight to find Silver Wing."

And to test him further, knowing that she wouldn't do such a reckless thing, she turned and started to walk away.

Soon she felt a hand on her elbow. She turned and found Father John walking beside her.

"I shall stay the night with the child," Father John said, walking inside Silver Wing's longhouse with Audra.

"She should sleep the rest of the night without needing to feed," Audra said, grabbing a rifle, then hurried to the door again. She stopped and smiled at Father John. "Thank you. I am so grateful."

She ran from the longhouse, saddled one of Silver Wing's most trusted steeds, slid the rifle into the gun boot, then swung herself into the saddle.

She held herself low over the saddle as she rode across a wide-open range, then slowed the horse's pace when she came to a canyon. She knew of three places to search for Silver Wing: the valley of the butterflies, the hot springs, or back at his wigwam close to his Appaloosa herd.

She would first look for him at Butterfly Valley.

Riding onward, trying to recall the way as she looked for things familiar to her, she became disoriented. She wasn't sure where she was, or how to even get back to the village. She was traveling in circles.

Now, so far from the village, she could no longer see the reflection of the glow of outdoor fires.

Tired and thirsty, and with no water nearby, Audra drew her steed to a shuddering halt. She dismounted and tethered her horse to a low-hanging limb of a sycamore tree. She knelt and dipped up enough night's dew from the thick grass to wet her lips.

She crawled beneath a juniper tree, then fell into an exhausted, frightened sleep.

The wail of a closeby wolf awakened Audra. Again, she recalled Silver Wing's tale of the wolves. She was so afraid her knees were almost too weak to carry her to her horse.

Finally she swung herself into her saddle and rode onward. She reached a canyon wider than the others she had ridden through tonight. Cautiously, she looked from side to side, the shadows of the pines tremoring as the wind picked up speed.

Again, she heard wolves. She looked over her shoulder and saw their outline high on a bluff, their eyes lifted to the sky, their cries sending goose bumps up and down Audra's flesh.

Sinking her heels into the flanks of the horse, the hem of her dress hiked up past her knees, her toes curled comfortably in her moccasins, she traveled onward at a hard gallop, then slowed the horse's pace to a slow lope when on the floor of the canyon the trail straightened and followed a dry wash between towering cliffs. At a narrow defile Audra was forced to slow her horse even more. The walls closed in until it seemed she could touch both sides at once.

Then she suddenly rode into a wider clearing, where

canopies of cottonwoods and willows were nourished by gushing springs.

As she topped a rise she drew a quick, tight rein, and stopped when she saw a lamplight up ahead, and then made out the shape of a cabin.

The moon's glow also revealed a huge corral of Appaloosa hoses not that far from the cabin.

A warning rushed through her. Surely those were the other horses stolen from the Nez Perce. Could Harry have been telling the truth after all? Were the men inside that cabin responsible for the death of the Nez Perce and the stolen horses? Or . . . had Harry and his men had two hideouts all along?

Needing answers, Audra rode onward and stopped a few feet from the cabin.

After securing her steed, she daringly sneaked up to the cabin and peered into one of the windows.

She found something different from what she had expected. There were no men there, but instead several women and children. One woman was sitting in a rocking chair holding a baby. The others were asleep on blankets on the floor.

No longer feeling threatened, and curious about those women, Audra knocked on the door.

The door slowly opened, revealing one of the women Audra had seen sleeping on the floor. In the moonlight Audra could tell that the young woman was hardly any older than herself, yet was unkempt, her tattered and torn clothes reeking of perspiration.

"Who are you?" the woman asked, looking from side to side to see if anyone else was with Audra. When she saw that she was alone, the woman again

focused on Audra. "What do you want here? How
did you get here? How did you find the cabin?"

Audra looked past her. The lamplight inside the
cabin revealed to her that the rest of the women, and
their clinging children, had awakened and were now
huddled together behind the rocker, where the woman
still slowly rocked back and forth, her eyes frozen
on Audra.

Audra wasn't sure what to say. So she decided to
be honest, yet leave out her suspicions.

"I was looking for someone, the . . . man . . . I
love," Audra murmured, seeking to get on their better
side by speaking of a man she loved, rather than a
Nez Perce chief . . . for the Appaloosa horses in their
corral were Nez Perce horses!

"I . . . got lost," she murmured. "I have no idea
where I am or how to get back home."

"Come on inside," the young woman said, stepping aside.

"Thank you," Audra murmured, stepping past her.

Inside, she could see how alone and frightened the
women and children were.

"I'm Mary," a middle-aged woman said as she
stepped away from the others. She offered a hand.

Audra took it. She winced when she felt the boni-
ness of the woman's hand. She gazed into a gaunt
face. The woman's eyes were sunken. Her hair was
tangled and dirty. Her clothes were yellowed with age
and reeked as did the other's.

"I'm Audra," Audra said, twining her fingers around
Mary's hand.

"Please sit?" Mary said, sliding her hand from Audra's. She nodded toward a chair at the kitchen table.

"Yes, thank you," Audra said softly.

Mary sat down across from her. "Most of our husbands came down with measles," she confided. "And even though they were very ill, they found the strength to leave to search for a doctor." Her eyes lowered. "My husband, Roy, already died. He's buried outside beneath a tree."

The young woman who had met Audra at the door came and sat next to Audra. Her crisp green eyes shined with tears.

"My name is Chris. My husband's name is Jimmy. He's one of those who had measles when the men left us here all alone," she cried. "We women didn't want to come here to this lonely place. We wanted to stay in our homes. But our husbands forced us to come with them. They said they didn't trust leaving us alone while they . . . while they . . . stole horses from the Nez Perce. Lord, they even killed an Indian, and while scalping him, they became exposed to the measles. Now even we, the women and children, are exposed. We're afraid that we're all going to die."

"And we're now afraid that our husbands aren't going to return to us," Mary said, drawing Audra's eyes quickly to her. "They're probably too sick to. We are all alone in the world without the men."

"You say that you are lost," Chris said, reaching a hand to take one of Audra's. "Surely you can find your way and help us find our way out of this death hole!"

"I truly have no idea where I am," Audra murmured. "I have no idea how I got here. But at sunrise I will try again to find my way back home."

She paused, then looked from woman to woman. "But I must tell you, that if you want to go with me, you will be taken to the Nez Perce village," she said, drawing gasps from them all. "You see, that is where I make my home."

"You . . . live . . . with Indians?" Mary said, shocked.

"Yes," Audra said softly, hoping none of them would be threatened by this fact.

"I've never had anything against Indians," Chris said, drawing her hand away from Audra's. "I'll be happy to go with you to their village. Anything is better than here."

"And then we can find our way back to our homes," Mary said, coughing into her hand. "I'm so afraid of staying here. I hate this place."

"Will the Nez Perce treat us badly because of the sins of our husbands?" Chris asked softly, her eyes pleading with Audra.

Audra reached a gentle hand to Chris's pretty face. "The Nez Perce are a gentle, forgiving people, and no, I don't believe they will punish you for what your husbands have done," she murmured. "But you won't be able to go into their village. You will have to make camp somewhere close by until the threat of measles has passed."

"That's fine with me," Mary said, rising from her chair.

Mary turned to the other women. "What say you?" she asked. "Do you want to try and find your way out of this hellhole with this lady? Do you want to seek help from the Nez Perce? They can surely help us find our way back to our true homes."

Everyone agreed.

"Now that that's settled, how about a cup of coffee to warm your insides," Mary asked, limping to the fireplace, lifting a coffeepot from the hot coals at the edge.

"That sounds wonderful," Audra said, accepting a tin cup of the coffee as Mary handed it to her.

Audra sipped it for a while, then asked the question that had been eating away at her. "Is Harry Weston one of the men who has gone for the doctor?" she blurted out, watching their reactions closely.

"Harry who?" Mary asked, forking an eyebrow.

"Harry Weston," Audra said, again looking from woman to woman. "He's supposed to have a group of men with him who've been stealing horses."

"None of us know the man," Chris said, drawing Audra's eyes to her.

Chris's eyes were telling the truth. And this truth revealed to Audra that there were two gangs of horse thieves in the area. She was relieved that Harry wasn't a part of this gang. At least he hadn't killed and scalped Red Bonnet.

Yet he was still a horse thief, and somehow managed to escape the day of the fire!

"Here's a blanket for you to sleep on tonight," Chris said, bringing a ragged blanket to Audra.

"You are all so kind," Audra said, nodding a thank-you as she took the blanket and lay it on the floor beside her.

"Best we get back to sleep," Mary said, stretching out on her blanket near Audra.

After drinking the rest of her coffee, Audra stretched out on the blanket. The woman who still held the child rocked back and forth. She was the only one who hadn't offered any response to Audra's questions. She seemed to be in another world, lonely and lost to what she had surely been at one time when she was young, vital, and in love.

Tired and bone-weary, Audra lay down on the blanket, then smiled at Chris as she brought her another blanket and stretched it out over her.

She watched everyone drift to sleep as she lay awake wondering where Silver Wing was. Would she be able to find her way to the Indian village in the morning?

And if Silver Wing was home, safe and sound, what would his reaction be to seeing her gone? Surely he would come searching for her! Although she had no luck finding him, he knew the land as well as his name and he would know how to find her!

Feeling more at ease with this thought, she drifted off to sleep.

29

Thy love is such I can no way repay
The heavens reward thee manifold, I pray.
———ANNE BRADSTREET

Feeling refreshed yet ready to confess that he should have never scolded Audra about allowing Rose Bud to sing the church hymn, Silver Wing rode into his village at the break of dawn.

His pulse raced as he gazed at his lodge. The smoke spiraling from the chimney gave him cause to believe that Audra was up and holding *Lap Lap* before her morning feeding. He would feast on that sight, then would draw them both into his arms.

He would vow to Audra that he would never again dictate to her what she should or should not do.

She was a wise woman.

She should be free to voice her opinions and act them out without always worrying about someone being there to question her decisions.

He would tell her that his love for her was without conditions.

He did not want her to feel as though she must flee him as she had felt so strongly about fleeing the convent.

Drawing a tight rein before his lodge, he smiled toward the closed door.

But when Audra didn't come to the door as Silver Wing expected, his smile faded. Had he hurt her so deeply by his behavior that she would not even welcome him back into her life?

Had his prayers the long night through been for naught?

Had his foolish behavior caused the loss of his woman's love?

Perhaps even . . . her respect for him?

His spirits lowered, he rode around to the back of his lodge and dismounted. Taking the reins in his hand, he led his steed into the village horse corral.

Then he went back to his longhouse and went inside.

He stopped when the fire's glow revealed the white holy man sitting on blankets beside the fire, slowly rocking Little Butterfly in his arms. Audra was not there.

Father John turned with a start and gazed at him.

"Where is Audra?" Silver Wing asked, his eyes narrowing. "Why are you here in her place?" His jaw tightened. "Who gave you permission to hold Little Butterfly?"

"I am here because Audra asked me to sit with the child while she went out to search for you," Father John blurted out, now holding the child still in his arms. "She's been gone for too long, Silver Wing. She left in the middle of the night. I truly believe something might have happened to her. She's been out there all of this time, alone."

"And you let her go?" Silver Wing said harshly. "You let her go *xoyim-xoyim,* alone?"

"You know her now almost as well as I, which means that you know that if she sets her mind to doing something, she will find a way to do it," Father John said, rising, taking the baby to her cradle.

He swung around and faced Silver Wing. "I think you'd better get together a search party quickly, and go look for her," he said sullenly. "As it is, it might already be too late."

"Why did you not do this yourself?" Silver Wing said, his eyes gleaming angrily. "You should have awakened my warriors long ago with the news that Audra did not return."

"Would you truly expect me to go to any of your warriors' lodges and ask anything of them, when I know how they feel about me?" Father John asked seriously. "No, I didn't feel free to. I just depended on the Lord to bring her home safe. I had hoped that she had found you and that she was safely with you."

"Why did she not ask my warriors to accompany her on her search for me if she was so concerned about my welfare?" Silver Wing asked, his voice drawn.

"She did, and she was denied their services," Father John said softly. "They said that you had chosen to go alone. They would not interfere with your decision."

"Because of their respect for me, they did this, and I understand," Silver Wing said, sighing. "But this time I wish they had not been so obedient to their chief's wishes. I wish they would have accompanied my woman."

"They will accompany *you* on your search for *her,*" Father John said softly. "I urge you, Silver Wing, to delay no longer, and pray that you find Audra. Although we have had our disagreements, I love her no less than were she my daughter."

Silver Wing questioned him with his eyes, for he knew that Audra was not aware of this man's deep feelings for her. If she had known this, perhaps she would not have had such a strong desire to leave this man's holy place. Then Silver Wing never would have had the opportunity to meet her and fall in love with her.

And now?

To possibly have lost her after only having found her and the love she gave him?

"I will leave now," he said hurriedly, but took a moment to gaze down at Little Butterfly.

"I will bring her back to you," he whispered, leaning down to brush a soft kiss across the child's brow.

He then turned and went back to his cache of weapons. He grabbed his rifle, fastened his leather sheath with his sharp knife at his left side, then positioned his quiver of arrows on his back.

Grabbing up his bow, slinging it over his left shoulder, he walked quickly to his door.

"God be with you, my son," Father John said, his voice breaking as he stood with his hands clasped tightly behind him, his eyes wavering as Silver Wing stopped, turned, and stared at him.

"My son, God *will* be with you," Father John said softly. "He *will* help you find our loved one."

Having no time to argue which god would be riding

with him today, believing his Great Spirit had a reason for having led Audra out there somewhere alone, and that she *would* be all right, Silver Wing sighed deeply, then spun around and hurried from his lodge.

After he gathered together many of his warriors, leaving some behind to keep watch on their village, they rode off in a hard gallop.

Silver Wing's black hair billowed in the wind behind him as he thought about where Audra might have gone to find him.

There were three places he knew that they had shared.

The place of butterflies.

The hot sulphur springs.

And his wigwam.

He would try Butterfly Valley first!

He swung right on his horse and rode at a harder gallop, troubled by something else now. He had not stayed away from his people for as long as Audra had said that he should. The fire had brought him back to his village.

And once there, among his people, he had stayed.

That was another reason for his private prayers last night . . . to pray he had not exposed his people to a disease that might kill them.

His prayers had been many last night, but now Audra was uppermost in his thoughts. Should she die, he would be at fault. He was not sure if he could live with such guilt. Already he had lost so much. One more heartache might be one heartache too many!

They arrived at Butterfly Valley.

Silver Wing's heart sank when he found that Audra wasn't there.

They went on to the hot sulphur springs.

Again, he did not find her.

He went back to his wigwam.

Again, he didn't find her.

His men sitting quietly around him on their steeds, Silver Wing on his, he scanned the horizon with his eyes. He saw the many Appaloosa horses, the lovely mountains, their slopes covered with wildflowers.

"The mountains," he whispered, softly kneading his brow. "Would she search for me where she might think I had gone to commune with the Great Spirit? Was she this fearless to go this far alone with the night animals lurking, seeking food?"

His heart sank to think that she might have been this daring.

"Follow me!" he cried to his warriors, again taking off in a hard gallop across the spacious land of waving green grass.

He traveled to one high butte and then another, neither one giving him any signs that Audra might have been there.

And then he found himself traveling in a canyon he had never seen before.

His throat dry, his stomach aching from hunger, his fingers raw from having gripped the reins so hard for so long, he slowed down the pace of his steed and rode cautiously onward, for one never knew who might be hiding in canyons.

Sometimes Blackfoot sought such hiding places.

Sometimes evil white trappers would go there with their kill.

Evil white men who stole horses from all Northwest tribes could hide them there! Yes, suddenly he saw a corral of horses—Nez Perce horses.

He stopped and stared, as did his warriors.

"They are ours," Tall Shadow said, sidling his horse closer to Silver Wing's. "Do you believe Harry Weston and his men have had time to steal this amount of horses from our herd?"

"Where there are horses, there is a hideout," Silver Wing grumbled. "Let us find the horse thieves. Surely we *will* find Harry Weston and his men. This time we will not bother keeping them as captives. We will hang them immediately!"

Riding onward, they drew tight reins when they saw the cabin up ahead, snuggled beneath tall cotton-woods.

When Silver Wing saw a lone Appaloosa he recognized from the village, grazing close to the cabin, tethered to a tree, his anger seethed.

"Harry Weston is here," he said, his voice drawn. "He burned our lodges then stole one of our most valued horses for his escape."

But then his eyebrows forked when he realized that there should be more than one horse there. Several white men had escaped that day. Not only Harry.

Then, who *was* there, and where were the others? he wondered, as the morning sun crept higher, this time casting long shadows from the high butte behind the cabin over it.

He raised a hand, commanding his men to stop. He

slid from his saddle, grabbed his rifle from the gun boot, then looked from man to man. "I will go to the cabin alone," he said tightly. "I will fire the rifle when I want you to join me."

After they nodded, Silver Wing scampered away through knee-high green grass.

When he reached the cabin, he crept around to one side and looked through a window.

He saw the women and children asleep on the floor, and then Audra lying among them. Relieved, he went inside and bent down beside Audra. He grabbed her into his arms and hugged her.

The abruptness of Silver Wing doing this startled Audra, and she screamed.

Everyone else awakened in a panic.

The women saw the Indian holding Audra.

They screamed in terror.

The children rushed into their mother's arms, also screaming.

When Audra looked up and saw who had truly awakened her, she could hardly believe her eyes. "Silver Wing, is it truly you, or am I dreaming?" she blurted out.

"Tee-men-a, this is no dream," Silver Wing said, gently touching her face, then raking his fingers through the tight red curls of her hair. "I am here. I have found you."

"You found *me*?" Audra said, forking an eyebrow. "Does that mean that you went back to the village and you discovered me gone?"

"Yes, I arrived there at daybreak," Silver Wing said thickly. "I started an immediate search for you."

He looked slowly around him at the women and children, then questioned Audra with his eyes.

She leaned away from him and smiled at the women. "He is a friend," she murmured, reassuring them. "This is Silver Wing. He is the chief of the Nez Perce your husbands have stolen from. He . . . is . . . my man. We are going to be married."

Still they clung to one another, their eyes wild.

"Please don't be afraid of Silver Wing," Audra reassured. "Remember I told you that his people would not hold anything against you for the sins of your husband's."

One by one she could see them relax.

The children even seemed to understand as they moved from their mothers and sat down together, their eyes wide as they watched Audra and Silver Wing.

Audra hurriedly explained everything to Silver Wing. The husbands of these women were the ones who had killed Red Bonnet and all but one of the men had left. Audra quickly set his mind at ease by telling him that this man would never bother anyone or steal horses again. He was dead.

The other men were all deathly ill with measles.

"Can the women and children go to the Nez Perce village?" she asked softly. "They are innocent of the crimes against your people. They are scared. They are hungry. And I doubt that the men will find a doctor. Surely they will die while looking."

Silver Wing looked from woman to woman, and child to child, his heart going out mainly to the chil-

dren whose hunger showed in their gauntness and
their pleading expressions.

He gazed into Audra's eyes. "They can come under
the protective wing of the Nez Perce," he said softly.
"But they cannot take lodging among my people.
They will be housed and fed close by so they will be
safe from harm. We must not risk any of these white
people carrying the measles to my people."

His eyes wavered as he took Audra's hands. "My
woman, in my haste to see about my people, I forgot
to be cautious about having been exposed to the disease myself," he said. "Should they . . ."

She placed a gentle finger to his lips, sealing the
words she knew he did not wish to speak. "You did
what you had to do," she murmured. "I understand.
They understand. Your love for your people would
have never allowed you to stay behind and not help
when you saw the smoke in the sky."

"I could not have stayed away."

She gave him a warm hug, then helped the women
and children pack up their meager belongings in their
ragged travel bags.

Slowly the procession of women and children on
horses rode out of the canyon as some warriors were
left behind to round up the Appaloosa to take back
to their herd.

Audra rode beside Silver Wing, only now aware of
how unkempt she was after her long time away from
the village. But now that she and Silver Wing were
together again, she looked forward to a bath in the
river, to a delicious bowl of stew, and to tonight when
they would share his bed of blankets.

So lost in thought, she did not notice how Silver Wing was occasionally wiping his face. But when she heard him emit a low groan, she looked quickly and flinched. His face was very flushed, and his eyes were glassy.

"Silver Wing, oh, Lord, you look as though you have a fever," she blurted out.

Her gaze swept downward.

She gasped when she saw a few red blotches on his neck. "Silver Wing, oh, Silver Wing, you have the measles," she said, a keen fear sweeping through her.

Understanding the meaning in this, he wheeled his horse around and rode away from the slow procession of women and children. He knew that they had already been exposed by their fathers and husbands, but his men who had been riding with him had now been exposed! Guilt lay heavy on his heart.

"Please don't go far!" Audra cried after him. "I'll come to you after I explain things to your people about why these white women and children are going to make camp close to your village!"

Hearing the panic in her voice, and knowing how worried she had been when he left her behind only last night, Silver Wing drew a tight rein and stopped.

He turned his horse around and smiled at Audra. "I shall wait for you," he said, yet feeling so ill he was hardly able to stay in the saddle.

His head felt like a dead-weight on his shoulder.

His skin was so hot, he felt as though the sun was beating from within it!

Not wanting to alarm Audra anymore than she already was, he willed himself to stay tall in the saddle.

When she was no longer looking, he hung his head in a hand.

The pulse beat at his throat was like thunder roaring in his ears!

As quickly as she could, Audra went on into the village and explained everything to the Nez Perce people.

Father John, Dennis Bell, and the other four priests left with supplies for the women and children.

Audra was touched deeply by how Father John so lovingly hugged the children, then embraced the women, talking softly and encouragingly to them, while the other five men began building temporary lean-to's and a fire.

She turned and felt a deep love for the Nez Perce women when they brought large parfleche bags of food and left them for the women to get.

Father John took an empty parfleche bag and walked with several of the children to the creek to get water not far from the new camp.

Relieved that the Nez Perce held nothing against these innocent women and children, Audra rode off toward Silver Wing, praying that he wouldn't die.

She counted on the fact that he was a strong man with as strong a will.

When she reached him and saw just how feverish he was, for the red rash now consumed his whole face, doubt spread through her like wildfire that just maybe his strength, his strong will, or his faith, this time, might not be enough!

30

I call thee from every leafy bough,
But thou art far away and cannot hear.
——JONES VERY

After seeing how ill Silver Wing was, Audra had left him to inform his people, especially his shaman, about his illness. He did not want Rainbow to come to him, but instead to go and pray for him at her private place of communing with their Great Spirit. He felt that prayers would do him more good now than any medicinal herb that she might give him to drink.

Shivering, Silver Wing wanted to pray himself. He did not have the strength to climb high to a butte for his prayers. But he could build a sweat lodge. A small one would suffice since he would be taking a sweat bath alone this time instead of with many of his warriors.

Groaning with each step he took, finding it harder to stay on his feet as each moment passed, Silver Wing cut two pliant limbs from a cottonwood tree. He bent them and tied them in a circle. He then built a frame of other bendable limbs over these poles and covered them with pelts and blankets, leaving an opening facing the east.

He then took wood inside the sweat lodge and surrounded it with stones. He brought more stones into the lodge and piled them close to the fire pit.

With what little strength that remained, he went to the stream and filled a parfleche bag with water and took it back to the small, quickly made lodge, then brought a burning twig from his outdoor fire and set the dried pieces of wood aflame.

Trembling, his teeth chattering, Silver Wing removed his breechclout and moccasins.

Naked, he then sat cross-legged on the earthen floor of the sweat lodge.

One by one he placed the stones into the leaping flames until they were all piled together.

He hugged himself as he waited for the stones to get hot.

He closed his eyes and hung his head, dizzy now from the temperature raging through him and across his flesh.

Finally the stones were hot enough.

He lifted the parfleche bag, turned it upside down, and poured the water on the hot rocks.

Steam rose in cloudy puffs from the rocks, soon filling the small sweat lodge, enwrapping Silver Wing like a gray, shimmering blanket.

As he sat there with the steam entering his pores, he lifted his eyes heavenward and prayed to *Tah-mah-ne-weg.*

He continued praying until the steam began to evaporate.

Then, even more weakened now, the steam having sapped what strength remained, Silver Wing slid his breechclout on, grabbed his moccasins, crawled from his sweat lodge, and collapsed on the ground just as Audra rode up and dismounted.

Panic seized Audra when she saw how lethargic he was.

He lay crumpled on the ground. His body was gleaming red, and his eyes were bloodshot, seeming unable to focus as he looked at her.

"Silver Wing!" she cried as he attempted to get up and then collapsed again, his eyes now closed, his breathing shallow.

She ran to him and cradled his head on her lap. "Lord, you're worse," she said, her voice breaking as she ran her hand across his scorching brow.

She gazed at the sweat lodge, not sure what it was, or how it had gotten there. Surely Silver Wing had been too ill to build it, yet there it was.

"Did . . . you . . . tell Rainbow?" Silver Wing said, his eyes slowly opening as he tried to focus on Audra. "Did you . . . tell . . . my people?"

"Yes, I told everyone," Audra said, her voice breaking again. He was now covered with the red rash. She had never before seen such a case of measles.

"The children," Silver Wing said, his voice barely audible. "I . . . have . . . endangered the children by . . . being . . . around them when . . . I . . . should have stayed away."

"Please don't worry about anything now except getting well," Audra murmured. She brushed a soft kiss across his scorching brow. "Silver Wing, I'm so afraid for you."

"I have much willpower and faith," Silver Wing

said, then closed his eyes when his teeth began chattering together so hard Audra thought they might break.

"I've got to get you back to the wigwam," she said, frowning when she saw how far he was from the wigwam. He was too heavy for her to pull.

"Do you have enough strength left to get to the wigwam?" she murmured, gently caressing his feverish brow. "I need to get you there out of the sun and wind. You should be covered with many blankets to help sweat out the fever."

"I took a sweat bath in the sweat lodge," Silver Wing managed to whisper through his teeth that continued clicking together.

She glanced at the small dwelling, now understanding what it was. She had heard of Indian sweat lodges. The most important bath for Indians was the sweat bath. For the most part it was a place built for spiritual purposes.

She had heard tales of warriors bragging that after using steam baths they were known to outrun deer and outwalk their horses.

Some said they went through enemy lines and would not be seen.

She now realized that this steam bath today was used to give her beloved the power to outlive the raging temperature that was enveloping him.

"I don't know how you had the strength to build the sweat lodge," Audra said, sighing. "Do you have enough left to help me get you to the wigwam? I can take care of you better there. I . . . I . . ."

She started to say that she didn't want him to get

pneumonia, which would quickly complicate things. But she decided not to alarm him.

"I can get there on my own strength," Silver Wing said, easing his head from her lap.

He moved slowly away from her as he pushed himself shakily up from the ground.

Audra's eyes widened, and she placed a hand over her mouth to silence a gasp as she watched him walk unsteadily toward the wigwam.

She then rushed to him and placed an arm protectively around his waist. She tried not to show how hard it was to hold him up. His body seemed to be a dead-weight as he leaned against her.

Finally she got him to the wigwam and comfortably on his bed of blankets and pelts.

"I will be back soon," Audra said, grabbing a wooden basin. "I'm going to go and get water."

Hardly able to think clearly now, or see Audra through his clouded vision, Silver Wing slowly nodded.

Then he closed his eyes, swallowed hard, and fell into a deep, troubled sleep. In a dream he saw so many familiar faces. His mother . . . his father . . . his wife. They were standing amid beautiful white clouds smiling at him, but not reaching out for him.

He was exceedingly happy and grateful to see them, yet he did not venture to go to them. He feared to do so would mean that his time on earth was finished. And he still had so much left to do.

And his lovely, sweet woman, whose hands he now felt on his brow, needed him.

As did *Lap Lap.*

He moaned and reached a hand up and gently

touched Audra's face. "I stay with you . . ." he whispered, yet loud enough for Audra to hear.

"Yes, yes," Audra whispered back. "Please stay with me. Hang on. Oh, Silver Wing, this surely will soon pass, and you will be strong and well again."

She moved to her knees beside him and wrapped his hot body more snugly with blankets. "I'm here for you," she murmured. "I will not leave you again until you are well. Get well, my love. Get well."

Again, she sat down beside him.

With a cool, damp cloth she bathed his brow, and then lowered the blankets enough to run the cloth over his broad, muscled chest.

She winced at the sight of the red blotches on his flesh.

She remembered when she had the measles, and they were nothing like this.

And she didn't recall having such a high temperature.

Never had she been as worried over anything as she was now over the man she loved.

When he began talking, his gaze hazy, yet focused on her, Audra sat closer and held his hand. "You should sleep," she murmured. "That is the best medicine now for you. Rest. Sleep. And soon it will be behind you."

"I must say something that bothers me," he said weakly. "As you know, white people are to blame for the measles that are now in the Nez Perce Oregon country. They . . . they . . . have brought the dreaded disease purposely to poison the Nez Perce so that the tribe will become too weak to defend what is ours."

"I know that it must look that way to you, but,

Silver Wing, no man would chance such a plan as that," Audra murmured. "In order to make the plan work, the men themselves would have to be inflicted with measles. As you now see, you have to know that no one would purposely become ill with the disease in order to give it to someone else."

"Perhaps . . . perhaps . . ." Silver Wing uttered. "But still I see it as a scheme against my people."

He then closed his eyes and drifted off to sleep again.

"Yes, I'm sure you do," Audra whispered. "And who could blame you? The whites have tried everything to rid their world of all skin colors that are not like their own."

His temperature still raged on and on.

Audra wiped tears from her eyes as she looked heavenward. "Lord, please don't let him die," she whispered.

She hoped that both hers and Rainbow's prayers were being heard, for she knew that Silver Wing needed all of the help he could get.

She leaned over him and pulled him into her arms. "I love you so," she whispered. "More than life itself."

She slowly rocked him. "I won't let you die," she said softly. "I just *won't.*"

31

There is sobbing of the strong,
And a pall upon the land.
——HERMAN MELVILLE

Weary from hardly any sleep for two days and nights, Audra gazed at Silver Wing, tears in her eyes. He was sleeping fitfully, moaning and stiffening as he tossed from side to side.

His temperature raged onward.

His body was consumed by blotches of red.

Audra now doubted that he would live.

"Please get well," she sobbed.

She reached for one of his hands beneath the blankets and twined her fingers through his.

The heat of his flesh against hers made her cringe. She had only moments ago given him a complete sponge bath. The bath of cool water had not even awakened him, nor had it lessened his fever.

Audra refused to believe that Silver Wing would be in her life for such a short time. Would she have to give him up? God could not continue taking the good parts of her life from her. First her mother, and now . . . ?

A soft voice outside the lodge startled Audra. Rainbow.

During Silver Wing's last moments of consciousness, he had asked Audra to send for Rainbow. She seemed immune to the disease for she had been exposed to measles now more than once and had not gotten them.

Knowing she must welcome her inside the small wigwam saddened Audra.

Not because she disliked the shaman.

But rather she shunned the duty that brought Rainbow here now.

Silver Wing had asked her to give Rainbow a message for him. His message made her heart crumble, it was so heartbreaking and final.

A verbal will.

He . . . wanted to . . . make . . . a verbal will, which meant that he truly thought he was going to die.

Swallowing hard, Audra still didn't respond to Rainbow, even after Rainbow spoke her name three times outside the wigwam. Audra didn't want to even think about such a thing as a verbal will, much less face it head on.

"Allow . . . Rainbow . . . to enter."

Silver Wing's voice drew Audra's eyes quickly to him.

He hadn't been awake for hours.

She hadn't heard his voice for so long!

"Oh, Silver Wing, I'm so glad you are awake," she said, flinging her arms around his neck. She cherished this moment when he was finally lucid enough to speak. "Oh, Lord, it's been so long since you were awake, darling."

"My *Tee-men-a*," Silver Wing said, his voice barely a whisper, but loud enough for her to hear.

Afraid to let him go, that he might disappear again into the dark void of unconsciousness, Audra still clung to him.

When he managed to slide an arm around her, holding her endearingly close, Audra was almost moved to tears with the joy of his gesture.

But she held back the tears. While he was awake and aware of everything, she wanted to continue proving to him that she was strong and courageous, for she knew that was how he had always seen her.

But now, when his life lay in balance, it was so hard not to burst into tears and show him just how vulnerable she was as she was faced with his possible passing.

"I have . . . summoned . . . Rainbow for . . . a purpose," Silver Wing said, his voice louder, yet still weak and drawn. "You know that purpose. Let . . . us . . . get it behind us, my woman."

"But a will?" Audra murmured, still clinging. "You don't need to have a will for years, Silver Wing." She swallowed hard. "You're going to be all right. Please believe me when I say that you are going to be all right."

"*Tee-men-a,* I must prepare for my death, which I now see as ultimate," Silver Wing said, easing his arm from around her.

He reached a tremoring hand to her hair and wove his fingers through the curls. "Your hair," he murmured. "It has grown so much. Ah, how soft it is against my hot fingers. And the color. It is such a vibrant shade of red. When it grows to your shoulders, ah, how I would love to have seen it."

Hearing him talking in the past tense, as though he was not going to be a part of her future, weakened Audra's strength.

She waited for him to drop his hand down to his side, then leaned away from him and gazed softly down at him. "You will see my hair when it is fully grown out," she said thickly. "I promise that to you, my darling. You will see it even when it is gray."

Silver Wing managed a smile. "Even then I will enjoy running my fingers through it," he said, his voice breaking.

"Now that's more like it," Audra said, smoothing the blanket over his arm and hand, bringing it over them. "I like it when you speak to me as though you still have hope for our future. We *will* be together, you and I, for many, many moons to come. We shall enjoy laughter of our grandchildren together. We shall enjoy the sunshine and flowers!"

Sighing, his smile fading, Silver Wing closed his eyes. "Do not delay any longer bringing Rainbow to me," he said, his voice now almost a whisper. "Sleep summons me again. I can . . . hardly . . . fight . . . it off."

Audra flicked tears from her eyes that she just could not hold back inside her.

She bit her lower lip, then went and held aside the goatskin flap for the shaman.

"He is awake now," she murmured. "He has asked for you."

Rainbow, her thick black hair dragging the ground

behind her, came into the wigwam and sat down beside Silver Wing. "My chief, I am here," she said, her
voice showing the strain of the moment. "I will now
hear your verbal will if you will speak it to me."

Silver Wing slowly opened his eyes. He gazed over
at Rainbow. "My shaman," he said, his voice drawn
and even more weak than before. "In my dreams I
am standing at the road of the hereafter. I . . . have . . .
seen so much, I have . . . seen my loved ones that
have gone on before me, yet they have not beckoned
to me. I did not go *to* them. I am ready now, though,
to go if it is our *Tah-mah-ne-weg's* Great Spirit's
bidding."

Audra almost choked on a sob as she turned her
eyes away from her beloved. She wiped the tears from
her eyes, then turned and gazed at Silver Wing again
as he struggled to get his breath, then began speaking again.

"It is . . . time . . . for my verbal will to be spoken,"
he said softly. He turned to Audra and saw her despair. He ached inside to know that he was causing
her such pain and wished it could be otherwise.

But he had fought this battle as long as he felt he
had the strength to. The fight was almost gone from
within him. His moments were now numbered on
this earth.

"*Tee-men-a,* hold my hand?" he whispered, scooting
a trembling hand from beneath the blanket and reaching it out toward Audra.

Audra smiled through her fear and sadness and
twined her fingers through his.

She tried to see past the heat of his flesh and just enjoy the wonder of his hand in hers.

She tried to envision the good times when they were alone and laughing . . . embracing . . . kissing.

Was it truly over?

Would they never share such wondrous moments again?

Would they not even be able to stand over Little Butterfly's crib together and glory in her presence in their lives?

Would they truly never share the birth of their own child?

Those questions made her so sad. If Silver Wing died, she would find a way to join him!

"All that I worldly possess, but my cache of weapons, will go to my woman and our child, Little Butterfly," Silver Wing said, his eyes moving slowly from Audra to Rainbow, who did not take visible notes, but instead engraved what he said in her memory. "My weapons will be Tall Shadow's. He will use them well."

He swallowed hard. "A drink," he said, licking his parched lips. "Before I . . . continue . . . I need a . . . drink."

Audra reached over and grabbed a small basket of water. She lifted this to his lips. She made sure to give him small amounts of water at a time so that he would not choke on it, then withdrew the basket and sat it down beside her.

Tears flowed from her eyes as she continued to listen to him, her heart breaking more with each word, for she knew that he didn't expect to live. And she also knew that when a man lost hope, he also lost his will to live!

Silver Wing closed his eyes, sucked in a slow, quivering breath, then again looked at Rainbow. "My people will inherit my love and devotion, that which they will carry with them until the end of their time," Silver Wing said, his voice breaking. "Tell them all that when they look at the stars I am there looking back at them. Tell . . . them . . . I have been blessed to have been a . . . part . . . of their lives."

He gasped, took a deep, shaky swallow, then said, "When . . . my last breath is taken on this earth, I pass on to my friend Black Fox my . . . my . . . *Wey-ya-kin*, Guardian Spirit."

Audra again turned her eyes away from him. What he had just said was too final for her. She could no longer hold back a torrent of tears. Her body shook with sobs.

But when she felt Silver Wing's hand tighten in hers, as a sort of reassurance, she wiped her tears away and again looked down at him.

"My woman, I . . . will . . . always be . . . with you, and . . . and . . . Little Butterfly," he said, then closed his eyes again, his head rolling to one side.

Audra's eyes went wild as his hand went limp in hers. She looked anxiously at Rainbow. "Please don't tell me that he's dead," she cried. "Tell me he's just gone back to sleep."

Rainbow placed a gentle hand to his throat to see if there was still a pulse there. When she found it, although it was slight, she gave Audra a reassuring, soft smile. "He has not left us yet," she murmured.

Her smile faded. "But prepare yourself for the end as he has prepared himself."

"He just can't die," Audra cried, her insides aching. "It's not fair. He is so young. He's so loved."

"He is everything to his people," Rainbow said, again gazing at Silver Wing. "Without him there will be such emptiness . . . such heartache . . ."

Audra nodded and watched Rainbow leave, then she sat closer to Silver Wing and watched him sleep.

Tears flooded her eyes again as she recalled their precious moments together.

Had she known their future would be so short-lived, she would have never left him for a moment.

She would have stayed at his side.

Nothing would have drawn her away from him.

Then her eyes widened. *"Lap Lap,"* she said, her voice breaking. "Oh, what of Little Butterfly?"

Then she remembered what Silver Wing had said as he had been speaking his verbal will to Rainbow. When he had mentioned Little Butterfly, he had referred to her as being "their" child, which meant he still referred to the child as being his and Audra's.

"I will care for Little Butterfly as though she were born of our love," she said, placing a gentle hand on Silver Wing's cheek. "I will keep you alive inside her heart. I will always talk to her about you. I will tell her just how much you loved her."

When his lips quivered into a smile as he still slept, Audra knew he had heard what she had just said.

"My darling, my darling . . ." she whispered.

She shivered when she recalled having thought earlier that if Silver Wing died, she would find a way to join him.

She now realized how wrong she had been to make such a vow as that to herself.

She had someone to live for.

Little Butterfly!

32

Give all to love;
Obey thy heart.

——RALPH WALDO EMERSON

After bringing a fresh supply of food to the women and children who still camped a short distance from the Nez Perce village, and hearing their pleas for change, Father John went to sit in council with the Nez Perce warriors. Tall Shadow was the spokesman now in the absence of his chief.

He glared at Father John. He still found it hard to trust this man, even though he had proven to be gentle and no threat to the women and children.

The fact that he had kept his word and had not spoken of his religion to Tall Shadow's people made Tall Shadow listen today with an open heart.

"The women want to leave now and start life anew without their husbands," Father John said, sitting beside the softly burning embers of the council house fire, his legs crossed beneath his black robe. "I have come to speak in their behalf. Could some of your warriors escort them to the Dalles Trading Post?"

"If the women and children leave, where will they

go?" Tall Shadow asked, his eyes narrowing. "Are they not defenseless without husbands?"

"They will be the first to admit they fear their futures without their husbands, but their plans are to find their way to their parents' homes, or to kin who will take them in and care for them," Father John said. "Once they are at the Dalles Trading Post the responsibility of traveling from there will be their own. But they seem confident enough of their plan."

Tall Shadow looked from warrior to warrior, who sat in a wide circle around him and Father John.

When each one nodded a silent approval of Father John's request, Tall Shadow again gazed at Father John. "Go to them and tell them to prepare for the journey to the Dalles Trading Post," he said thickly. "They will have a safe escort there."

"I thank you for the women and children," Father John said, rising to his feet. He started to walk toward the door, then turned and gazed at Tall Shadow again. "I would like to ride with you to the trading post. I believe my presence will help ease the concerns of the women and children."

"Concerns about what?" Tall Shadow said, moving to his feet, casting a tall shadow over the priest. "Or should I say *who*? Do you believe the women and children have no trust in the Nez Perce? Do you believe they fear being alone with us?"

"No, I didn't mean to imply that at all," Father John said, his face paling. "It's just that they have grown to know me. At least for a while they will find comfort in the presence of someone they know."

He didn't want to say that they wanted him to accompany them because he was a holy man and God would be closer to them. Father John made certain not to refer to his religion at all as long as he stayed with the Nez Perce.

He had even begun thinking about not leaving at all. He wanted to build a mission in this area, but not to convert the Indians, but instead to preach to the settlers as they came to the Northwest Territory.

And for certain they would come. No land as beautiful and as giving as this would be overlooked for long by white people.

He envisioned a vast population here one day. They would need guidance about how to live peacefully among the Indian population.

He had been thinking hard on how to convince Silver Wing that this would benefit his people, yet with Silver Wing so ill, he now wondered if he would even get that chance.

"Then, you may accompany them as well to the trading post," Tall Shadow said, interrupting Father John's thoughts. "Make haste, though. I wish to get this behind me. My heart is heavy over my concern for my chief. Rainbow returned with the sorrowful news that Silver Wing has worsened. Should he die . . ."

Tall Shadow's words faded away into a nothingness, for he did not wish to even think about the possibilities of his best friend dying. It didn't seem possible that Silver Wing *could* die. Thus far he had seemed invincible!

"Dennis Bell wants to accompany us, also, to the trading post," Father John said, having noticed how

Tall Shadow failed to complete his sentence about the possibility of Silver Wing dying. Father John had prayed often that this would not happen. He feared a retaliation against him and his friends, for surely the blame would be cast on them.

Especially Dennis Bell. That was another reason Father John wanted to make sure Dennis Bell was away from the village should Silver Wing pass away. Of all people to be blamed, surely it would be Dennis for having, personally, brought the disease into the Nez Perce village!

"Yes, Dennis Bell can also ride with us to the trading post," Tall Shadow said, walking with Father John to the door. He opened it and stood aside. "Go. Ready the women and children. I shall tell Dennis Bell that he will be leaving soon for the trading post. I shall have horses prepared for the travel."

"Thank you, Tall Shadow," Father John said, reaching a hand out to clasp it on Tall Shadow's bare arm, but instead jerking it away when Tall Shadow stepped away from him to elude such a touch from the white man.

Father John gazed with wonder into Tall Shadow's eyes, then turned and left with the news for the women and children.

Tall Shadow left the council house and told Dennis Bell that he should ready himself for travel.

Soon the warriors who were accompanying the small procession toward the trading post rode somewhat behind the women and children and Father John and Dennis Bell. This distance assured them protection from measles.

Father John rode stately on an Appaloosa, the hem of his robe fluttering in the breeze.

Dennis Bell, well and strong now after his bout of measles, rode beside Father John. He glanced often at the women and children, who rode a short distance behind them. They all looked frail and unkempt, their clothes dirty and tattered. It was obvious they had all been neglected by their husbands and fathers. They seemed so alone in the world . . . so forlorn.

For certain Dennis felt that they had made a wise decision about not wanting to be a part of the horse thieves' lives again. Surely in time they would all find a much better life, elsewhere.

Father John looked over at Dennis. He followed his line of vision and saw that Dennis was quietly troubled about the women and children.

Father John edged his horse over closer to Dennis's. "God will provide for them," he said, reaching a comforting hand to Dennis's arm. "They are going through trials and tribulations now. But God will make things right for them."

"If they live long enough," Dennis grumbled. "They all seem so weak . . . so . . ."

A noise at his right side in the forest startled Dennis so much that he forgot what he was saying. He gazed into the dark shadows, then drew a tight rein when he saw a man sitting on a horse watching the procession, obviously having tried to stay hidden. His horse neighing to those that rode past had given him away.

Harry Weston rode out into the open. He was soon surrounded by the Nez Perce, their arrows notched onto the strings of their bows and aimed at him.

"Please have mercy," Harry gulped out. "As you can see I am alone. I . . . I . . . have separated myself from the others. I want to return to San Francisco. I was wrong to ever come here and become involved in the illegal activities."

He hung his head. "I have abandoned the life of crime that has proven to be so undesirable for me," he murmured.

He lifted his head, and with desperate, pleading eyes, looked at Father John. "Please don't let them hurt me," he cried. "I want to return to San Francisco. I want to start life anew. Tell the Nez Perce that I apologize for any wrong I have done to them. Tell them if they let me go, they will never hear from me again."

"Can you not speak for yourself to the Nez Perce?" Tall Shadow said, sidling his horse closer to Harry's. "Are you not man enough to face those you have wronged?"

Harry's eyes widened. He gulped back a tight knot of fear in his throat. "I do apologize to you for what I have done," he said, his voice tight with fear. "Please let me go. How can I be a threat to you now? I am only one man. And once I return to San Francisco, I promise never to return to your land again. I was wrong to want the horses so badly."

"How can you expect the Nez Perce to let a man go who has done so much wrong against their people?" Tall Shadow grumbled. "Not only did you steal our horses, you also are partly to blame for the death of our brethren, and for the fire that destroyed so much of our people's lodges."

Harry's face drained of color. "I have told you that I am innocent of anything that happened except for stealing horses," he said, his voice drawn. "Someone else killed Red Bonnet. Someone else burned your lodges."

Father John sidled his horse closer to Tall Shadow's. "What he says is true," he said solemnly. "He had nothing to do with the death of Red Bonnet. Nor did he even know those who burned the village. That he and his men were set free because of the fire was something that was not planned but taken advantage of only because they feared for their lives should they have stayed."

Having heard and seen what was transpiring between the Nez Perce and Harry Weston, Chris, the woman who had the courage to speak up, walked up close enough to Tall Shadow to speak her mind.

"What Father John has said is true. My husband and his men are the ones who are guilty of everything you are condemning this man for," she murmured. "I don't know this man. He has never rode with my husband and his friends. That makes him innocent of setting the fire or killing and scalping your friend, now doesn't it? He is a stranger to me and my husband. He . . . is . . . innocent."

Harry sighed heavily. He smiled down at Chris. "Thank you," he murmured. "Thank you for speaking in my behalf. I will forever be grateful."

Tall Shadow had absorbed all that had been said. He did see now that the man was innocent of everything except stealing the Appaloosa, and that was an unspeakable crime in itself.

He looked over his shoulder in the direction of his chief. Tall Shadow wanted to get this all behind him so that he could return to his village and await word of Silver Wing's condition. He was wasting time here listening to this horse thief. It did seem that setting this man free was a more practical thing to do under these circumstances. No one wanted to be bothered with him and having to decide his fate should he be imprisoned among his people again.

As Tall Shadow saw it, his people would be best served if this man *was* gone and only a sordid memory.

"All I want is to leave this wild, unfriendly country," Harry blurted out. "I again apologize for the trouble I have caused your people."

"Let him go," Father John murmured. "And let *him,* along with Dennis, take the women and children on to the trading post so that you and your warriors can return home. I'm sure you are anxious to know the welfare of your chief. Leaving the women and children in the hands of these two white men would give you the opportunity of being where you want to be. I would like to return to the village with you to be with my friends."

Tall Shadow glowered at Harry. "You will do this?" he said flatly. "You will see that the women and children arrive safely at the trading post?"

"Yes, I will," Harry said. He glanced quickly at Father John. "Along with Dennis Bell, I promise to make sure they arrive there, Father John. I promise."

Tall Shadow's gaze moved to the Appaloosa horse that Harry rode, and then he gazed at the others upon which the women and children sat. "The horses will be sent for later at the trading post," he said tightly. "You be on the next ship that arrives at the trading post, no matter where it travels next. I want you away from my country and people. Go far, for should I ever see your face again, one of my arrows will find its way quickly in your heart."

So happy that he was being set free, Harry beamed. "I'll do anything you say," he said. "Thank you. Thank you."

Father John sidled his horse close to Harry's. He placed a hand on his shoulder. "This is as far as I go. I will not be there to see if you keep your word. But you know that you must," he said tightly. "And you had best see to the safe arrival of these women and children to the trading post, or I will manage to find you someday and make you pay for lying to me . . . a man of God."

His eyes wide, Harry nodded anxiously.

Dennis Bell rode over and reached a hand over for Father John. "I had always hoped we'd meet again, but never would I have thought it would be under such interesting circumstances," he said, chuckling low. He clasped his hand to the priest's. "Until we meet again, my friend."

"Yes, until we meet again," Father John said, his voice breaking. "Be careful, Dennis. Who is to say what this deranged man has up his sleeve. Keep a watch at all times."

"You don't have to tell me that twice," Dennis said, casting Harry a troubled glance.

"May God keep you safe," Father John said, easing his hand from Dennis's.

Dennis nodded and rode off, Harry beside him, the children and women behind them.

Father John watched the women and children proceed on their journey with the two men. For the women and children's sake, and especially Dennis's, Father John hoped that he had chosen wisely when he had encouraged the Nez Perce to let Harry go.

He hoped that it wasn't wrong for him not to accompany them himself. Yet he had the need to return to the Nez Perce village to be with his four friends who were vulnerable without him. Should Silver Wing die, for certain they could become the target of the Nez Perce's vengeance!

33

O, what a smile! a threefold smile
Fill'd mc that like a flame I burn'd;
I bent to Kiss the lovely Maid,
And found a Threefold Kiss returned.
———WILLIAM BLAKE

Snuggled against Silver Wing, exhaustion having taken its toll, Audra had finally slept through the night.

When a cool hand touched her cheek gently, her eyes flew open and gazed at Silver Wing, who was smiling almost mischievously at her.

It was his hand that had awakened her!

And it was cool to the touch!

That had to mean that . . .

"Your fever has broken!" she cried, her eyes brimming with a sudden joy.

Silver Wing reached both hands out for her, his vision now clear, the throbbing of his temples due to the raging temperature having subsided.

He feasted upon her with his eyes, loving her so much he ached, for he would never forget the long hours she had sat vigil at his side. She had tried to hold back tears to appear strong and courageous, yet when she had turned her eyes away from him, she would cry.

He had wanted to comfort her and tell her that he would be all right.

"*Tee-men-a,* come to me," he whispered, placing his hands at her waist, drawing her down beside him.

He turned to her and held her close, his cool lips feathering soft kisses across her brow, her cheeks.

Then he kissed her with a long, deep kiss that made his want of her twofold.

But he knew that he was too weak to make love. That would have to wait until he was stronger. The waiting would enhance the moment they truly were able to hold each other, their bodies rocking and swaying as the passion heated between.

As Silver Wing's hands crept down, across Audra's body, and he felt how frail it had become, he leaned away from her and looked at her more closely. "You have lost much weight," he said, his gaze now absorbing the gauntness of her cheeks and how her eyes were sunken and black beneath.

Silver Wing sat upright, and he gripped her gently by the shoulders, his eyes suddenly troubled. "You said that you could not get measles, that you had already had them, yet you look as though you are not well," he blurted out. "Are you coming down with measles, after all? Will you have to go through the trauma my body has just gone through? If you are already weak, your body might not be able to fight off the ravages of the disease. You . . . might . . ."

Audra gently slid a hand over his mouth to silence him. She smiled reassuringly to him. "My darling, I am just tired, that's all," she murmured. "And I haven't told anyone, especially you, but I am having trouble holding my food down after I eat breakfast each morning. I attribute that to nervousness over worrying about you.''

She leaned into his embrace and snuggled closely against him. ''But now that you are well, I am certain I won't be ill like that any longer,'' she murmured. ''You have to know how distraught I have been over you being so ill. When you spoke the verbal will, it was perhaps one of the worst moments of my life. I knew then that you did not believe you would recover.''

Again, he held her away from him. His gaze went to her stomach, then he gazed into her eyes again. ''How many mornings have you been ill at your stomach?'' he asked softly, a twinkling in his eyes Audra did not understand.

''Several,'' Audra murmured, cocking an eyebrow when his gaze shifted once again to her stomach. She was truly in wonder when he slid a hand down and gently placed it over her stomach.

''Why are you doing that?'' she asked softly, searching his eyes when he gazed into hers again, a slow smile quivering on his lips.

''Has your body experienced its menses since we made love that first time?'' he asked, confusing Audra even more by such a question as that.

''Menses?'' Audra said, forking an eyebrow. ''What does that mean?''

''Blood that comes to women's body one time each month,'' he said softly.

Audra smiled bashfully. ''I see,'' she murmured. ''But no, now that I think of it, I haven't had my monthly flow, not since I have been away from San Francisco."

She questioned him with her eyes. "Why would you ask?" she murmured.

"You have said that no one explained to you about your body, or much of life, in general," he said lightly. "You said that your mother told you nothing about being with a man sexually."

"Yes, I told you that," Audra said, scarcely breathing as she wondered what was causing him to ask such questions at such a time as this. He had just gotten over a terrible disease. They should be rejoicing, not wondering about her and why she was ill in the mornings.

"Then, that means that your mother did not tell you about babies and how some women feel when they discover they are first pregnant," Silver Wing said hoarsely, his eyes again on her stomach as he gently stroked his hand across the buckskin dress, beneath which he was certain lay the wonders of a child.

"No, she never told me such things," Audra said, her voice now a whisper as he took both hands and slowly lifted her goatskin dress, then lay a hand directly on the flesh of her stomach.

She looked quickly up at him again. "Why are you doing that?" she asked, her pulse racing. "I'm very confused, Silver Wing. You are even somewhat frightening me."

"Do not be afraid," he said, sliding his hands away from her, smoothing her dress in place again. "My woman, I believe there might be more to your sickness than what you think is the cause."

"What are you trying to say?" she asked softly, her hands now resting on her abdomen, her heart pounding, for now she thought she might know what he was referring to. A baby. Could she be carrying a baby inside her womb? If so, it would be a joyous way to celebrate Silver Wing's recovery!

"*Tee-men-a,* you say your monthly flow has abandoned you since we made love and you are now ill in the mornings," he said, placing a hand at the nape of her neck, drawing her closer to him. "I do not doubt at all that you are pregnant with our child."

Overcome with joy, she flung herself into his arms. "These last several days, especially yesterday, when I thought you might be dying, I thought we had been robbed of the happiness we had found together," she cried. "But I was wrong! Now our happiness is real again! It is ours to bask in! It is even more so now that I might be carrying a child made from our loving one another."

"You *are* carrying our child, not perhaps," Silver Wing said huskily. He held her for a moment longer, then held her away from him so that he could look upon her again. "But there is something that must be done about the pregnancy."

"What do . . . you . . . mean?" Audra asked guardedly. "What must be done? I . . . thought . . . you were as happy as I that I might have our child growing inside my womb."

Silver Wing laughed and again drew her into his arms. "You misinterpreted what I said," he said softly, gently stroking her back. "What must be done is something as wonderful as you being with child."

Audra eased from his arms and gazed intensely into his eyes. "What could be as wonderful as that?" she murmured. "I can hardly believe the wonder of it. A baby? Growing inside my body? And that it is yours is so wonderful."

"A wedding ceremony must be performed soon," Silver Wing said, framing her face between his hands. "Go to Tall Shadow, who waits outside to know of my condition. Tell him that I have recovered. Tell him that I am taking a bride today and that he should go for Rainbow so that she can perform the simple, private ceremony that will make you my wife."

"We are getting married?" Audra exclaimed, her heart pounding. "Today, Silver Wing? You are marrying me today?"

"We are marrying each other," Silver Wing said, laughing softly. "You will soon be my wife."

"My husband?" Audra said, excitedly clasping her hands together on her lap. "Are you truly strong enough to do this? I wouldn't want to be the cause of you having a relapse."

"Marrying you will make my strength return even more quickly," Silver Wing said, chuckling. "Go. Give Tall Shadow the message. Then return to me. Together we will go to the stream and bathe. I must wash the sickness from my flesh before I take you for my bride."

"But should you use your strength to do that?" Audra said, afraid that he *was* jumping into doing too much too quickly. She was afraid that if he had a relapse, he might not fully recover after all.

"You have worried enough about me," Silver Wing

said softly. "You have no need to worry any longer." He beckoned toward the entrance flap. "Go. Give Tall Shadow my message. Also, tell the other warriors I no longer need their protection. I am lucid and strong enough to fill my bowstring with an arrow should it become necessary."

Audra started to argue the point, but knew that it would displease him, even make him feel less a man. She said nothing against his decision for she would still be with him. Although she had never even notched an arrow onto a bowstring before, she would if faced with danger.

"I shall only be a moment," she said, then left the wigwam.

Knowing just how weak he was, Silver Wing doubted that he could do all that he had boasted about, but knew that to recover as quickly as he wished to, he must force his lapsed muscles to move.

As he pushed himself up from the bed, his knees quivered while he slowly made his way to the wigwam entrance.

Sweat pearled his brow.

His heart pounded like distant thunder in his ears!

And by the time he finally achieved getting to the entrance flap, he heard the thunderous beats of the horses as his warriors left for their village.

"Are you certain you can do this?" Audra asked softly, watching his arms quiver as Silver Wing came outside into the morning sunshine.

"I am certain," Silver Wing said, huffing and puffing as he stopped to rest.

"Let me help you," Audra murmured, grabbing him by an arm, then slid an arm around his waist.

"Just steady me as I need it," Silver Wing said, his voice weakened by the struggle. "Help me to the stream. The cool water will invigorate not only me, but also my muscles."

"Just take it slow and easy," Audra encouraged.

Finally they reached the stream, where the limbs of cottonwoods hung over it like beautiful green umbrellas. "Let me hurry out of my clothes so that I can join you in the water," Audra said, hesitating at releasing her hold on him for fear of him falling.

As she slid her hand slowly away from him and he stood steady enough, she hurried out of her clothes.

Silver Wing's gaze swept over her, his hunger for her greater than his hunger for food.

Nude, the sun warm on her body, Audra helped Silver Wing out of his breechclout.

Holding him again around his waist, she led him into the water, its sting so cold she visibly shivered.

"It is cold, but welcomed," Silver Wing said as he noticed how Audra shivered. "Release your hold on me. I want to swim for at least a moment."

Questioning him with her eyes, not thinking this decision of his was too wise, afraid that if he was too weak and started to drown, she might not have the strength to save him, she started to reach out and encourage him against it.

But he had already dove headfirst into the deepest part of the water. She held her breath as she waited for him to rise back to the surface.

She sighed and said a soft prayer of thank-you when

his head bobbed quickly into the open, and he began taking smooth, even strokes through the water. She was amazed to see him this revitalized.

Wanting to be with him, to help him should he suddenly discover that he could not make it to shore, Audra dove in the water and swam over to him.

They swam, side by side for a while, then Silver Wing reached out for Audra and brought her over against his hard body. He anchored his feet on the rocky bottom of the stream and held Audra close, his arms enfolding her, his lips quivering as he gave her a long, deep kiss that made his body cry out with a renewed want of her.

Needing him, her body aching for him, Audra swept her hand down and twined around his manhood. She heard his intake of breath, and then heard his moan against her lips as he began to grow within her fingers.

As her fingers pleasured him, one of his hands reached down and began stroking her.

She leaned into his hand, her moans now mingling with his as their kisses became frenzied and heated.

Soon they both trembled with release as the pleasure reached its peak.

When she felt his chest heaving as he breathed, Audra eased from his arms and looked at him, in her eyes a soft apology. "I'm sorry," she murmured. "I shouldn't have initiated that. I should have . . ."

He slid a gentle hand across her lips. "I encouraged it," he said huskily. "But the next time, I will be the one who initiates the lovemaking, and it will be wholly done, not only with caresses."

"I love you so much," Audra murmured. "I have missed you so much."

"And you have me again for all times," Silver Wing said, again encircling her with his arms, drawing her against him. "My woman, it has been lonesome in my bed without you."

"I have been as lonely," Audra murmured. "That's why I came to your bed last night. I had such a need to snuggle."

"Your snuggling is what made me well," Silver Wing said, chuckling.

They left the water and just as they completed dressing, they caught sight of three horses approaching in the distance. One carried Rainbow, the others Tall Shadow and Black Fox. Silver Wing took Audra's hand and led her from the water.

"We are here!" Audra cried, waving at them so that they could see them. "We . . . are . . . here!"

"Hold me steady again so that I can make it back to the lodge," Silver Wing said as he walked toward the wigwam.

"I'd be delighted to," Audra said, laughing softly. "We have a wedding to attend. *Ours.*"

34

Ah, bear me with thee, smoothly borne,
Dip forward under starry light,
And move me to my marriage-morn,
And round again to happy night.
——ALFRED, LORD TENNYSON

Knowing that the Dalles Trading Post was just around a bend, Dennis Bell gave the women and children looks of relief. They didn't look like they could go much farther. Especially the children. They were whining and crying.

During this short time with Harry, Dennis had seen a side to him that he had never expected to see. No one could have been as gentle as Harry had been with the women and children. It was hard for Dennis to imagine Harry switching the children's legs at the Nez Perce village. Surely being so close to finally having something special . . . the horses and the land . . . had blinded him of the man he could be.

When a child started crying even now, Harry drew a tight rein, dismounted, and took him from his mother's arms to comfort him.

Dennis stopped his steed and slid from the saddle, to take a rest before taking the final leg of his journey. He had made his home at the trading post for many years now. He and Phil Harper owned it.

He smiled when he envisioned how happy Phil would be when he saw Dennis come into the trading post well and strong again. The Nez Perce had sent word to Phil that Dennis was ailing. Phil had sent word back that he would keep things going at the trading post until his partner returned.

The child no longer crying, but instead playing with the others as though things were normal, Dennis lumbered over to Harry and patted him on the shoulder.

"You've got a way with the children," he said softly.

Harry laughed awkwardly. "I know a few people who'd argue that," he said, sighing. "I was a foolish man to go into the Nez Perce village and push my way around there. I don't know what got into me."

"You've never had much in life, that's why," Dennis said, settling down beneath a cottonwood tree, crossing his legs at his ankles.

Harry sat down beside him, his eyes slowly raking across the lusciousness of the land. "This is a place men could die for," he said, mesmerized. "I almost lost my life over it. I owe my life to the Nez Perce for allowing me to return to my stamping grounds in San Francisco. That's where I truly belong. Not here."

"What are you going to do when you get there?" Dennis asked, stiffening when he thought that he heard a sound of muffled hoofbeats in the distance.

"I'm not sure," Harry said, frowning. "I'll find something. I want to make something of my life. I've wasted enough of it already doing things that didn't amount to beans."

Dennis turned his head with a start when again he thought he heard something.

Suddenly all hell broke loose when gunfire rang in the air.

Dennis's body bolted forward when a bullet entered his back. Before he drifted off into unconsciousness, he saw Harry's body lurch sideways when a bullet entered his side.

The women and children went frantic, screaming and running into the forest, but were soon caught and gathered together.

Clutching their children, the women's eyes were wide and wild as they gazed in fear at their husbands, two of their rifles still smoking from having shot Dennis Bell and Harry Weston.

"Why did you do that?" Chris cried, tears rushing from her eyes as she looked at the two unconscious men whose shirts were soaked with blood, and then at her husband Jimmy again. "They were helping us. Why would you shoot them?"

Jimmy stepped forward, grabbed Chris by an arm, and yanked her against him, his breath mingling with hers as he glared down at her. "And so you ran out on me, huh?" he snarled, his eyes filled with angry fire.

"Jimmy, you . . . never . . . returned," Chris said, swallowing hard. "We all thought you were dead. We had no choice but to leave."

"And so you just happened along those two gents for company, huh?" Jimmy shouted, squeezing his fingers painfully into her arm. "Not even caring if your Jimmy was dead or not, you took up with someone else who might give you something better? What'd the men promise you? Huh?"

"Freedom!" Chris cried. "Freedom from likes of

you." Tears filled her eyes. "They meant us no harm. They were taking us to the trading post. We were going to seek passage on the next ship to anywhere but here. Lord, Jimmy, *I* want to go back to Missouri. I want to see my ma and pa again."

"To hell with Missouri, to hell with your so-called freedom," Jimmy said, shoving his wife away from him. "You're goin' to stay with us. The measles didn't down us. We've got more to do before hightailin' it to higher Northwest country. We've some more horses to round up."

"Those you had are now in the possession of the Nez Perce," Chris said, smiling wickedly at Jimmy, and then the others whose eyes were narrowing angrily at her. "So seems you've got to start all over again, doesn't it?"

Jimmy slapped Chris across the face with the back of a hand, then threw her on the ground and spat on her.

The other women sobbed and begged for mercy, but their husbands ignored them.

"Please let us leave this horrid place," Chris begged, frantically grabbing Jimmy by an ankle as she still lay on the ground. "Please let us go. None of us want any more to do with you. We want to go anywhere but with you. I, for one, want to go home to my parents."

She scrambled to her feet and grabbed her three-year-old son and held him close. "They'll welcome me and little Jimmy with open arms."

"Slut, you married me for better or worse, sickness or health," Jimmy spat out. "I don't let anyone out of their obligations to me that easy. You'll go where I go. Do what I do. Do what I *say*."

He walked over and gave Harry Weston a kick. "Whoever they are, they're not goin' to do any more wife stealin', that's for sure," he grumbled.

He turned and smiled crookedly at his wife. "Want to kiss 'em good-bye?" he chuckled. "It'd do you good to get a feel of what a man dyin' feels like. Then you'd think twice about crossin' us men again."

"Yep, one more raid on the Nez Perce horses and then we'll move farther out of their country and find another place to do our hell raisin'," Jimmy said, taking his pistol from his holster, spinning the bullets in the chamber.

"You can't get away from Indians," Chris said, running her fingers through her long blond hair, pulling it back from her eyes. "Indians are everywhere in this Northwest country. There aren't only the Nez Perce, but also the Flatheads, Blackfoot, and Suquamish. One tribe might be worse than the last. And no tribe can be as gentle and forgiving as the Nez Perce. You're stupid to stay here. You'd best return to stealin' from banks in Missouri."

"Yeah, I'm sure you'd like to talk me into that, for once there, you'd turn us all over to a sheriff, wouldn't you?" Jimmy said, his teeth clenched. He glared at Chris. "There ain't no way in hell I'd ever give you that opportunity."

He gave her a shove. "Now, get off your high horse and you and the other women grab hold of the kids and get on the horses and let's head back to our new hideout," he said.

"Your new hideout?" Chris said guardedly.

"Yeah, now, git!" he said, giving her a rough shove.

Chris gave Dennis and Harry a downcast, sorry look, then gathered together with the women and children and mounted the horses, reluctantly following their husbands.

Grumbling obscenities to herself, Chris had to find a way to get back at her husband.

If she ever got a hold of one of the men's firearms, she'd wipe a few smirks off a few filthy faces!

35

Harry awakened and groaned when he felt a searing pain shoot through his side. With a shaky hand he reached up and cringed when he found his shirt soaked in blood.

Panting, he rolled over on his other side and winced when he saw Dennis Bell lying still on his stomach. Blood had spread from his back to the ground on each side of him.

"Damn," Harry whispered as he crawled an inch at a time over to Dennis. With trembling fingers, he reached up to see if Dennis had a pulse. He did, thank God. At least for now they were both still alive.

But not knowing the extent of their wounds, Harry wasn't sure how long either one of them would live.

"We've got to get to the trading post," Harry whispered, each movement causing more pain. He tugged on Dennis's shirtsleeve. "Dennis. Wake up, man. We've got to get help, or we'll both be dead by nightfall."

When Dennis didn't respond, Harry closed his eyes

and took a deep breath. He tried to recall the very moment he was shot, but nothing came to him. He couldn't even recall what he had been doing prior to being shot.

"Who?" he wondered to himself.

Then he recalled the women and children. His eyes opened wildly. He managed to lean up on an elbow to look around him, finding no one. Not even a trace of them having been there.

"Oh, Lord, what's happened to them?" he cried, wincing again when a sharp, searing pain shook him, body and soul.

"Where . . . am . . . I? What . . . happened?"

Dennis's voice drew Harry's eyes quickly to him.

He scooted closer to Dennis. "We were ambushed," he said, his voice dull with the onslaught of pain. "We are . . . lucky . . . to be alive."

Dennis looked over at Harry. "Who . . . did . . . this?" he asked, very aware now of the pain and his blood on the ground.

"It was an ambush," Harry repeated. "The cowards didn't . . . show . . . their faces . . . before shootin' us."

"The women?" Dennis said, his voice scarcely audible. "The children?"

"Gone," Harry said, then lurched with alarm when Dennis's eyes closed and he knew that he was unconscious again.

He gazed at Dennis for a moment longer, then knew that if they were going to make it out of this horrible ambush alive, it was up to him to make it happen. He alone would have to get them to the trading post.

"I don't know how, but I'll manage somehow,"

Harry whispered, each move he took more painful than the last as he reached over and grabbed Dennis by the arm. "If I have to drag you the entire way, by damn, I'll get you there."

Sweat beaded on his brow as he began dragging Dennis, each inch seeming like a mile.

"We'll make it, Dennis," Harry then whispered. "I'll prove to everyone I'm not the villain they have made me out to be."

But he was saving Dennis for another more important reason: he liked the man. And this man had already survived one close call with measles. Harry was not going to let a bullet do what the measles couldn't.

36

Breathed in her ear,
The "Wilt thou?" answer'd again and again,
The "Wilt thou?" ask'd till out of twain.
Her sweet "I will" has made you one.
——ALFRED, LORD TENNYSON

Glad to be back at the village, Silver Wing sat next to Audra among his people. They were celebrating his recovery and his marriage to Audra.

The sun was warm overhead. Eagles soared through the warm skies, their shadows reflected on the people beneath them, as though the birds were a part of the celebration, blessing it.

"Aren't they beautiful?" Audra declared. "What joy they must feel being a part of the sky and the clouds."

"The true joy is here," Silver Wing said, sliding a hand over and taking one of Audra's. She turned her eyes to him and smiled. "You are my joy, my *wife*."

"I love how you say . . . wife," Audra murmured, a shudder of rapture riding her spine. "I still can't believe it . . . that I am your wife and that I am carrying our child within my body."

She slid her free hand over her abdomen, the doe-skin dress laying soft and comforting against it. "I will be a good mother, Silver Wing," she murmured. "I shall always be there for our children. And I will be sure to talk to them. I will teach them things about life that I was never told. I will prepare them *for* life."

"As will I," Silver Wing said, slipping an arm around her waist, drawing her close to his side.

He looked away from Audra and smiled as young braves gathered together in the middle of the circle.

She had enjoyed watching the small girls and their games earlier. They had made circle of stones in which each represented a wish or prayer.

Over these stones, the girls prayed for strength and endurance . . . to carry her burden in later life, then specified what wish each stone represented.

Audra had been told that this was called a "Wish upon Rocks" game.

"The braves will now play the 'bone game,' " Silver Wing said, giving Audra a quick glance, then once again focusing on the children at play.

Audra saw how sweaty and tired the young braves seemed to be and knew that it was because of the footraces. They seemed to welcome the less strenuous bone game, laughing and talking among themselves as they sat in a small circle.

"The game is simple enough, but what they are gambling over is not," Silver Wing said, anxiously watching the first young brave guess in which hand a piece of elk bone was being held.

"What will those who are the victors win?" Audra asked softly as she saw the first young brave pick the right hand. She saw his smile of relief as he scooted farther back so that another brave would choose a hand held out before him.

"The game will be played around the full circle of young braves before anyone announces what they will give to those who win," Silver Wing said, frowning when one of his favorite young braves chose the wrong hand. This meant he might have to give up his valued pony, or perhaps the bow he had only recently finished carving.

"They now look so serious," Audra murmured as smiles were replaced with serious frowns.

"That is because there are now winners and losers, and those who lose will soon have to hand over something special to himself to those who win," Silver Wing said, flinching when another of his favored braves, already singled out to be a great warrior, lost.

"But I would think that those who are winning would be smiling," Audra said, glancing over at Silver Wing.

He gazed over at her. "Of course they will gladly take what will soon be theirs, yet they know the sadness of the loss of those who lose to them," he said thickly. "They would not want to part with their own prized objects. That is why they sympathize with those who do."

"Then, why play this game at all if no one comes out of it happy?" Audra asked, forking an eyebrow.

"It is the challenge they must experience, no matter the end result," Silver Wing said, then watched the players disband.

His eyes followed the two braves he favored and watched what they chose to give up. As he had thought, one gave over his favored pony. The other gave over his newly carved bow.

Then his attention was drawn to the circle again when both young braves and women entered it and began dancing to the drums and soft magical sounds of the *Flageolet*, flute, also used in courting.

Audra watched the young dancers in awe. She imagined Little Butterfly all grown up, dancing with the children.

Then her own daughter, born of her and Silver Wing's love, came to mind. Petite and beautiful, her face would be radiant with a smile, as she swayed and danced to the drums and flutes. She envisioned her with features of the Nez Perce, and long flowing hair. Her eyes would be a deep, lovely gray.

"You are far away in thought," Silver Wing said as he placed a finger beneath Audra's chin and brought her eyes around to meet his. "What were you thinking about? There is such a radiance in your eyes."

"I was envisioning our daughter," Audra said, filled with a warm joy at the remembrance. "It was as though she were already born and grown to the age of those who are dancing today. She . . . seemed . . . so real to me, Silver Wing, as though I could reach out and touch her."

"It is the magic of the dance and instruments that brought such visions into your heart," Silver Wing said. He drew her into his arms and gently hugged her. "You are becoming more and more Nez Perce by the day. Visions are a part of our daily lives. Wonderful visions give us the hope we have always built our lives around. You will envision many more things that will make you happy before you die."

"I don't see how I could be any more happy than

now," Audra murmured, drawing away from him when she looked past Silver Wing's shoulder and saw Father John approaching them.

"Someone is coming," she murmured, causing Silver Wing to lean away from her to see.

When Father John came and sat down beside him, his eyes revealing to Silver Wing that he had more to discuss today than the celebration, Silver Wing tensed.

"Soon a ship will arrive down the Columbia that could take me and my friends back to San Francisco," Father John said, looking past Silver Wing as Audra scooted farther out from Silver Wing so that she could also face Father John.

"That *could*," Silver Wing said, his voice stiff. "Do you not mean to say *will*? Your plans are to leave. I have never seen it as any other way than that. So what do you have on your mind that is different?"

"I've been thinking about so much these past weeks," Father John said, brushing the skirt of his long black gown around him on the ground. "I have grown close to many of your people. Our bonding comes from trusting one another. I am not anxious to leave them. Many have said they are saddened over my eventual departure."

"I have noticed that many of my people, in my absence, have grown to respect you," Silver Wing admitted. "Of course, you have to know that does not set well with me. I want nothing of you or your religion. When the ship arrives, you will board it. That is final, holy man. Final!"

"Please reconsider," Father John said, his eyes begging.

"I cannot believe you are asking such a thing of me," Silver Wing said, his voice tight. "I do not want white man's religion among my people. I was wrong ever to ask for the Bibles. It has gained nothing for my people except confusion."

"I'm not asking to stay among your people and live with them," Father John said. "I am wanting your permission to stay in the vicinity, only. I wish to build a mission in a place that is serene and beautiful . . . a place filled with God's presence. I wish to build it near Butterfly Valley."

Audra couldn't even believe that Father John was asking such a thing of the Nez Perce, especially Silver Wing. Father John knew that his presence here was only tolerated because the ship to San Francisco hadn't arrived yet. It was ludicrous of him to think otherwise!

"I will hear no more of this," Silver Wing said, angrily folding his arms across his chest. "Go and sit with your friends. Leave me and my wife, *and* my people in peace."

"Please hear me out," Father John pleaded. "What I want to do can help your people, not harm them. You have to know, Silver Wing, that white people will be arriving to your land, especially after they hear of its loveliness. This land has much to offer everyone, not only Indians. You know that things change. It *will* change here, Silver Wing, and there will be no way to stop whites once they begin coming and building homes."

"Because of people like you, that will be so," Silver

Wing grumbled. "You spread the word . . . they will come!"

"I won't spread the word to anyone," Father John said, sighing. "I will just be here when someone else does. I will have the mission ready for the whites. It will be there for the settlers to attend. I will teach them how to live among your people. Can't you see now that what I want to do is only for the good of your people? Not the bad?"

Audra held her breath, but she was surprised to hear Silver Wing's answer.

"You will not spread the word to my people about your God?" Silver Wing said, his voice drawn. "You will not encourage them to attend your church services? You will not invite them into your lodge?"

"I will do none of that," Father John said, his eyes anxious. "Can I build the mission . . . and still be friends with your people? It is . . . a . . . good feeling I have for your village."

"I have watched and seen the respect my people now have for you and your friends," Silver Wing said. "And I do know that the big water vessel with wings will bring more and more whites to my area. It would be good to have someone like you waiting to teach them things that would keep them as no threat to my people. Yes, holy man, I will agree to your staying. My warriors will even help you build your mission."

Stunned that Silver Wing had agreed to Father John's plan, Audra took a deep breath. Yet she knew that Silver Wing had been thinking about the way things were changing in the world, especially his. Since the outlaws had come so easily onto his land and wreaked such havoc, he realized it could happen again and again and his people would not be able to stop it. Soon they could be outnumbered and then what of the Nez Perce?

Yes, she saw the logic of what Father John suggested. She was even touched that he cared this much for the Nez Perce.

And she knew that he was a man of his word. He *would* not interfere in the Nez Perce's lives unless they wanted him to.

"But, Father John, the mission cannot be built anywhere near Butterfly Valley," Silver Wing quickly interjected. "That is a sacred and mystical place to the Nez Perce. No white man's lodge should disturb its serenity."

"There are many places as beautiful where I can build my mission," Father John responded appreciatively. He clasped a hand onto Silver Wing's shoulder. "Thank you, Silver Wing. I will never give you cause to regret what you have agreed to today."

Father John smiled gently at Audra, then rose and went back to sit among his friends.

Audra watched him talking anxiously to the other priests. She saw how their eyes lit up. She could tell by their expressions that their joy was genuine and that they could be trusted.

"Come with me," Silver Wing said, taking Audra by a hand, urging her to her feet.

Audra questioned him with her eyes, looked back at the celebrating Nez Perce, then went with Silver Wing to their longhouse.

She watched him bolt the door, then smiled as he turned and swept her into his arms.

"I need to be alone with you," he said huskily. "I did not want to stay at the celebration to be delayed by someone else coming with ideas about this and that. I need you, Audra; no one else."

She twined a loving arm around his neck. "I will always be here for you," she whispered, then shuddered with ecstasy when he kissed her, his one hand snaking up the inside of her dress, leaving ripples of desire in its wake.

When he swam his fingers beneath her cotton undergarment and touched her where she ached for him, then began slowly caressing her, she almost went mindless with ecstasy.

She closed her eyes and floated into the wondrous moments of bliss. And when he thrust a finger inside her, touching her where all of her sensual feelings seemed to be centered, she gasped with pleasure and felt the warmth begin to spread through her in waves.

And when Silver Wing laid her on their bed of blankets and pelts and he hurriedly undressed her, she welcomed his hands, lips, and mouth everywhere that he knew to arouse her even more.

Almost arriving to that place of no return, when her body would become fully encased in blissful tremors, she opened her eyes and gently shoved Silver Wing away.

"Please remove your breechclout," Audra whispered, her heart racing. "I want to touch you. I want to fill you with the same joy I am feeling."

"I already feel it," Silver Wing said huskily as he

stood over her and slowly slid his breechclout down past his hips, and then down his muscled legs.

He kicked it away from himself, then sucked in a wild breath of rapture when Audra reached for him and twined her fingers around his manhood.

She watched his eyes become hazy with pleasure as she moved her hand on him. She could see his body stiffening and knew that he was already nearing the ultimate of bliss with her hand only having given him a few strokes.

Smiling down at her, Silver Wing took her hand away, then knelt beside her and cupped both of her breasts with his hands.

His tongue flicking over her nipples caused Audra's breath to catch with desire.

She closed her eyes and rolled her head when his tongue left a wet, warm path downward until he came to her swollen nub.

She could feel his fingers parting her fronds of hair and then she melted away when he swept his tongue over her, leaving her breathless and wanting.

Although she was floating with rapture by being loved in what she still saw as a forbidden way, she was glad when he rose over her and quickly thrust his manhood deeply inside her and began moving within her rhythmically.

Locking her legs around him, her arms twined around his neck, she rocked and swayed with him, welcoming the bliss that soon enveloped them both. They clung and tremored, then rolled away from each other. Panting, they lay on their backs.

"I never thought my life could be labeled as 'perfect,' " Audra murmured, moving to cuddle against Silver Wing's long, hard body. "But it is, Silver Wing. I don't wish for a thing, You have given it all to me."

"You are the true gift giver," Silver Wing said, turning to face her, forming his body against hers. "What you have given to me is beyond what I ever imagined being with a woman could be."

He gently touched her face. "And to think that you are now carrying our child," he said softly. "It is a thing of miracles . . . how we met that once, and then again. Had you not been brave enough to flee the convent and board that ship, we would have never known the wonders of these stolen moments with one another."

"I was so afraid while hiding on that ship," Audra said, visibly shuddering. Then she giggled. "And never had I smelled anything as vile as myself after so many days without a bath."

He bent low and licked one of her breasts. "You taste of honey now," he whispered. "And you smell of forest flowers the butterflies seek during thcir time at Butterfly Valley."

Audra leaned up on an elbow. "I think you are so kind to have given Father John the chance to have his mission," she murmured. "Now, had I been asked." She paused and placed a finger to her chin. "No, I'm not sure what I would have said. I wouldn't have been able to give an answer as you did."

"While I was ill and drifting in and out of consciousness, I had much come to me that normally would not," Silver Wing said thickly. "I saw things I would have never seen. I experienced feelings I would have never experienced. It has given me insight into many things I would have never otherwise known. And seeing the logic in what Father John said is a part of those times when I was alone with my thoughts and visions of the future."

"How do you see the future?" Audra murmured.

"When I look across the land, I see many white eyes," Silver Wing said, his voice drawn. "It will happen. Has it not everywhere else where Indians owned land? There is nothing that can stop what white man calls 'progress' from happening here. I am not a man of war. And our people are too few compared to the white eyes who are many."

"I wish it could stay just like it is," Audra murmured, again cuddling close. "Your land is such a peaceful, wonderful place. And, ah, the horses. How beautiful they look grazing on the lush, tall grass. If settlers come into the area, the horses will be as it was with the buffalo. They will be crowded out. They will disappear."

"I will keep a corral filled with many," Silver Wing said. "Nothing will keep me from my horses. Nothing."

He swept her up over him so that she straddled him. "But enough talk of things that could destroy my hope for the future if I allow it," he said thickly. He reached up and held her breasts within his hands. He thrust himself up inside her. "Let us think of nothing but now."

Audra closed her eyes and held her head back as she felt the pleasure encompassing her again like the warm rays of sunshine were flooding her senses.

Yes, there was now, Audra marveled to herself, beautiful, wonderful now.

37

The sun was gone now; the curled moon
Was like a little feather fluttering.
——DANTE GABRIEL ROSSETTI

Stars were like millions of wishes overhead. Like a sparkling round diamond in the dark sky, the moon was full and bright.

A fire burned high into the heavens as the Nez Perce nestled around it before heading on home from their successful fishing expedition.

Hiding her fatigue from Silver Wing, Audra sat beside him on a blanket. She had done her part today in securing in woven baskets the many salmon her husband had caught with his iron harpoon and fish spearheads.

All but the elderly and the women whose children were too small to make the journey had traversed many little valleys and crossed many creeks and streams to get to that perfect place where the salmon were forging their way to their spawning ground.

Their salmon harvest had been a huge success, and soon the Nez Perce smokehouses would be filled with the tantalizing aroma. The salmon would be prepared to keep for the long winter when food was scarce.

Audra had already been taught how the smoking would be done. Particular wood was used for the process. It might be willow, alder, bear wallow, or thornbush. Awaiting the salmon catch, drying racks were already strung halfway up within the smokehouse.

After the salmon was prepared and left there for smoking, it usually took three days and nights for the process to be completed.

The Nez Perce men were the fishermen.

The women assisted in splitting, drying, and storing the salmon.

To entertain themselves as they rested, their bellies full of salmon they had cooked over the outdoor fire, their thirsts quenched by juniper tea, tonight the Nez Perce took turns talking of their legends.

Fascinated by it all, Audra listened intensely. She wanted to be able to tell her children the same legends of their forefathers.

Her eyes widened, and she found herself lost in a story as Rainbow stood up and took her part in the legend telling tonight.

"According to legend, *Its-welx,* the huge monster, swallowed all animal beings and imprisoned them in his stomach," Rainbow said, smiling as what she said drew low gasps from the children. "The Coyote, our sly, legendary hero, permitted himself to be swallowed by the monster. While inside the monster's belly, he slew the monster and freed all the creatures. He then took the pieces of the monster's body and threw them in every direction, each time naming a particular tribe and their physical characteristics. The heart he left in this area, and from it sprinkled the blood saying from this the noble *Nee-me-poo,* Nez Perce, are created."

As Rainbow sat down, everyone applauded, then their attention was drawn to Tall Shadow as he rose to his feet and began his tale. . . .

"Many, many moons ago there were huge birds that could pick up and fly away with a human being," he said, smiling down at the children who came and huddled at his feet, their eyes wide with wonder as they gazed up at him. "These huge birds were called *Khoosa.* And this is true, my children, for my great-grandfather was one among those who found the huge bones of such a bird at Tolo Lake, a lake named after a Nez Perce woman named Tolo."

Then Tall Shadow sat down, and Silver Wing rose tall and noble above his people, the children then scampering to him and settling down at his feet, their eyes anxious.

Silver Wing wove his fingers through one of the young brave's long, thick hair, in his heart seeing his own son as one who would one day sit and listen to legends of his people.

He cast Audra a quick glance, his heart warming when she smiled sweetly up at him. He marveled over her carrying his child within her womb. Finally he would have a son, or daughter. Either one would be as loved as the next. Having a child born of their love was what mattered.

"Tell us, Silver Wing," a child begged. "Tell us your tale."

Silver Wing nodded. He moved his hand from the child's hair, then gestured toward the northern sky.

"My story is of the first horse," he said thickly. "Stories came from the North that the Shoshone had a wonderful animal, a great white mare from which all the horses of the tribes descended. It was said that it was taller than a buffalo, and very swift. Men soon learned that this animal could carry heavy loads. They then learned that they could get on the back of that great white beast and ride him. Our people went to see this animal. They discovered that everything they heard about it was true. They discovered that there was not only one great four-legged beast, there were many. They traded and brought back to our villages many of them. One was more beautiful than all the others. It was a white mare and was heavy with foal. When the foal came, it was beautiful also. The foal was a she-horse, and the people went again to the Shoshones and returned with a stallion. From these the great Appaloosa warhorses came."

Suddenly the serenity of the camp was disturbed by a lone blast of gunfire, and then a cry that pierced the darkness.

It made everyone rush to their feet and look guardedly to the east where they had heard the sound.

Afraid, the cry having sounded like a human in pain, Audra rushed to Silver Wing and clung to his arm.

"Someone has been injured, or . . . or murdered," she said, trembling.

"That was not the cry of a human," Silver Wing grumbled. "That was a bear. When wounded, a bear cries in a high-human wail of pain. And my people are not hunting tonight, nor do the Blackfoot hunt this close to Nez Perce territory. That leaves only white men."

"Would they be foolish enough to come this close to where you are making camp to go on a hunt?" Audra said, still shaken from the alarm of having heard the sudden gunfire.

"The hunters made sure they were not close to our village as they killed the bear," Silver Wing said, reaching a hand to his sheathed knife at his left side. "They did not expect my people to be this far from the village, where they could be caught firing on the mighty creature."

"But the men surely saw the glow of the campfire," Audra said softly.

"They are not that close," Silver Wing said. "The gunshot echoed from a distance. So did the bear's cries. And those who hunt it took quite a chance. Most night creatures even run from the great bear's shadow, much less approach it as a possible meal. Especially the grizzly bear. It puts fear in the hearts of the most fierce animals."

Tall Shadow came to Silver Wing. "Someone hunts by the light of the moon tonight," he grumbled. "And they do not hunt for such animals as deer. They have downed a bear."

"Yes, and we must find the one responsible for the kill," Silver Wing said, rushing away from Audra toward his tethered horse.

Audra ran after them. She grabbed one of Silver Wing's hands, stopping him. "Can't you wait until morning?" she asked, fear in her eyes. "If someone is out there killing things in the night, might you become a target?"

"If we allow them to continue hunting tonight, even you might become the target," Silver Wing said, then drew Audra into his arms. "When hunters become lost in the challenge of the hunt, they do not worry where their bullets might stray."

"I'm afraid for you to go," Audra said, hating it that she was looking so cowardly, yet she now had someone else to worry about. Her child. The child needed to come into this world and be held also by its father!

There was also Little Butterfly. Her very existence depended on Audra *and* Silver Wing!

"We will search for a while, but we will not go too far because we do not want to leave you women and children alone for too long," Silver Wing said, gently framing Audra's face between his hands. "If we do not find the hunters soon, we will come and resume our journey home. Then tomorrow, when the sun is high and tracks can easily be followed, my men, under my lead, will resume the search. The white men do not know the land as well as the Nez Perce. Now that we know they are out there, this close, they will not get away for long with their bear kill."

"Please be careful," Audra murmured, leaning up on her tiptoes to brush a soft kiss across Silver Wing's mouth.

"Stay close by the fire with the others," Silver Wing said, gazing down at her. "The women will resume tales of our ancestors. That will help guide your mind from worries of a husband."

"Nothing will keep me from worrying," Audra said, stepping back as the other warriors came with their bows and arrows and stood waiting for Silver Wing.

She watched them all go to their horses, mount them, and ride away.

Then she returned to the circle of women and children, and sat down with them.

"Do you have a tale to share with us about your ancestors?" Rose Bud innocently asked Audra.

Audra was taken aback by the question, for she had nothing interesting to tell them. Her mother had never shared anything of her family or ancestors with her.

She thought for a moment, then remembered a story that her mother had told her on a day when her father had gone drinking and whoring.

It was just before her mother had gotten ill, her voice soon silenced forever.

"There was a young boy called Jack," she murmured. "He had planted beans in his garden. One day he noticed that one stalk was growing much faster and healthier than the others. It grew and grew until it reached up into the clouds. It was so strong, Jack began to climb it. When he got to the top of the beanstalk, the clouds now below him instead of above, he found a huge giant in a huge castle. . . ."

The children were mesmerized. Audra continued talking, but her heart was with Silver Wing. . . .

Silver Wing and his warriors rode through the night. The moon gave off enough light to find their way through the forest, across valleys, and into deep canyons.

Just when they were about to give up their search,

Silver Wing drew a quick, tight rein, leapt from his horse, and knelt down over the remains of a huge grizzly bear.

All that was missing were its great paws!

Someone had slain the bear only for the paws, which were known to be a favorite delicacy of white men!

"They will pay," he grumbled as Tall Shadow knelt down beside him, his eyes wide as he also looked at the gruesome sight—at the waste of such a beautiful animal.

"The ones who did this are not true hunters," Tall Shadow said, his voice drawn. He glanced over at a bush that was heavy with berries. He looked at the bear's mouth, the juices dried around it.

"They who killed tonight caught the bear off guard as they traversed the night to do other dirty deeds," Silver Wing said, his voice tight with anger. "The bear, who usually senses men's approach, was enjoying his feast of berries too much to smell or hear the approach of white men."

"The men," Tall Shadow said, moving to his feet. He looked into the distance. "Do you believe they are the outlaws whose wives stayed at our village for a while? Do you think the measles did not kill them?"

Silver Wing rose to his feet and stood beside Tall Shadow. His thoughts went instantly to Harry Weston. If Harry Weston had not kept his word and instead backtracked and joined this gang, Silver Wing would make the man die a slow death!

"Let us get our women and children, as well as our salmon catch, safely home, and then prepare ourselves and our horses for warring," Silver Wing grumbled. "This time the whites will not get off so easily. This time the warring will be as it was when our forefathers fought those they despised!"

"I will smile as I paint myself and my horse for war," Tall Shadow said, doubling his fists to his sides.

They looked at the dead bear a moment longer. Silver Wing thought of the grease that could be taken from this body, and the meat, but felt that the bear had been too defiled tonight already and would not add to its disgrace.

He most certainly would not remove its eyes, that which was the custom after an animal was downed. When a kill was made, the hunters punctured the eyes out before it was butchered, otherwise the animal might see what was being done to him and the next hunting party would not be as successful.

He smiled as he thought of those men who were carrying the bear's paws in their bags. The bear's eyes would jinx them now, no matter what sort of hunt they would be on . . . be it for horses, or whatever else. Nothing good would come to them from the bear kill.

Silver Wing would personally make sure of that!

38

The delight of happy laughter,
The delight of low replies.
——ALFRED, LORD TENNYSON

In the Nez Perce village excitement ruled as the warriors prepared for warring against the white outlaws.

Drums boomed.

Dogs barked.

Children gathered to watch the warriors getting ready.

The elder warriors talked to the preparing warriors to raise the war spirit within them.

Audra was with the women as they took the catch into the smokehouse, busying themselves to get their minds off of their men leaving at daybreak . . . for these white men not only had committed a crime against the bear, but also had stolen several Appaloosa.

As Audra helped clean the salmon, she kept glancing through the opened double doors at the warriors, who were now stripped to their breechclouts and moccasins. She found Silver Wing among those mixing powdered tints with water and grease, to make the war paint for their skin.

Audra was drawn to the door, as the men began

fastidiously applying the paint on each other's bodies. Since the Nez Perce was not a warring tribe, she hoped this would be her only opportunity to witness these preparations.

She saw how a red streak went down the part in the center of the warrior's hair.

The forehead was smeared solidly with an orange color, known to be the symbol of strength.

Dots and lines of yellow, red, green, and black covered the cheeks, eyelids, and body, in various patterns, representing every individual's own guardian spirit.

Audra's eyes stayed transfixed on the men as they now placed feathers and symbolic decorations in their hair.

She caught her breath when she saw Silver Wing put on an eagle feather war bonnet. Before, he had always looked noble in appearance, but now with the long, beautiful feathered war bonnet gracing his head, the feathers hanging down to his waist, he was majestic!

Audra's gaze was taken elsewhere when young braves brought the painted warriors their personal steeds. The warriors painted their horses, the white steeds showing the striking war designs the best.

The head and neck of each horse were streaked yellow and red.

The mane was blackened.

The body was covered with meaningful stripes, circles, and zigzag lines.

Their tails, clubbed in knots, were tied short and painted red and decorated with colorful streamers.

And yet the warriors were still not finished with

decking their horses out for the occasion. From the horses' heads, festoons of feathers, streamers, and trinkets became the animals' war bonnets. Then rawhide bridles were looped to the underjaw of the horses. Man and animal blended in a single, wild apparition of colors and decorations.

"It is now time to join the men," Rainbow said as she gently took Audra's hand. "Come. See how the women say their good-byes to their loved ones."

A maiden came and offered Audra a bag of food rations and a pair of moccasins.

Audra gave Rainbow a quick, questioning look.

"These items are for you to give to your husband," Rainbow explained. "All women give such farewell gifts to their husbands. These are highly prized by our warriors and precious to them."

"Thank you," Audra murmured as she turned a soft smile to the maiden and took the moccasins and bag of food. "You are so kind to help teach me things of your people."

The maiden smiled, then went to the far side of the smokehouse, picked up another bag and pair of moccasins, and hurried outside. Audra watched her go to her husband and hand them to him as he sat proud and tall in his saddle.

"Go now to your husband," Rainbow said, nodding toward Silver Wing as he sat proudly on his decorated white steed.

Audra hurried to Silver Wing. She forced back tears as she reached her gifts up to her husband. She just couldn't allow him to see that she was afraid, yet she knew that white outlaws were good at ambushing. Her husband could be taken from her in a blast of gunfire!

"Ride with caution and care," Audra murmured as Silver Wing smiled down at her and received her gifts with a proud heart.

She looked nervously at his large bow slung over his shoulder and at the quiver of arrows. She wanted to say that she didn't think his bow and arrows would be enough to fight men who had powerful rifles. Her husband owned such firearms, yet she knew that he trusted the skill of his bow and arrow more than he trusted firearms.

And he had explained to her that the arrow sent a silent message through the air.

The rifle's report announced the bullet's arrival!

"Please be careful," she then said. "Those men could be anywhere. They might even this moment be watching from a bluff. If they know what your plan is, you could be . . ."

"You worry too much for a woman who is heavy with child," Silver Wing said, interrupting her. He leaned low so that only she would hear what else he had to say. "And do not show so little faith in your chieftain husband. It makes him look small and unimportant in the eyes of his people."

"I'm sorry," Audra rushed out, her eyes wavering. "I didn't mean to imply anything like that. It is the white men I do not trust."

"Go now and join the women in their singing as we warriors leave to find those who are the scourge of the earth," Silver Wing said, bending lower to brush a kiss across her brow. "I will return soon the victorious. It is time for we Nez Perce to rid our lives of *Yi-hell-lis,* scum of the earth!"

"I love you so," Audra murmured, then ran back and stood with the women as they formed a circle a few feet away from the saddled warriors. Only moments ago, while preparing the salmon for smoking, Rainbow had explained the *Kihl-lo-wow-ya,* "Serenade Dance," to her, which would be performed by the women as the men departed for warring. It was a farewell to the warriors.

Some women broke away from the circle and stood in the middle. As the drums boomed and rattles shook, those women began to sing while the others danced in a slow standing fashion, their feet shuffling and lifting, yet taking them nowhere.

The fringes of Audra's goatskin dress shook and swayed as she joined in the dance, yet her eyes were elsewhere. She fought back tears as she watched Silver Wing and the others ride away on their painted, proud steeds.

The dancing and singing continued until the men were lost from the women's sight.

Busy hands helped troubled hearts as the women went back to the smokehouse and resumed preparing the fish.

Audra could hardly stand these moments of anticipating the arrival back home of her husband. She had to believe that he *would* return safely. He surely would not place himself in danger, not with him having a wife who was with child, and also Little Butterfly, awaiting his return!

She looked around her as she helped clean the fish.

She saw the same looks of apprehension on the other women's faces and even heard some of them praying quietly while others sang soft, low songs.

Rainbow came and stood beside Audra again. "Let us talk of babies," she said, trying to draw Audra's attention from the worries at hand.

"Yes, babies," Audra said, sighing contentedly at the thought of the child laying inside her womb, growing each day into someone who would be beautiful and so dearly wanted.

She would give this child all of the love that her mother never had time to give Audra.

And Silver Wing would be the best of fathers whose mind would never be clouded from the consumption of rotgut whiskey!

Yes, Silver Wing *would* return and be there for their child's future . . . and for *theirs*.

39

Take up the quarrel with the foe;
To you from failing hands we throw
The torch; be yours to hold it high,
If ye break faith with us who die,
We shall not sleep.
——JOHN MCCRAE

Silver Wing and his warriors returned to where they
had found the slain bear. Silver Wing smiled cunningly
when he saw a trail of blood that led away from the
kill. It was obvious to him that whoever had killed the
bear foolishly hung its dripping paws at the side of
his horse.

"Follow me!" Silver Wing cried to his men as he
led his horse onward, now not only following the
blood trail but also the crushed grass left downed by
the outlaws' horses.

As the sun rose higher and higher in the sky, Silver
Wing rode onward and onward.

Then when the trail led into a long, deep canyon,
he dismounted and led his horse by foot for a while,
his men following his lead.

They all stopped suddenly after climbing a rise in the
land. Below them were their prized Appaloosa horses,
and a crude shack made quickly of cedar timber.

Still saddled, several horses were tied to a crude
hitching post rack.

Silver Wing counted twelve horses, which meant twelve outlaws.

His gaze shifted elsewhere, and he saw an outdoor fire.

A huge black pot hung over it, wafting the aroma of meat.

"Bear meat," Silver Wing grumbled to himself, quickly sliding his bow from his shoulder.

He meticulously slid an arrow from the quiver at his back.

He glanced over at Tall Shadow, who knelt on one side of him, and Black Fox, on his other side.

"Pass word along to our warriors to follow me," Silver Wing whispered to Tall Shadow, and then to Black Fox. "We will surround the cabin. We will surprise those who are inside it. They will soon be dead or will be our captives."

Tall Shadow nodded.

Black Fox nodded.

After everyone knew the plan, they slid down a small incline and ran in the shadows of trees until they reached the back of the cabin.

Silver Wing nodded to first one warrior and then another until soon the cabin was fully surrounded.

It was considered a dishonor for a Nez Perce warrior to be struck in the back. This indicated he was running away.

If one was to retreat, it must be done while facing the enemy.

Silver Wing and his men never retreated. They always faced their enemy head on!

Silver Wing then went to the door and kicked it

open. His arrow was now notched on the bowstring. Eleven other warriors followed his lead. Silver Wing and the warriors ran inside the lodge.

Surprising those who were inside, Silver Wing smiled cunningly when he saw that he had succeeded at getting to the men before they had reached out for a firearm.

Silver Wing looked past the cowering men, who were only half dressed, and saw children and women huddled together in a corner.

It was apparent they had been sleeping.

He quickly recognized them. These were the same women and children he had taken in and cared for.

His eyes were quickly drawn elsewhere when one of the men fell away from the others. He knelt to his knees and clasped his hands together in a pleading manner. "Please don't kill us," he cried, his eyes wide with fear. "Especially *me*. Let me go. I'm not here willingly. After the men killed and scalped the Injun, I wanted out. But they wouldn't allow it. I'm their captive. Please . . . believe . . . me!"

Seeing the cowardice of this man, Silver Wing pitied him, yet he would not be pulled into such an act as that, especially when the other men snickered and called him a liar.

"Get back with the others," Silver Wing said, motioning with his bow and arrow for him to do this. "You will suffer the same treatment as the others."

Silver Wing waited for the man to crawl back to the others, then rise slowly to his feet, his eyes brimming with tears as he shivered uncontrollably from fear.

"Women and children," Silver Wing said thickly, "you are free to go outside."

Silver Wing reached out for one of the children as the boy started to rush past him. "You are one of the children who camped near my people's village," Silver Wing said softly.

The boy nodded.

"How is it then that you are with these men when you and your mothers were escorted to the trading post?" Silver Wing asked. "And if you are with these men, where are the two men who were supposed to escort you to the trading post? Dennis Bell was one of the men. Harry Weston was the other."

His gaze swept past the child and hurried across the faces of the men in the cabin. He was relieved not to find Harry Weston among them, or he would feel foolish for having trusted the man.

"They are both dead," the boy blurted out, causing Silver Wing to flinch as though he had been shot.

Silver Wing fell to his knees and laid his bow and arrow aside. He clasped his hands onto the frail shoulders of the child. "They are dead?" he said thickly. "Both . . . are dead?"

"Shot dead by . . ." the boy said, then stopped short when an outlaw behind him shouted at him to keep quiet, the threat enough to still the child's words.

Silver Wing looked past his shoulder again at the men and found the one who had spoken out of turn. He nodded at Tall Shadow. "Take that man outside," he grumbled. "Remove his clothes. Tie him to a tree!"

"No!" Jimmy cried, struggling as Tall Shadow grabbed him by both arms, shoving him toward the door. "You cain't do this to me. Let me go, you Injun savage!"

The word "savage" fueled Tall Shadow's anger even more. "The true savage is you," he breathed out heatedly. "You who kill bears only for their paws, and you who steal horses that are not yours, and you who treat children and women as you do, do not deserve another day of breath on this earth."

"Don't kill me!" Jimmy begged, then groaned with pain as Tall Shadow gave him a shove that sent him out the door, landing on his face in the dirt.

"Tell me more, young man, about how Dennis Bell and Harry Weston died," Silver Wing said softly, his grip lightening on the child's flesh.

"Mommy and I were sitting beneath a tree resting when . . . when . . . we heard the first gunshot," the child said, now sobbing. "It happened so quickly. Mr. Bell and Mr. Weston were shot so quickly. They . . . were . . . left for dead."

"Does that mean you aren't certain they were dead?" Silver Wing asked, hoping Dennis Bell's life hadn't ended so needlessly. He had no feelings one way or the other for Harry Weston, except that he didn't like to see anyone die by someone who so cowardly ambushed to kill.

"There was much blood," the child choked out. "So I imagine they are dead."

Silver Wing rose slowly to his feet. He walked slowly around the room, looking at each man individually, then he stamped to the door. He turned and glared at his warriors. "Bring them all outside," he said. "We will unclothe them and tie them all to trees.

We will leave them at the mercy of the weather and prowling animals."

Sobs and cries broke out among the men as they were half dragged out of the cabin.

Silver Wing gazed at the women and children, who still huddled, their eyes wild.

"You will be taken to the trading post as you earlier requested," he said, stepping up to them. "But this time I promise that you will get there without anymore interferences."

He saw the relief that flooded the eyes of both the women and children.

Then he turned and watched the outlaws being tied to the trees, their naked flesh white against the bright rays of the sun.

Silver Wing slowly smiled, yet deep inside him he was sad for the loss of Dennis Bell. He was a man with a good heart who never harmed anyone. For this man's death, he hoped these outlaws would suffer twofold as they slowly awaited their death on their prison trees!

He glanced at the men's scalps. For the first time in his life, he desired scalping white men, but he would not dirty his hands by touching the flea-infested, greasy hair of any of them!

He was a much better man than that!

40

My love is such that rivers cannot quench,
Nor ought but love from thee, give recompense.
——ANNE BRADSTREET

The salmon now smoking in the smokehouse, Audra
was inside her cabin, bathed and in clean clothes, pacing. She had never felt as helpless as now when her
husband was out there somewhere, vulnerable to those
who killed so easily.

She had taken a short nap after getting Little Butterfly to sleep, and in her fretful dreams she had seen
many lurking wolves high on a bluff, their forms black
against the sky.

Then, in her dreams, the wolves had talked to her
and told her they knew where Silver Wing was. . . .

Audra had awakened with a start, cold sweat damp
on her brow.

Not wanting to think about what such a dream
might mean, afraid to know, she had left her bed
quickly and began nervously pacing.

She stopped and gazed over at the cradle, where
Little Butterfly still slept so contentedly, without a
worry in the world, so trusting of everything and
everyone.

"One day you will have to know that there are many evil men in the world," she whispered. "I will protect you as long as I can from them. I hope I will always be here for you."

But she knew that life had its ugly twists and turns. She *could* be taken anytime from this child. Hadn't Audra's mother died too soon in life? Hadn't the child's true mother been taken much too soon?

"I just don't know . . ." Audra whispered, a sob lodging in her throat. "So much is left to chance . . . to one's true destiny!"

The sound of a horse arriving at the village made her stop with a start and stare at the closed door. "One horse?" she whispered, paling.

Her throat tightened, for if the warriors were arriving successful, there would be many horses!

Not . . . only . . . one!

Audra ran from the cabin, then stopped short when she saw that it wasn't an Indian. It was a white man.

And as he rode closer to her, revealing his face, she was stunned.

Not so much over who was arriving, but by the blood soaking his shirt.

"Dennis Bell?" she whispered, then broke into a run and met his approach.

"Lord, Dennis, there's so much blood," Audra cried. "Why?"

"My wound has reopened," Dennis said, his brow covered with nervous sweat. "Audra, help me from the horse. I've much to tell you."

By then several more women, as well as children and the warriors who had stayed to protect the village, surrounded the horse as Audra gave Dennis a helping hand from the saddle.

"Thank you," Dennis gasped, reaching for his back, the pain grabbing at him in quick snatches.

"Come into my lodge," Audra murmured, allowing Dennis to lean against her.

Once inside with Dennis comfortably on a blanket beside the fireplace, Audra carefully removed his shirt, and grimaced when she saw the blood-soaked bandage.

"Tell me, Dennis," she said softly as she went to get a basin. She poured water into it from a parfleche bag, then sat beside him again. "Tell me what happened."

"We were ambushed on our way to the trading post," Dennis breathed out, his eyes closed as he turned on his side and Audra slowly bathed his wound. "Both Harry and I were left for dead. The men who did this were the women's outlaw husbands. They apparently survived the measles. They . . . took . . . the women and children away and left me and Harry for dead."

"Good Lord, they are certainly the most heartless bunch I have ever heard of," Audra said, succeeding now at removing the blood. She flinched when she saw the puckered wound on his back. "And poor Harry. He had tried to do something good for the first time in his life."

"And he *did*," Dennis said softly. "If not for him, I'd be dead even now. He . . . he . . . had the strength to help me on to the trading post. And then . . . he . . . collapsed."

"Why did you come back here when your wound is so bad?" Audra asked softly.

"Because I wanted to warn Silver Wing about the outlaw gang," he said thickly. "They are bloodthirsty sons of bitches. They'd as soon shoot you as look at you. I wanted Silver Wing to know they are still in the area. They are going to steal more horses. I know, because as I lay there pretending to be dead, I listened to their plan. And they forced the women and children to join them. I pity them. Who is to say how they will be treated, especially knowing they were deserting the men?"

"Silver Wing already knows about the men," Audra murmured. "He and many of his warriors are out even now searching for them."

She quickly explained why.

"I hope the warriors have eyes in the backs of their heads," Dennis said, his eyes slowly closing. "Those men . . . those men . . . are vicious."

Audra was glad when Rainbow entered the longhouse with her medicines for Dennis, for it helped her to get her mind off her husband for at least a while. But she could not shed the worst of her fears. Could the outlaws find a way to best the Nez Perce, even after the warriors might think they had bested the outlaws?

"I've got to go and find him," Audra suddenly said, rushing to her feet. "I must warn him!"

Rainbow stumbled to her feet. She grabbed Audra by an arm. "You cannot do that," she said softly. "The child. Audra, you are with child!"

Audra's eyes wavered as she slid a hand over her

abdomen. "Yes, the child," she said, tears filling her eyes. "You are right. I must think of my unborn child."

"Have faith that Silver Wing is doing what is best," Rainbow said, gently leading Audra back down on the blanket beside Dennis. "Busy your hands. Help apply my herbal ointments to this man's wound."

Dennis smiled up at Audra, then reached a hand to her arm and patted it. "She is right, you know," he murmured. "Silver Wing *can* take care of himself, *and* his warriors. I have never known as strong an Indian as Silver Wing.

"Even now I am certain Silver Wing is quite in charge of things," Dennis reassured. "I imagine he already found the men and has decided how they will pay for their crimes."

"I wish he would bring back their scalps," Rainbow murmured, drawing a gasp from Audra.

"You don't think he . . ." Audra stammered as she questioned Rainbow with her eyes.

"Never," Rainbow said, smiling back at Audra. "He is a man of principle. Taking scalps is beneath him."

Audra sighed.

41

Take this kiss upon the brow!
And, in parting from you now,
Thus much let me avow.
——EDGAR ALLAN POE

Audra prepared the evening meal for Silver Wing, confident that he would arrive home safely.

"Roast pheasant," Audra whispered, smiling at the generosity of a young brave who had brought her what he had caught on his morning hunt.

She had known that the gift of pheasant was not so much for her but for Silver Wing to feast upon when he returned from his search, and hopefully capture, of the murdering thieves.

The pheasant, stripped of its feathers and beheaded, lay before her in a heavy black roasting pan, looking more like a chicken than a wild bird. Audra continued stuffing it with berries and nuts.

She remembered her mother had used grapes instead of berries, but since grapes were scarce today, the wild berries would suffice.

In fact, Audra thought that just perhaps the berries would taste better than grapes. It would give the bird a more tangy flavor instead of sweet.

The pheasant finally ready for baking, Audra slid

the heavy lid over the pan and carried it to the fireplace.

Having already prepared a place for the pan amid the hot coals at the edge of the fire, she scooted the pan into them, then stepped back and smiled at how soon everything in the longhouse would be filled with the fragrances of the slow-cooking pheasant.

When Silver Wing stepped inside the lodge, he would know that his wife had expected his victory, which they would celebrate in their own way in the privacy of their lodge when the moon was high and bright in the heavens.

"Where are they?" she whispered, glancing toward the door.

She had listened intently for the return of the horses until her head ached.

It seemed an eternity now since their departure.

And although she had promised Rainbow that she wouldn't go and search for Silver Wing, Audra knew that she would not be able to hold back for much longer.

She *would* go and look for him.

If anything happened to him . . .

Her heart skipped a beat, and her breath caught in her throat when she thought that she caught the distant thundering sound of horses' hooves.

She scarcely breathed as she stood listening, her body stiff, her heart pounding.

The booming sound of the hooves grew louder and louder.

And then there were the warriors' shouts of victory that wafted like sunshine across the land to the village!

Breathless with relief, Audra lifted the skirt of her buckskin dress and began running through the village, the people coming from their lodges soon following.

Victory songs broke out everywhere.

The beat of the drums began rhythmically.

Children shouted.

Dogs barked.

By the time Silver Wing and his warriors finally arrived at the outskirts of the village, everyone who had been left behind was there to greet them.

Seeing the throng of people awaiting him and his warriors, Audra among them, Silver Wing drew a tight rein and stopped his horse.

His eyes locked with Audra's, he leapt from his horse and ran to her.

Grabbing her, he laughed into the wind and playfully swung her around, then swept her into his arms.

"And how is our daughter Little Butterfly faring? And our new child?" Silver Wing asked, gazing into her eyes. "Have you all missed Silver Wing?"

"Very much," Audra murmured. "Oh, so very, very much."

"But I am home now and untouched by bullets," Silver Wing boasted, proudly squaring his shoulders.

Then his eyes brightened. "It is done," he said, his voice carrying to everyone, who was now quiet and watching his chief with his wife.

He looked around him and shouted, "It is done," again and much more loudly. "Those who have wronged us are paying for their sins against the Nez Perce!"

The other warriors dismounted their horses.

Young braves hurried to them, took their reins, and led the horses away, toward the corral.

"How are . . . they . . . paying?" Audra dared to ask, her breathing now shallow as she awaited Silver Wing's response.

He smiled at her. "No scalps were taken, if that is what you are thinking," he said, chuckling. "They are paying in a much simpler way. They are tied naked to trees. They will be there until they die."

Audra paled at the thought of the men tied to the trees in such a way. It could take days for them to die, yet it was a more decent way than having been scalped and left on the ground like Red Bonnet, flies buzzing over his bloody remains.

Then Silver Wing went somber as he slid Audra from his arms so that she stood before him, his hands gently on her waist. "But the news I discovered was not good," he stated quietly. He hung his head and sucked in a deep breath as he thought about Dennis Bell and how he did not deserve to die.

Then he looked up at Audra again, only scarcely aware of Father John approaching at his left side. "The women and children did not make it to the trading post. The men who are tied to trees today are their husbands and fathers. These men came upon Dennis Bell and Harry Weston escorting the women and children to the trading post. These children and women witnessed the deaths of Dennis Bell and Harry Weston," he said. "The outlaws gunned them down without hesitating. Both men are dead."

"The outlaws only thought they were dead," Father John said, stepping up beside Audra. He smiled at

Silver Wing and held out a handshake of welcome, which Silver Wing accepted. "They survived the shooting." He glanced over his shoulder at his lodge. "Dennis Bell is here. Rainbow has treated his wound."

Silver Wing's throat tightened. "Is Harry Weston here, also?" he asked, his voice revealing his disapproval.

"No," Father John said, easing his hand from Silver Wing's. "Harry is at the trading post. His condition is not the same as Dennis's. He is alive, but due to his brave struggles, draining his own strength to help get Dennis to the trading post, he is having to take more time to recuperate."

"Dennis came here to warn you about the outlaws and their heartless practice of shooting anyone on sight they wish to shoot," Audra murmured. "He worried about you getting ambushed." Tears filled her eyes. "I'm so glad you bested the outlaws first."

"Yes, they are no longer a threat to anyone," Silver Wing said. He smiled into the crowd of Nez Perce. "We have much to celebrate! Let us begin!"

The singing began as everyone started back to the center of the village, where a huge fire would be built and much dancing would occur.

Audra's pheasant would join the other women's food as a feast would be shared by all. It would be the best of times for everyone!

"I must go to the river and remove the war paint and the scent of those white men from my skin," Silver Wing said thickly as his men came and stood around him, waiting to join him. "But first I will go and say hello to Dennis Bell. It is good to know that the outlaws' bullets did no final damage to his body."

He turned and nodded at his warriors. "Go to the river," he ordered. "I will soon join you."

They nodded a confirmation to him, then ran off together, their happy voices wafting in the air behind them.

Silver Wing slid Audra from his arms, then arm in arm, Father John walking beside them, Silver Wing and Audra went to Father John's lodge, where Dennis was asleep on a bed of blankets.

Silver Wing knelt down beside Dennis, his gaze going to the bandage wrapped around his back. He thought of the men tied to the trees and smiled.

Dennis's eyes slowly opened. He smiled at Silver Wing and slid a hand over to his arm. "I'm so glad you're all right," he said softly. "I came to warn you. You . . . you . . . were already gone."

"And all is well," Silver Wing murmured. "The men will no longer be a threat to anyone."

"They're dead?" Dennis gulped out.

"No, but in time they will be," Silver Wing said, his eyes gleaming.

Dennis didn't ask what he meant by that.

Instead he sat up and moved around so that he could bend over and put his shoes on. "I need to get back," he said. "I'm worried about Harry."

"You care this much about Harry?" Audra asked, her eyebrows forking.

"That man saved my life," Dennis said matter-of-factly. "I want to get back to the trading post and make sure he's being taken care of."

Father John knelt down beside Dennis. He slid an envelope in his hand. "Will you see that this goes out with the next mail from the trading post?" he asked softly.

"Certainly," Dennis said, sliding the letter into his rear pocket. He reached for his shirt and slowly slid it on.

Father John turned to Audra. "I'm sending word to Sister Kathryn, asking if she can come on the next passenger ship from San Francisco and be with me at the new mission," he said softly. "I'm also asking her to see if sweet Sarah would like to accompany her."

Then he looked over at Dennis again. "And while you are at the trading post, please send out word to those who might have skills to help build the mission," he said. "I hope to get it done as soon as possible. I don't like putting such an imposition on the Nez Perce by staying here."

Suddenly Silver Wing smiled, his eyes twinkling. "I do not think you have the need of sending word out for laborers for your mission," he said, chuckling. "There are men already available for you."

"Who?" Father John asked, forking an eyebrow.

"Instead of leaving the white outlaws to die on the trees, why not put them to good use?" Silver Wing said, giving Audra a sidewise glance when she gasped at his suggestion.

"These white men can pay for their sins by building a holy man's mission," Silver Wing then said. "Those who cooperate and repent could be set free. Those who have to work by force will find imprisonment awaiting them once the mission is completed."

The irony of the plan, forcing the deadliest of out-laws to build a place of worship, made Audra smile. How clever.

Father John rose to his feet and placed a hand on Silver Wing's bare shoulder. "Thank you," he said softly. "I am humbled by your kindness."

Silver Wing gave Father John a lingering gaze, then helped Dennis from the lodge. "Several warriors will escort you to the trading post now," he said softly. "Unless you wish to stay for a while longer and join the celebration of victory."

Dennis gazed over at Audra, who smiled and nod-ded at him.

Then he smiled up at Silver Wing. "I would like to join you, but just for a little while," he said. "I need to see if Harry is doing all right."

"Whenever you wish to leave, just tell us," Audra said, then watched as Silver Wing ran toward the river.

She looked back at the longhouse, where pheasant was already filling the spaces with its delicious aroma.

Also, she needed to check on Little Butterfly. It thrilled her to know that things were finally all right with her world.

She had so much to be thankful for!

42

If ever two were one, then surely we,
If ever man were loved by wife, then thee;
If ever wife was happy in a man,
Compare with me, ye woman, if you can.
——ANNE BRADSTREET

Winter had given way to spring. The wind carried the sweet scents of flowering plants and greening trees across the land. Birds flooded the morning with their songs, while newborn fawns steadied their wobbling legs.

Silver Wing saw rebirth everywhere. It was time for him to remind his warriors of their obligations.

Audra and Silver Wing's baby was two years old . . . a son they had named Yellow Fox.

She and Silver Wing were on a blanket at Butterfly Valley. They could see the tall steeple of Father John's mission in the distance.

Audra had visited the mission yesterday to greet Sarah and Sister Kathryn.

She was glad to see that Sarah was no longer frail. She was robust with rosy cheeks and eyes that always smiled.

As for Sister Kathryn, she was the same and was to be respected for being so devoted to her religion.

Audra laughed to herself when she thought of who else had joined Father John at the mission.

Harry Weston.

He was no longer a mere gardener, though.

He was learning from Father John the art of priesthood.

Audra found it hard to grasp every time she saw Harry now in his long black robe. Somehow he didn't fit the role of priest.

But that was because she knew the worst about him.

"Look at our son and daughter chasing the butterflies," Silver Wing said as he drew Audra over against him, his arm gentle around her waist.

"Nothing could be as beautiful," Audra said, sighing.

"You are," Silver Wing said, turning to gaze at Audra.

He lifted a hand behind her and filled it with the heaviness of her long, red braid, where one lone eagle feather hung from the end loop of the braid.

"And your hair is more beautiful each day," he said, mesmerized.

"For certain no one will ever take scissors to it again," Audra said, glorying in having her full head of hair back, and even more. She wore it braided some days, and loose and flowing down past her waist on others.

She always smiled to herself when she saw the Nez Perce children gazing at her hair, marveling over its brilliant red color.

"Like the sunshine," some would say as they would come up and touch it.

Or others would say it was like flames of fire!

No matter how it was described, it was just good to have it back!

Today she wore a beautifully beaded doeskin dress. Her skin was tanned almost as dark as her husband's copper body. The freckles that dotted her nose brought almost as much attention as her hair.

"Life is perfect," Silver Wing said, brushing a kiss across her brow. "You have made it so, my wife."

"You have made it so for *me,* my husband," Audra murmured, gazing into his dark gray eyes, so filled with love for him at this moment she felt as though she was aglow with it.

"We make our lives what we put into them," Silver Wing said. "With you in mine, I am a man of much happiness and pride."

"With you in mine, I am forever and ever filled with joy," Audra murmured, then melted inside when he yanked her close and gave her a long, deep kiss that made the butterflies that fluttered around them blush crimson.

Through her moment of ecstasy, Audra tried not to think about the dark side of life, fearing that even their love for one another would not be enough when his Nez Perce people became surrounded by too many whites who would slowly steal their horses and land.

For now Audra would cherish what they had, and not linger on what might be, especially for their children, whose futures were truly uncertain!

Dear Reader:

I hope you enjoyed reading *Silver Wing*! My next book in my Indian series is *Thunder Heart* and will be in the stores in time for Christmas.

Many of my readers are collecting my historical romances. For those of you who are collecting the books in my Topaz Indian series and want to know about my backlist and future books, please send a legal-size, self-addressed, stamped envelope to the following address for my latest newsletter and bookmark—

CASSIE EDWARDS
6709 North Country Club Road
Mattoon, Illinois 61938

Thank you so much for your support of my books. I truly appreciate it!

Always,

Cassie Edwards